THE
NEAR DEATH
EXPERIMENT

by

Steve Glassman

Tropical Press

Library of Congress Cataloging-in-Publication Data

Glassman, Steve
　　　Near Death Experiment /Steve Glassman. 1st ed.

　　　　　　p.　　cm.

　　　ISBN 0-9666173-7-1

　　　1. Glassman, Steve

　I. Title.

　　LCCN: 2001087467

Cover Design: John Wilton

Manufactured in the United Sates of America

TROPICAL PRESS
P.O. Box 161174
Miami, FL 33116-1174
www.tropicalpress.com

For Dugie and Brendan,

two who passed too soon

Acknowledgment

The effectiveness of this novel hinges on the credibility of its science, especially in matters dealing with citrus diseases. The author thanks Dr. Tim Gottwald of the USDA Agriculture Research Station in Orlando for providing information on the citrus canker, regarding which he is one of the world's leading authorities. In particular, the author would like to thank Dr. Gottwald for suggesting the extremely clever means by which the Goins family attempted to contaminate the entire Florida orange juice crop. Thanks, Tim. Your help was invaluable.

THE
NEAR DEATH
EXPERIMENT

1

Rupert J. "Bru" Bruton, Ph.D., stumbled on the threshold going out of the country market somewhere between Daytona Beach and Orlando. He toted a sixteen-ounce Old Milwaukee. As he levered the top, a county prowl car swung off State Road 415. It rammed up to the curb, the radiator grille stopping a quarter inch from Bru's knees. Bru looked at the deputy through the windshield. He sported a wide-brim hat, pencil-line mustache, jug ears. His eyes were hooded, like some pop-eyed beetle, by sunshades. Bru considered chucking his beer in a trash can. He decided, *Fuck it.* He took a swig of the Old Milwaukee and slung himself in his ten-year-old Fiesta. He laid down a patch of rubber shooting onto 415.

Humped cattle with long curved horns grazed on the Saint Johns River bottom among tall palm trees. A black cloud drifted across the sky. Thunder rumbled. Sprinkles of rain came slanting down. A motorcycle shot around Bru's Fiesta, followed by another and another--it was Bike Week in Daytona. The bikes just kept zooming around Bru. The last cyclist, in an antlered helmet and a red fu-man-chu mustache, tooted his horn and pointed at Bru. Bru saluted him by hoisting the Old Milwaukee. It was a smart-ass gesture, with no pretense at fun.

Bru was pissed. He'd been made a fool of at that meeting in Daytona. The man he'd gone to see was named Goins, pronounced Go-ins he'd been snootily informed at the run-down art deco mansion on the beach. The gangly, hairy-eared old Goins--he had to be in his late seventies, maybe more--had told his servant to bring Bru something to eat. Then the old man had swiped half the sandwich off

Bru's plate. Before Bru could say boo he grabbed the other half, the part Bru had taken a bite out of, and swallowed that too. And this Goins was supposedly the richest man in the state, counting his fortune in the multibillions.

Then there was his daughter, Elizabeth, dressed in the Florida heat in a business suit for no reason Bru could discern. She invited him into her cubbyhole office and suddenly the front of her blouse flew open and her tits, big as medicine balls, had lashed at Bru's face. Her hands prospected in his lap as she tried to relieve Bru of the stack of file folders the old man had given him and which were now safely ensconced on the car's backseat. Bru's family jewels still smarted from her mincing action down there.

Bru slugged down beer. Still something nagged at him, something bigger than that bottle of thalidomide he found in Elizabeth's bathroom medicine chest when he'd gone in there to cool off. Something even bigger than Kimberly, Elizabeth's daughter who seemed the only normal person in the place. His heart went out to Kimberly--she reminded him of his daughter Amber.

Then he knew what was bugging him about that research Goins wanted him to do. It was the hundred fifty thousand dollar bonus--if the old boy liked Bru's report on the toxicity of 1-2--DCA in orange juice containers, or rather its nontoxicity. The deal was Bru was suppose to show the compound which was an incidental byproduct in the manufacture of orange juice containers was perfectly safe. Otherwise, Bru'd get a measly fifty thousand, barely enough to cover the lab fees. A strange way to do science. But a great way of doing business, of making sure you got the science you wanted.

A motorcycle horn tooted. Bru looked out the driver window. He started, spilling beer in his lap. Parallel Bru in the oncoming lane was the guy in the antlered helmet and fu man chu. Could he still be there? Or had he fallen

2

behind and then pulled ahead? Whatever, a string of cars was pushing toward him. The motorcyclist was jabbing his finger and hollering something. He was pointing at Bru's rear tire. His voice was slurred by the windstream. The lead car, a vintage Oldsmobile or Buick, wasn't but ten car lengths away. It swung wide onto the shoulder but was not cutting its speed, afraid of being rearended by the caravan behind. Bru stomped on the brakes. The old Fiesta sighed, the brakes spongy. Bru wheeled onto the shoulder, pulling over as far as he could. The wheel vibrated in his hands as the motorcycle shot to safety into the lane ahead. Bru's passenger tires, going off the pavement onto the shoulder, shuddered. The Fiesta skidded, the brakes locked. The rear began to fishtail, then brake shoes unfroze. The rear end kicked back in line. The car plowed to a stop.

Ahead, Bru noticed the brake light of the antlered biker's motorcycle flash on. The motorcycle cut to the right and dove down the steep bank into the ditch. He executed a 180 degree turn. A rooster tail of mud and water shot up. The motorcycle tore up the bank and charged down the shoulder towards Bru. Bru slipped out the door. A quick peek showed the driver's rear tire was fine.

The motorcycle was coming on fast. The bike braked violently. It skidded broadside and went over. Bru ran around to the front of the car. The biker jumped from under the cycle. He was a tall fellow going up to six two at least. He was rail thin and swaddled in biker's black leathers, jacket and chaps. He reached under his jacket and produced a tire iron.

"Leave my girl alone," he coughed at Bru in a wasted voice. He flailed the tire iron in the air. Bru, not having an idea of what this seeming maniac was talking about, ran reflexively to the rear of the car. The man charged after him, stopped midway, and smashed the iron into the back window. He turned his back to Bru and leaned against the car.

Bru hollered. He ran toward the man. Before Bru could get to him the man swung at the driver window. Shards flew. The man turned. He waved the tire iron at Bru. He heaved the tool at Bru. It came twirling about ten feet up, swishing like a helicopter rotor. It rustled into the tall ditchside vegetation.

The man said, "Oh shit," and cocked his arm. Bru arrived just as the fist let go. Bru threw his left arm up and deflected the blow. There was astonishingly little force in the guy's swing. Bru's momentum carried him into the man. The guy thrust backwards. Bru grabbed him by the throat of his leather jacket to keep from falling. Bru managed to get his feet under him, and then the man in the motorcycle leathers started to go down. Bru pulled him up and drew back his arm.

Smack him before he clobbers you, Bru told himself. The guy found his balance and let one fly at Bru. It caught him just under the eye. Bru smashed back against the Fiesta, losing his grip on the biker.

Suddenly the silence, punctuated by the grunts of Bru and his assailant, was shattered by the pipes of a flotilla of bikes. The cycles roared by--zaroom, zaroom--two abreast. Seeing the fight and the overturned bike, like many parts of a single body, their brakes lights pulsed red simultaneously. The antlered biker ran to his cycle. He uprighted the machine, and hit the starter button, which whirred furiously. The bike roared to life. He hopped onto the saddle and the machine stormed off on one wheel. The guy showed Bru his teeth wrapped in a fu-man-chu mane of red hair as he roared by.

2

"What the hell goes on here?" a big guy in leathers demanded. Five other bikers of both sexes peeked out from behind him.

Bru told him, holding his hand to his face. He wondered if he was going to get a shiner out of this. Actually, Bru reflected Elizabeth's tit had smacked him with almost as much force as the skinny biker's fist.

The big biker wandered over to the car window. "Shee-it," he proclaimed. He smelled of motor oil and too long unwashed jeans. But he had an honest if scarred face. A red bandana was tied around his forehead. His hair was graying. "I think this guy is telling the truth," the big fellow hollered. "Come on you guys, let's go after that son of a bitch. Heidi, look after this dude until we get back." Bru watched the bikers dash, well, limp for their machines, as they were all overweight and most bore the scars of injuries. But once they mounted their sleek Harleys, they roared off with a grace and speed that the fu-manchu guy hadn't shown.

Heidi, a busty, ditchwater blond of about twenty-six, looked at Bru and smiled. "How well do you want me to take care of him?" she asked nobody in particular. "How about doing a line of coke?" The offer was accompanied by a cocktail waitress curtsy, the kind that gives the consumer a chance to ogle the cleavage, of which there was an abundant supply.

Before Bru could answer a sheriff's car pulled in behind Bru. The blue lights were going. A heavy-set little guy with a round face and Howdy Doody ears popped out. He had a pencil-line mustache and a Harry Truman Stetson, eyes shaded by sunglasses. "What's going on here?" he harrumphed.

Bru told him.

"You stopped for a biker you didn't know?"

"He indicated I had a flat."

The deputy shook his head and paced beside the broken windows. "What's them things on the backseat?" he asked indicating the file folders.

"Some work of mine," Bru said.

"How about I see some identification?"

Bru fished his driver's license out of his wallet. The deputy slipped it under the clip of his board.

Thunder rumbled in the sky and a few fat rain drops zinged down. A chill crossed the back of Bru's neck, even as dazed and disoriented as he was by the near auto crash and that brush with the biker. What was it about that sheriff that made him seem familiar? Then Bru got it. He was the deputy in the parking lot of the market. The beer--what happened to it? It spilled, foaming on the floorboards. Bru tried hard to give a shit about the cop busting him on account of it. He was spared the effort by a fire hose opening in the sky. Water poured down in torrents.

The cop pushed the driver's license back to Bru. "I'll be in touch if need be."

Bru wondered how he was going to get in touch, seeing he never took Bru's information. But rain was drenching down. Taking a file folder, Bru swept the glass on the seat onto the road and slid behind the wheel. Rain pummeled him through the broken windows, onto the back seat where the file folders were. Bru piled the manilla folders on the seat beside him. The female biker stood by the passenger door.

"Let me in," she said. "We'll do that line and have

6

some fun."

Bru cranked up the Fiesta and drove away, leaving Heidi stranded in the rain. Bru had no use for drugs or strange women. He looked forward to seeing his wife, Leta.

3

Deputy Hank Smith stomped on the gas. He didn't want those two-wheeled vigilantes to do any harm to the biker, a gent by the name of Leroy who he had under surveillance. Everyone of the two-hundred horses under the hood of his Ford Taurus snorted to life. He went through the village of Osteen with the needle reading eighty-five miles per hour.

A couple of miles farther on, in the sunlight again, Deputy Hank saw bikers clustered on the side of the road. He turned on the siren and edged the rapidly charging cruiser onto the shoulder. The bikers scattered like hens in a chickenyard. He pulled behind two tall bikers squared off. Leaving the blue light going, he exited his vehicle, hitched up his standard-issue belt, and adjusted his Harry Truman Stetson. The corner of his mouth curled into a Warren Oates grin, showing the teeth that Deputy Smith had surgically corrected--corrected to be jagged and uneven.

"Can't you give us a minute here, officer?" the beefy one said. "I'm about to teach this here fellow the rules of the road."

"Was it you that forced that Fiesta off the pavement?" the deputy asked. The big guy in the bandana didn't answer. "If not, scram," the deputy said. "And take your friends with you."

The gypsy-looking bikers mounted their machines, leaving Deputy Hank and Leroy. "Let's see some I.D.

here."

The beanpole biker coughed a couple of times and pulled a laminated card out of a leather wallet on a chain. Hank glanced at the card, saw the name and address were phony. He took the information down and handed the card back to Leroy.

Leroy slouched and dug in his breast pocket and produced a single cigarette. Leroy dug again and came up with a kitchen match which he struck on his thumbnail. He lighted his cigarette, which slanted out of his mouth at a jaunty angle, and gusted smoke through his soup-straining fu-man-chu into Deputy Hank's face. *Getting that i.d. back made him cocky,* Hank thought. *He thinks he's getting off scot free.*

"It's lucky for you I'm late for an appointment. Otherwise I'd run you in."

"Yeah, tough break," Leroy said.

Hank got back in his cruiser and turned toward Osteen, leaving Leroy slouching on the side of the road smoking his cigarette.

Hank thought he was indeed fortunate. Now that he was heading back toward Daytona, he'd learned what he needed. He no longer had to keep Leroy under surveillance. And the man had led him out to this far flung area. Hank had a chore that needed tending hereabouts. He turned onto an asphalt road that followed a canal down to a subdivision on the swampy shores of a large lake. The yard trees were sabal palms and cypresses hung with moss. Hank flipped on the light bar as he turned into the driveway of a house with barred windows. He swaggered to the door. He hammered his fist against the panel.

Presently the door cracked and revealed two surprised eyes in an intellectual face, long and narrow. Perhaps the only pair of slacks being worn at that hour in the entire subdivision--even Hank had on drill shorts--clothed him. The upper body was covered by a white shirt buttoned to the collar. The man gave the impression of an intelligent farmer. "What can I do for you?" he asked cooly.

"Your security service requested officer assistance."

"The alarm's not even armed during the day," the man said.

Hank folded his hands as if in prayer and pressed the wedge of fingers into the crack in the door. He pushed his way into the house. "Close that door and rig the system," Hank ordered.

The man regarded the deputy for a moment then moved down the hallway into a brightly tiled room. To the right Hank could see what in most houses would be the living room. This room was fitted out as an office. The windows were draped, and the neon glow of an oversized monitor showed file cabinets and metal shelves with journals boxed in cutaway cardboard cartons. Hank sauntered into the brightly lighted kitchen. The light came from french doors which gave onto a patio deck. Through the french doors Hank could see a wooden dock snaked its way through cypress trees to the open lake.

Hank strode purposefully to the french doors. He removed a pistol with a very short barrel from his trouser pocket. The grip of the weapon was wrapped with rubber bands. He flicked the butt against a pane of glass, shards of glass arrayed into sunlight like slivers of diamond. A siren began to howl.

The man staggered. His eyes blinked. "The old man sent you," he said. "You're Deputy Smith."

"And you're William Arbuthnot. If you got the sense the good lord borned you with you'll get me a garbage bag and give me all your citrus canker files."

The telephone pulsed. "Don't you want me to get that?" Arbuthnot asked cooly. "It's the alarm company wanting the password."

9

Hank wagged his head from side to side.   T h e
phone ceased pulsing. Only the alarm wailed. But it was the
mild non-pulsing of the telephone that hung in the close,
white atmosphere of the kitchen like the knell of doom.
Arbuthnot's air of intellectual superiority collapsed. His
face drooped and seemed to wrinkle. Even his hair, an
aristocratic silver at the temples, seemed now completely
gray and wilted to rat-like tufts. "1,2-DCA is the stuff that
everyone can be sent to Old Sparky for--"

Hank laughed. "You're not going to have to worry
about it. Because you're going to be already dead."

"It's not fair. I do all the work and the old man
gets..." Arbuthnot turned and tried to run. The leather soles
of his wingtips scraped the terra-cotta tiles of the kitchen
floor. They slipped and he slid, losing his balance.

Hank frowned. He squeezed off a shot. It went
wide into a cabinet door--a mixing bowl exploded and flour
dust sifted into the air. Hank cursed.

Arbuthnot lay sprawled on the floor, his knees and
hands working furiously to get up. Hank padded up to the
prostrate, struggling form and pressed the snub barrel into
the grayish tufts of hair below Arbuthnot's wisdom knot. In
desperation, the tall thin man lurched, his arms flailing. The
.32 bucked in Hank's hand. Arbuthnot's wrenching motion
knocked the barrel askew. The slug tore a furrow in the
side of the scalp. Brains and blood exploded onto the wall--
and on to Hank's hand.

The little pistol bucked again. The slug opened a
hole the size of a pencil in Arbuthnot's back. The man was
poised on all fours, straining with the strength of
desperation. Sweat was beaded on the line of Hank's
mustache and his underarms were giving off a stink. The
pistol yipped. A hole opened in the white shirt, just above
the last now blood-streaking one. Arbuthnot collapsed onto
his face. Smith grunted and stepped forward and on bent

knee put the remaining four slugs into Arbuthnot's formerly so brilliant brain. He casually dropped the pistol next to the body.

He stood back and looked at the blood and gore on his hands. "Sweet Jesus's mother," he grunted and went to the sink and washed his hands with warm water and a dollop of liquid soap from the Dial dispenser. With his foot, he opened the cabinet door and discovered a roll of paper towels. He dried his hands on two panels of Scotty Fluffies, put the discarded towels in his pocket and looked with dismay at the mess on the floor. Flour and blood had formed a medium that partially recorded his footprints. He spooled off several more panels of towel, scraped the soles of his shoes clean. A box of Hefty garbage bags caught the deputy's eye. He peeled off four of them, closed the cabinet door, and went into the office, doubling the plastic bags on the way.

Two complete drawers bore the legend, "Citrus Canker." He rapidly transferred the files to the Hefty bags. Then removing the cards on the drawers, he sauntered to his prowl car, opened the trunk and deposited both bags. He slammed the lid and turned around to see a patrol car with the words "Village of Palmdale," stenciled on the doors glide up to within a foot of his bumper.

The car door swung open and a burly man in his twenties clad in black shorts, teeshirt and baseball cap emerged. The word "police" was written in white across the crown of the cap and the front of the shirt. "What's up?" he asked Hank, looking at the trunk of the sheriff's cruiser.

"Murder," Hank said.

"No shit," the tee-shirted cop said, no longer interested in the trunk of the deputy sheriff's car.

"I'd say murder one, from the looks of it. Whoever did that knew what he--or she--was doing." The local cop made sort of a gagging noise then charged toward the door of the house. "Hey," Hank called. "You mind getting your car out from in back of mine first? This here ain't my jurisdiction. I'll just mosey along and leave you with the glory of solving this here case."

The younger policeman was brought up short. He reversed into the street and waited as Hank calmly started up his car and backed onto the asphalt. As he passed the local cop, Hank pointed a finger and nodded. Then he promptly forgot all about the younger cop.

4

Bru, lugging his pile of file folders, followed the middle-aged man with silvered hair in a tuxedo into the main dining room of the Jardin d' Espirit, the most expensive and maybe even the best restaurant in Central Florida. The pile carpet was so deep snowshoes would have helped negotiate it. Dinner here had been his nominal boss Jerry's idea. The plan was to celebrate the Goins contract.

The waiter installed Bru at the most visible and best table in the room. In an ice palace devoted to preening and fantail display, the most obvious table was naturally the best. "Mr. Wiley," the maitre d' said, "asked us to present this to you."

A wine steward in a white dinner jacket unwrapped the towel to show a magnum of Krug champagne. The wine steward made to open the bottle. Bru held up his hand. "Wait until Jerry and Rhonda and my wife arrive."

"Mr. Wiley said you were going to say that. You don't have to drink it. But we have to open it." The steward unwound the wire wrap and extracted the cork with a gentle poof. He poured Bru a sip. Bru wasn't sure what wine etiquette required him to do, as Bru hadn't been served many two-hundred-dollar bottles of champagne. He murmured approval. The wine steward filled his glass and left.

Bru took a gulp of wine. Had it just been Bru's imagination that the mysterious assailant had thrust something through the back window? The only thing that he could have planted was a file folder. Bru opened the top folder which bowed a bit, as though stuffed against a man's side. The folder enclosed a copy of a scientific paper. A note at the top of the paper said: "Bruton--Check this out." The paper bore a weird title, "Genetically Altering the Citrus Canker." The author's name was William Arbuthnot.

Why was a paper on such a strange topic in old man Goins's 1,2--DCA files? Bru read the abstract of the paper. What this guy was trying to do was Nobel-prize-winning stuff. At the end Bru found a footnote thanking Dr. Humbert Khoury, an old prof of Bru, for his help. Dr. Khoury had won the Nobel prize in physiology in the mid eighties for work in this very field.

What the hell was going on here?

Bru drained the champagne glass and refilled it. He shook his head. Just nine months before Bru had lived a disgustingly normal existence. Back in those days Bru had felt bucking for tenure at the Seven Sisters clone he had taught at in Orlando gave his life an existential edge. God knew it was tough enough--at work there had always been demands for a little more than he could deliver. Then at home there'd been the usual family crises--such as when Bru was certain Leta was having an affair, which blew over with a blind eye turned.

Bru took another sip of wine and thought what a great, golden, now unattainable age that had been. And then suddenly their daughter Amber died. Suddenly the entire world tilted. Suddenly it didn't matter whether those payments were made or whether he were tenured. Or even that he'd been handed his walking papers at Lawson College--which he had been. He looked at his watch. Leta had hinted to Bru that she wanted to see him alone before Jerry and Rhonda arrived. *So where was she?* Ever since the unthinkable had happened, since Amber had died of the ear amoeba--an organism peculiar to Florida and usually contracted only by teenage boys swimming in shallow lakes--Leta had been a puzzle to him.

A burst of excitement brought Bru out of his reverie. Jerry and Leta had entered the dining room.

5

Jerry stopped at every second or third table to shake hands. The distinguished faces that drove those very expensive cars in the parking lot stirred to attention and beamed at Jerry, pleased that the most notorious defense attorney in Central Florida should stop to let some of the Marvin Belli--Racehorse Haynes--F. Lee Bailey luster wear off on them. Or perhaps those nice old faces--who Bru was sure had nicely functioning bowels because they resembled the folks in the laxative ads--preferred to think they were congratulating the defeated state attorney who had tried to hold the line against pornography.

Leta appeared to enjoy the attention too. Her perfectly round face, with those high Slavic cheekbones, radiated pleasure. It had been many a month since Leta had beamed. Finally, the triumphal party made its way to Bru's table. "Is it a yes or a no?" Jerry wanted to know.

"I guess it's a yes," Bru said. "Where's Rhonda?"

"So Goins went for the full six figures?" Jerry said.

"Only fifty thousand," Bru confessed.

"Hm," Jerry snorted. The wine steward filled glasses with bubbly.

Leta flew to Bru, pressed her cheek against his and made smooching noises. She was a fine-looking woman, one of those who grew better with age. Now in her late thirties her figure was as trim as ever, her dark blue eyes had grown even more mysterious, and she still had hair that was never mussed. That was one thing she shared with those early bird diners, the never-mussed hair of those born to money, although in Leta's case it came mostly from the fear of looking like the abused child of an alcoholic.

Leta moved between Bru and Jerry, actually a touch closer to Jerry. The head waiter handed her a glass of champagne. Jerry already had one. *The teetotaling Christian, drinking?* Bru raised an eyebrow.

"To that great philanthropist and humanitarian, Billy Goins," Jerry said.

"Here, here," Leta said.

They gulped the wine down and the waiter refilled the glasses.

"Armand, I'd like to order now." A liveried busboy arrived and began removing the formidable arsenal of eating utensils marking the fourth place at table. "Why don't we just ask the chef to surprise us? Jerry said and winked, "It's only forty-five dollars an entree."

"Where'd you say Rhonda is?" Bru asked. Jerry and Leta grinned an embarrassed smile at each other. Bru drained the glass and, not anxious to tackle the Rhonda situation, pressed a different question, "What do you know about Goins?"

"My firm has done some work for him. The old man has the reputation of being a cob." Then Jerry turned and patted Leta's hand. Bru wondered how he could have let himself get maneuvered into the corner he was in.

15

Jerry really seemed to have changed. In grad school days, Bru hadn't--as he'd told old man Goins earlier--really liked or respected Jerry even though he was Bru's rival for Leta. Back then Jerry was the kind of guy called "too clever by half." He came from some citrus and ranch town lost in the middle of the peninsula. His origins showed in his heavy country accent and his bent, despite his professed atheism, to frame any discussion in terms of the Bible and god, which he always pronounced "gawd" like a hick preacher. The fraternity hazing accident came like a gift out of the blue. Jerry disappeared. Bru and Leta started sleeping together, and shortly afterward they conceived Amber and married. They found jobs in Orlando. After a time, they learned Jerry had too. He seemed the same wily old Jerry. His slimeball clients earned acquittals at appallingly high rates. Then Jerry switched and ran for state attorney. He promised a morality crusade, once elected.

He delivered on that promise by closing down neighborhood video stores, and that brought Bru as president of Advocates for the First Amendment into the streets--and Jerry back into their lives. He turned the cheek by showing up one day at Bru's office at Lawson College. He understood exactly why Bru had to protest his censorship actions. As a lawyer and constitutional scholar, Jerry himself--or so he told Bru--had some doubts about his own censorship position. "It isn't always easy being a Christian," he'd told Bru. "I think my scruples are going to cost me this job."

Jerry lost the election. Bru and Leta didn't see how they could refuse going to a bowing-out party. Then had come the death of Amber, and Jerry and Rhonda just couldn't do enough for Bru and Leta. The service had been held in the Wiley family church. Later Leta had taken to attending services with the family, something Bru had never expected he could approve of, but given Leta's despondent state anything was a step up.

Next came Bru's dismissal from Lawson, and Jerry once again showed up in person in Bru's still-cramped and untidy office. He'd long since wanted to establish an ecological wing in his office, he'd told Bru. With Bru's excellent credentials, notably that Ph.D. in microbiology, he could do a job nobody else was capable of. By the end of the year, he'd be making more than he ever thought of at Lawson.

"When will Rhonda arrive?" Bru asked again.

"She won't be joining us," Jerry said.

"Why not?"

"We'll get to that in a minute, but right now let me see the contract," Jerry said.

"Would I be asking anyone to violate a professional confidence to let me in on what is wanted here?" Leta asked.

"Of course not, dear," Jerry said, looking to Bru.

"Have you noticed that most concentrated orange juice--either already reconstituted or frozen--now comes in plastic containers?" Bru said.

"Sure," Leta said.

"Some kooks have started a campaign against those new containers, claiming they have high concentrations of 1,2--DCA and that those concentrations are causing the so-called KiDS epidemic sweeping the nation."

"One of the students in my school came down with what her parents were claiming was KiDS," Leta said. "The school nurse just laughed. She says 'KiDS' stands for nothing and was made up by media hype artists drumming up a story."

"In a nutshell that's what Goins claims too. He hired me to disprove those rumors," Bru said.

"How'd he expect you to do that?" Leta asked.

"By having tests run on the 1,2--DCA content in the plastic containers and researching the toxicity of 1,2--DCA.

17

Its full scientific name is 1,2-Dicitrolaminealdehyde. Evidently the lunatic fringe fastened onto it as a bad boy because of 'aldehyde' suffix. He claims the suggestion of formaldehyde gets them going."

"So why do you seem down in the mouth about this deal?" Jerry asked.

"How about because on my way out the door, the old man dropped his wooden leg and a pistol flopped out."

Leta giggled. "Get serious," Jerry said.

"I am dead serious," Bru said. "How about because the old guy wouldn't tell me why he wanted the report written."

"Why he wants the report is his business," Jerry said. "You don't have to defend murders for a living to know that."

"All right, well how about because he didn't give me a contract," Bru said. "More importantly, Goins didn't fork over any up-front money. He was pretty cheesy about it too--claiming he wasn't feeling good and letting that leg drop and having me escorted out fast. I figure the lab work could come to almost fifty thousand bucks. Does he really expect me to put that on my credit card while I'm waiting for him to pay up?" Then Bru told them about the enormous bonus--if he produced the results Goins wanted.

"You're right. That doesn't sound good," Jerry said.

Bru related the particulars of the motorcycle attack and the mysterious appearance of a paper on a citrus disease.

"Jesus," Jerry said. "My brother lost his farm on account of the citrus canker. All you need is one irregularity to walk away from a deal. Already, you've turned up a bundle. So the deal is off."

"No," Bru said, "the deal is on. I'm going to do it."

Jerry looked at Bru quizzically. "You mind explaining that."

Bru shrugged. "It's what's on the docket. You got to do the work you got." Actually, Bru had two reasons, neither of which he felt like blurting out to Jerry right now. For one, he had a gut instinct--or a hope--that if there was a connection between the biker's attack and the Goins' contract, there might also be a link between this Goins' deal and Bru's being turned out of his job at Lawson, remote as that might seem. The other reason had to do with curiosity, the kind that killed the cat. If he took the job, and got more or less financially on his feet, he suspected a big change would occur in his life, one that would occur soon, very soon, like immediately.

"All right," Jerry said, "I'll get on the horn tomorrow and tell the old fucker to send us a contract and a check if he wants that report. In the meantime you just sit on your hands. No money--no movement. And for a dead certainty, stay away from that citrus canker thing. If someone wants you to be their cats paw, they are going to have to pay for it--up front, the same as Old Man Goins. What were the stipulations you discussed with Goins?"

Bru repeated what he'd already told Jerry adding that Goins insisted the final draft had to be over two hundred twenty-five pages and less than three hundred. Also it had to be finished in a month.

"I'll see if I can't get more money on the barrel head. You say lab costs will run up to forty or fifty thousand. You ought to get that much for yourself as well. I'll ask for one-fifty. Maybe he'll come across with seventy-five or eighty thousand." Jerry looked up from the napkin he was jotting notes on.

Then, as if on cue, both Jerry and Leta turned to Bru. Neither looked happy. "Rupert, Leta has something to tell you."

Bru looked at Leta expectantly, almost as if he hoped for good tidings.

19

Leta laughed nervously. "I need some space, Bru."

A waiter butted into Leta and Bru's conversation. Bru hoped he had misunderstood--never minding that he'd known, more or less, the blow was coming. "Space, like moving out?"

"Exactly like that, honey."

"What about Jerry?" Bru asked. "Does he need some space too?"

Jerry looked more shamefaced than even the best courtroom lawyer-actor. "I thought it was all over between Leta and me," Jerry said. "I was certain no force on earth could make me abuse my family. I will accept eternal damnation rather than forego Leta." Jerry was staring at his soup bowl.

Bru wondered if maybe there was something better in his bowl. He looked. Nope, just limp onions and greasy croutons. "Is that the way you feel too?" Bru asked Leta.

"We had seventeen very good years, Bru. I'll always love you, and you will always be my husband in a way no man can ever replace. Please don't try to cling to something that is no longer possible."

"There's no reason you can't continue working out of my office," Jerry said.

Work out of his office? In his mind's eye Bru saw himself stalk to his car, storm to the home he and Leta shared in Winter Park and retrieve the M15 General Westmoreland had presented to Bru's father on retirement. Bru was to carry it after he graduated from the slot at West Point Westy had secured for him. But he hadn't gone to West Point. So he'd inherited it after his father had died. He saw himself leveling on Wiley's chest then turning to Leta. Bru drew himself up with a painful grimace. He could not shoot Leta--Amber's mother--even in a daydream. For as downcast as her announcement made him, for just an instant before he became fully aware of the cost, Bru had been happy for her. Bru picked up his spoon and lapped at the soup. Bru attacked it as though he hadn't eaten in a month.

The waiter cleared the soup dishes and Bru thought, It's time to leave. He twisted in the chair. Pushing himself out seemed to require more energy than he had available. The waiter returned with the next course, four freshwater crayfish with a drawn butter sauce.

The main course arrived. The group ate in silence, except when Bru asked for a second glass of wine from the bottle of red at Jerry's elbow. In an odd way, Bru derived some comfort sitting with Leta and Jerry at that moment. After all, they were the closest friends he had.

6

When Billy Goins heard the knuckles rap against his study door, he shoved the copy of *Fortune 's* list of the World's 200 Richest under the untidy mess of papers on his desk. The door pushed open and he groaned, "Oh, shit."

Elizabeth's face registered hurt. At the same time she assumed the stoic air of an unduly put-upon but loving daughter. That look earned an "Oh, fuck." Billy liked it a lot better when they both admitted flat out that they flat out couldn't stand each other.

"Kimberly is waiting at table," Elizabeth said, giving her special bright, chipper look. "We're going to try to live like a family--a happy family." Billy took in the business suit, black skirt and jacket, and snorted. Her blouse with just the faintest trace of a ruffle was buttoned modestly at the throat as though she wouldn't just as soon be running around with her tits hanging out.. A liberal pasting of face powder had all but dusted away worry lines around her eyes and mouth. An expression of overwhelming concern and solicitude suffused through her face.

"Is Joo-an there too?"

"Yes," Elizabeth said icily. "Juan, your little majordomo, is there too. Let me give you a hand, father."

Billy clambered to his feet--or rather foot as he had only one real one and an artificial limb. Elizabeth glided forward and put her arm around his waist. "I'm not a cripple," he snarled.

Kimberly sat at Billy's right, Juan to his left. Elizabeth occupied a chair, not at the foot of the table, but next to Juan.

"Good evening, grandpa," Kimberly said with a Colgate grin.

Billy grinned back at her. Any time Kimberly was nearby he was pleased. How could anything that sweet and beautiful have issued from his body--even at the remove of one generation--especially via that whore of a mother. The old man very badly wanted to bend over and touch Kim's hand and pull her to him and kiss her. He would have liked to have stroked her long, blonde shepherd's-crook tresses. He settled for, "Hi, snookums."

"Thank you, Heavenly Father, for blessing the world with--" His heart strained to say Kimberly, but some restraint deep in his bowels wouldn't allow him. He ended with, "the Free Enterprise system."

"Help the plates, please, Father."

Billy spooned black-eyed peas and sausage from the Limoges bowl onto the Spode china plate Kim handed him. Next to that he put a dollop of mustard greens--canned, not fresh--and garnished with sidemeat, not sugar or vinegar. "Grab a hunk of cornbread, dear," Billy said to Kimberly.

He fixed his plate and then, leaving the others to shift for themselves, put his elbow on the table with hand on neck and tucked into his food. When he finished, he asked, "Do you want dessert, honey?"

"No, grandpa. Can I go study?"

"Of course, dear." The old man pressed his finger to his cheek. Kim rose and kissed the spot. "'Night, grandpa." She turned and made for the door. Just before leaving the room, she added, "'Night, Juan, Mother."

"She's really going to watch television," Elizabeth said. "I saw her looking at her watch."

"She'll never have to pick up another book as long as she lives," Billy said.

"That won't make any difference to that one," Juan put in. "She has something between her ears. She's a chip off the Goins block."

Billy noticed Elizabeth's lady-of-the-big-house manner crumble. She rolled her eyes at the ceiling.

Like a dagger in the heart, Billy thought. *It's those closest to you that are most likely to hurt you.* That's why he never let anyone get close to him, not since Liz's mother, and of course Kim, but Kim didn't count.   Juan, that buttoned-down and buttoned-up anal twerp, was the closest thing to a robot possible to find. He had made a mistake letting Liz--or Elizabeth as she featured herself nowadays-- come back, one of the few such mistakes he'd ever made, although in her case he'd made the mistake over and over. She was making like the perfect homemaker, clearing the table, her face showing concentration and forbearance. Suddenly she became aware of Billy's stare. She set the plates aside and smiled nervously, folding and unfolding her hands in her lap.

Billy banged his fist against the table. "One of you two is fucking with me. And I don't like it."

"Whatever could you be talking about, Father, dear?" Elizabeth asked, eyes agog.

So's it's her, Billy thought, going on the first-hen-that-cackled theory.

"You know damn well what I'm talking about. I mean that letter you or your boyfriend sent me about the citrus canker. I guess you all think I'm going to go all spongy at the knees if someone just mentions that little adventure."

"I declare, Father, you are speaking gibberish."

"We did pretty well in grove land back in the eighties. Maybe I should have just left the citrus scams at that. But I didn't, and you are all going to have to live with it."

Billy had the perception he was talking too much-- telling too much. Not the sort of thing he usually did. He was notorious for keeping his lip buttoned. But it wasn't every day that those nearest and/or dearest tried to gouge him.

He cast an auger-eye at Juan. The little faggot smiled primly and blinked his eyes rapidly. *Jesus, could he be the one behind this squeeze?* Billy didn't really believe that possible. But the butter-wouldn't-melt look on Juan's acned face seemed too studied.

Juan had grown up dirt poor in a dirt hut in the Zacapa desert in Guatemala. As soon as he was old enough, Billy's spies had learned, he stowed away on a banana boat. He jumped ship in New Orleans without a word of English to his name. He got a job in a hotel Goins owned and stayed at occasionally. There he caught Billy's attention.

Juan had begged to be allowed to be Billy's houseboy. He went to night school. Billy had smiled at his See-Dick-and-Jane-Run books and the simple bookkeeping texts. The poor bastard hadn't a chance of really making anything of himself, Billy had thought.

It took him more than a decade, but Juan had mastered English--well enough that he began calling himself

24

Joo-an and was able to puzzle just about everyone as to his origins. Likewise, he showed exemplary business acumen. Twice, Billy had offered to set him up as a senior vice president of one of his corporations with the understanding he would become CEO shortly, but each time Juan had refused. He wanted only to stay at Billy's side. When his homeland became a real democracy with no death squads, he would go back to Zacapa and be the richest man in town. That's all he wanted. And Billy believed him. He could have had so much more, so many times, and he'd refused.

Elizabeth--or rather the asshole she hung out with-- was behind that extortion plot. To look at her she seemed the proper southern lady. But that was just the money he wasted sending her to those finishing schools.

"Tell us, Father, exactly what has you so upset," Elizabeth said.

"I got a letter, made from words cut out of the newspaper, saying I was behind the citrus canker scare in the eighties."

"What is the citrus canker, for goodness sake?" Elizabeth said.

"An armed intruder killed William Arbuthnot, the author of that scam this afternoon," Billy said. He scrutinized Juan and Elizabeth closely. He wanted to see which one would betray pleasure that he had confessed to implication in a crime. Neither showed undue interest.

"I declare, Father," Elizabeth exclaimed.

"If you fuck with the bull, you get the horn," Billy warned.

"But what had this Arbuthnot person done to you, Father?"

"Arbuthnot is not important. I've taken precautions in this orange juice affair. The report of that fellow Bruton will deflect suspicions long enough to get all the pieces in place."

25

"You are not making any sense whatsoever, Father?"

"Oh, yes, I am. And if things really get out of hand, I will give them Bruton's head on a platter. It was no accident that he was turned out of his job. The president of Lawson College received one million dollars for his endowment fund. Shortly afterwards our friend Bruton, found himself unemployed. This guy's daughter had died a few months before, and he hasn't quite got over all that. He's dazed and confused, which makes him an even better candidate for my plans."

Elizabeth pushed her chair back from table. "May I have permission to leave the room?"

She waited as though to be excused. But Billy knew what she was really waiting for. The punchline. To find out how he had framed Bruton. "Last fall right after Newcombe and I struck up that agreement, I had Bruton hired on as a consultant at the Port Saint Joe Plastic Works. Newcombe thoughtfully provided Bruton's social security number, facsimile of signature and other information. We paid him very good money to spike the plastic works with 1,2--DCA. I also took the trouble to use this information to open a commodities account for Mr. Bruton at a brokerage firm. At this moment, he is the proud possessor of one million dollars in orange juice futures. If the price of o.j. goes up to where I expect it will go on the spot market, those contracts will be worth somewhere between fifty and one hundred million dollars. Although he will be very rich, I'm afraid Mister Doctor Bruton will have a great deal of explaining to do--from his jail cell."

Elizabeth circled the table and kissed her father. "You have such a dear sense of humor," she said, "although I must admit I don't quite understand what you're talking about. If you don't mind, I'll finish clearing the table."

Billy Goins erupted in laughter. His sides shook. He put his hands on his ribs. It was the first good cleansing laugh he'd had in a long time. "Are you trying to pretend you didn't call Bruton in and have a discussion with him this afternoon, claiming you had a class with him at the University of Florida."

"I did, Father. I had a frightful crush on him."

Billy snorted. Elizabeth was a piece of shit. But she had one talent and that was getting around men. He'd never known anyone she'd not been able to have her way with, and that included himself. He shook his head thinking of the times he'd allowed her to weasel her way back into his good graces. "I don't want to hear you're fucking with Bruton, Elizabeth. Stay away from him."

"Father, please. I just happened to notice his name was on your appointments calendar. It was a simple coincidence."

"I've made a fortune by not believing in coincidences. And you'd better hope you are not trying to use him to shake me down, because you might end up in the frame with him. Nobody, but nobody, can beat a guy with three billion dollars in the legal system in this country, especially an out-of-favor daughter without a nickel to her name. Think about that!"

Billy stopped talking. His palms were sweaty. He was wet under his arms and on his forehead. But this project was his crowning achievement. "By this time next year, I'm going to--" Billy's breath caught. It was his dream of dreams. "One year from today, I will have cornered the world's orange juice market."

"Oh, Father, you make me so proud."

"Don't give me that shit. One of you two is trying to fuck me up. And it's not going to work. If I don't have my way with o.j., I'll be dead broke and you will go down the tubes with me."

7

After Elizabeth left her still cussing father, she beat a hasty and by no means prim retreat to her landward-side room.

Once behind the door of the former maid's quarters, she shot the bolt. Like a snake shucking its skin, she shed the jacket of the suit she'd been imprisoned in all day. The garment sailed onto the floor. She wriggled out of her skirt and kicked it on top of the jacket. A toss of each foot sent her clumsy pumps onto the pile. Then off came her slip, camisole, bra and pantyhose.

She regarded her nude reflection in the mirror above the vanity. She decided she still looked overdressed with her formal up-put hair. She pulled a bobby pin out of her coiffure, threw the pin at the tin on the dresser, fished for another. First, she had to remove that pancake makeup from her face and get the window air conditioner going.

It was hell living in this climate without real air conditioning--the old man was too cheap to put central air in the place. She hit the button, and the machine thumped, then groaned, to life. Elizabeth smeared cream from a pot onto her face. She found a pack of cigarettes, shook one out, lipped it, and lighted up. Now the figure in the mirror looked more like herself.

Elizabeth twisted her body. Her feet faced the vanity but her torso showed in three-quarter profile. One huge breast peeked out from around her shoulder. The aureole was as large as a pasty, but the nipple was relaxed. She moistened her finger and teased the nipple. It sprung erect, poking out a plump full inch. Elizabeth enjoyed that view-- her face mucked up with cold cream, cigarette dangling from lips, and to top it off, a tasteful little tattoo just below the shoulder. The tattoo resembled a rose. A closer look showed it was a stylized image of a jam jar in the guise of a grandmother with the initials f.j. tatooed inside.

A gentle rap at the door. *Shit. Fuck.*

Elizabeth cranked the window open and jettisoned the burning cigarette. She pulled on a kimono. "Who is it?"

"Kim."

So much for the panic attack. Just her pasty-faced little brat. "In a minute." Elizabeth waited two minutes then unbolted the door. No luck. Kim was still there, looking pouty and out of sorts.

"I spied Leroy on a motorcycle on the beach today. He had on a helmet with horns on it."

"Couldn't be. He's in California. I haven't heard from him in months--years."

"It was him, mom."

"You stay away from that guy," Elizabeth lashed out. "He's mine and I don't want you stealing him out from under my nose like you have all the rest of them. This afternoon you had your cap set for that Bruton guy."

Tears welled in Kimberly's eyes. A drop, like a pearl, oozed over the dam and slowly slipper-slid down her cheek. "What are you talking about, mother?"

"You know what I'm talking about, you little bitch. Go away."

Elizabeth removed the rest of the bobby pins and began to viciously brush the spray from her hair. "Little snookums" was even better than Elizabeth. Unlike her father, Elizabeth knew of her own failures with men, but she had never known her daughter not to score a sureshot-- almost always on the guys Elizabeth had marked out for herself. After a time, Elizabeth quit stroking her hair and observed the effect in the mirror. Her hair hung in sexy tangles over her shoulders. Even better, she saw Kim slouch toward the door, as though expecting to be called back.

Never happen, Elizabeth thought. She closed and bolted the door. She put her face on, lots of eyeliner and Estee Lauder kohl mascara, and a shit brown lipstick to match the shit brown nails. Next went on the choker collar, black leather halter, and garter belt. She attached the fishnet stockings and squirmed into the black leather hot pants. She pulled on a pair of high-heeled black leather boots and her fringed black leather jacket, and she was all set.

The outfit didn't go so well with the two-door Chevy sedan she backed out of the basement garage, but some things couldn't be helped. The Chevy was the only wheels available as her skinflint father wouldn't provide a decent car. Now to get out of the dump.

Her father spent tens of thousands on the high-tech gadgetry, but the security people were minimum wage flunkies. The guard at the booth on the street, a youth in a Sam Browne belt with a toothpick in his mouth, pretended he couldn't let her out. "The chief's around for some reason."

Elizabeth flashed him some tit and pursed her lips in a sexy promise that both knew would never be redeemed. The electric gate creaked open. She had to park a half-mile away from the Boot Hill Saloon on Main Street, the epicenter of Bike Week festivities. Rendevousing there was dumb--it'd been Leroy's idea. On the street, bodies were eyeball to asshole, and a canopied outside bar had been set up, which was thronged. Inside the Boot, booths were packed and the bar stools were occupied, but there was wiggle room on what in any other dive might have been called the dance floor. There was just one problem. No Leroy.

In a lean-to off to the side of the bar a clot of

bruisers in leather caps and studded belts stood around a pool table holding an extension cord with two naked wires. A guy plugged the cord into his mouth. His eyes jerked, his body convulsed and he collapsed onto the floor. He flopped and wiggled. There came the smell of singed hair and charred flesh. A second guy in black leather retrieved the wire and stuck it into his mouth. His large frame buckled. He staggered, then regained his full stature. He shook his head and said, "Wow, man. What a high!" He collapsed and writhed on the floor.

Where was Leroy? She rushed to the Chevy, fighting panic, cruised up to Ormond, checked out the Iron Horse Saloon--nada. Next she I-95ed down to Edgewater and Earthquake Magoon's. No Leroy. Verging on hysteria, she pointed the lumbering Chevy down Park Avenue and then around Glencoe Road to the trailer park. Leroy's bike was parked out in front of his ramshackle cottage. The lights were off. The front door was locked.

Elizabeth reached under the seat and retrieved her scabbard knife. She tucked the leather scabbard in the waistband of her hot pants and made her way to the window. She put her ear to the crack and listened. You never knew who or what might be inside. She heard a rasping, irregular noise. Snoring. The sleep was not restful.

With the blade of the knife, Elizabeth probed the window sill, found a catch, worried it a bit, and bingo. Early doctrine formulated by the primo guru, Charley, held you should go in unarmed. In fact, Charley had sent his girls, Squeaky Fromme, Leslie Van Houten, and others of the immortal but now incarcerated first brigade, in through the front door in broad daylight. They'd enjoyed the passivity with which most homeowners greeted their boldness, as they helped themselves to valuables and cash-- usually stopping by the refrigerator for an eat-as-you- burgled snack. But that had been back in the sixties, before every jerk armed himself to the teeth. Following the procedure Leroy had drilled into her, she ducked over the window sill with the knife in her hand. Once inside the room, she stopped and crouched motionless by the wall. She listened.

She heard the labored suspiration of breath being pulled in and sucked out of a body. She groped the wall, found the light switch, and flicked it up. Leroy's wasted body slanted across the bed, his emaciated chest expanding enormously then collapsing to nothing with each wheezing breath. He had laid out his pharmacy on the table. A hypodermic syringe, two vials of pills, a teaspoon, a plastic baggie and a propane lighter. A pint of liquor was clenched between his legs.

Elizabeth frowned. The man could remember to shoot up and pop pills like clockwork. But he couldn't maintain the simple schedule to make the drug cocktail with the protease inhibitors and other AIDS drugs work. Elizabeth shook her head. The thalidomide--another drug he could remember to take because he liked the laid-back tranquilizing effect it had--was stopping the dreadful wasting away, at least for now.

She went to the table, picked up the vial, shook two of the capsules into her hand. Red with white stripes. She chucked them into the back of her mouth, extracted the liquor bottle from Leroy's thighs and knocked back a shot. She winced, remembering liquor wasn't the best pill chaser. She curled up next to him on the sprung and lumpy mattress.

Her anxieties began to go away. She took in Leroy's naked, almost hollow chest. She ran her fingers in the nest of hair between his nipples and admired his tattoo, same as hers, the old lady in the shape of a jam pot just above his heart. Her hand dropped to his belly. Leroy was the man who saved her from the man who saved her from that Miss

Gregg's Finishing School in Greenville, South Carolina. That had been a long time ago--a coon's age ago, considering the kind of lifestyle they had led. Her hand shot across his belly and below the belt line into his crotch. She got him in hand and worked his crank. It began to stir. She could feel that characteristic bend--Leroy had gotten moderately famous for his crooked erection. Some of the girls in the family claimed it made him a great fuck. Elizabeth supposed she shouldn't be fooling with his prick unless she had a rubber handy.

"Whatever you're doing, don't stop," he ordered. He pulled the bottle from his crotch, took a snort and tilted it above her lips. Elizabeth was feeling mellow. She needed to get laid. He fingered her crotch. She unbelted and unzipped him. He wasn't hard enough to get in. He pointed at his crotch and then at her mouth. He shook some pills from the vial into his mouth and swallowed. He rattled the vial in her face. If she didn't get him in her and get off, he might pass out again.

Suddenly she had another thought. "Hey, did you get our message delivered?"

"Yeah, I covered your fuck up on that."

"Bruton wouldn't let those files out of his hands," she said.

"The close shave came when a bunch of bikers chased me down. They just about had me when I was saved by, guess what, a deputy sheriff."

Elizabeth could hear her heart thumping in her chest. "Did he issue you a summons?"

"Nah. With a half million bikers around, you can get away with murder. How'd the old man react to that letter I sent him?"

"He called the little queer and me in and bragged about how he wasn't afraid of the citrus canker anymore, because he'd had the guy who did all the damage killed."

"Yeah, sure," Leroy said.

"Then he bragged he had Bruton fired by Lawson College."

"That's a good one, that he got Bruton fired. He doesn't have a clue that we were way ahead of him on that one."

Elizabeth wished she understood what that plan was, exactly, so she could carry it out in case--in case Leroy was unable to. Elizabeth loved Leroy. But she wondered if he was going to fuck this deal up for them. Did he have what it took to stand up to her father? "Explain to me again how you think you're going to get Bruton to do things my father can't?"

"Just keep doing what you're doing there, babe. That feels so goo . . ." His head fell back. He resumed a sonorous honking.

8

Car lights projected on the wall of Bru's bedroom and a moment later the *Sentinel* slapped onto the driveway. Bru hadn't slept a wink. He got up, dressed, and stepped into his study and booted up his computer. He clicked into the newspaper archives and did a keyword search for KiDS. He got about two dozen hits. According to the most recent article, medical doctors were confused by the symptoms-- nausea, stiff neck, alternating fever with chills--striking youngsters around the country. None of the scientists was willing to claim a connection between the cases. The article concluded by saying the death total for KiDS-like symptoms was fifty-five, all children under thirteen. Bru winced.

Then Bru did a keyword search on 1,2-DCA. This

time he had no hits. He went into the kitchen, made a pot of coffee and opened the paper to the classifieds. He went down the "apartments--furnished" column. Suddenly, Bru remembered the reason that cop who stopped on the highway yesterday looked familiar. He was Deputy Smith. Smith had gotten himself locally famous for popping off two people supposedly in the line of duty. The first was a father who had taken his daughter hostage with a plastic knife. The second was a middle-aged manic/depressive who had gone off his medication. Some members of the Advocates of the First Amendment had wanted to protest the second shooting.

Then abruptly Bru's mind flew back to the time he'd been a high school dropout crewing for a Keys lobsterman. His woman then was Ileana, and she was the only woman he had ever really loved in a full physical sense. She had a spray of black hair that hung in tight curls halfway down her back. Her nipples and lips were the color of eggplant. To keep her in cigarettes, beer and grass with the occasional line of coke, Bru had sometimes helped friends bring in a haul of square grouper--bales of marijuana. Life had been easy and cheap, if not exactly free.

Then Etienne had appeared. A Haitian with a missing tooth, no English (or Spanish) and b.o. that could shame a gorilla. She'd begun to grow vague and abstract. No, it wasn't Bru, she'd assure him. Then he'd discovered the funny pipe. She'd began losing weight, quit her job, and moved north to the ghetto of farm labor shacks Etienne ran in Florida City. One day a friend had told Bru she was peddling her butt in Homestead. Bru'd found her strolling along US 1 in a halter top and day-glow hotpants. He'd begged her to get in the car. She'd laughed. He'd offered her money which she took and insisted he take her to Etienne, whom she called her *conexion*. Bru'd raced up the Turnpike to his father's house off Miller Road in the

Kendall section of Miami, retrieved the M15 general officers pistol Westy had presented his father on retirement. Back to the collection of shotgun shacks he'd gone. He'd found Etienne loafing at the curb. "I sent yo woman back to work," he'd yukked as Bru leveled the service revolver on his heart and squeezed off one shot. A geyser of blood had leapt out at Bru. Etienne's bony body'd slammed against a light pole with a metallic clang and slid to the ground, his heart gushing lifeblood, his face going pasty and gray. A black woman standing by had run up, spit in Etienne's face and said, "Go now. Before the po-lice come."

He'd retrieved Ileana and taken her to his room, where they shacked (and she mainlined junk) while waiting for the police to arrive. The police didn't come. After a while, Ileana'd drifted away and Bru got his act together. He'd finished high school in a night program at Miami-Dade Community College and enrolled at the University of Miami. He hadn't gone out with another woman until he met Leta when he was in graduate school at Gainesville. Years went by. He'd heard a rumor that Ileana had died of AIDS. He didn't like the AIDS part, but he had to confess a distinct relief in learning the only person with direct knowledge of his great crime was out of the way. He had escaped that folly unscathed.

Or had he?

Abruptly, he scurried into the garage and poked through the crawl-space hole in the ceiling. He got down his old foot locker and the boxes his computer had come in. He emptied his dresser drawers into the trunk and put in the divider tray and dumped his toilet articles into it. Then he got some garbage bags and bagged up his suit and sport jackets and slacks. He went into the main part of the house and disconnected Leta's fax-answering machine and his computer and drove to the first circled ad.

The West Indian landlady showed Bru a converted

up and down stairs garage apartment. Bru gave Salome, the landlady, a check for $750--five hundred for the first month and two-fifty deposit, and she went happily off to work, leaving him in her kitchen to make phone calls to the utility companies. Then he dialed Michaelson Labs located in Minneapolis. Michaelson didn't pick up. Bru looked at his watch--it was a few minutes before nine, eight Central Time. He waited five minutes and called again. Bru told the agent, Connie who he had dealt with before, he was considering having every brand of concentrated orange juice container-- frozen or reconstituted--in the Twin Cities tested for 1,2-- DCA. When he said he needed the job completed as soon as possible, the price doubled. Bru told her he might call back later in the day and authorize the tests, depending on whether the job was officially let to him.

Then Bru, taking Goins's file folders with him, drove through the City Beautiful as Orlando liked to style itself-- past lakes and green swards--until he arrived at the parking lot of Lawson College's main library. Was he just being paranoid. Or did all the dots connect? If they did, old Nuke'em Newcombe would want to have a chat with him, once his presence on campus was known.

When Bru passed through the electronic security uprights, he saw the very person he was looking for, Miss Tibbs, the hair-netted head reference librarian. Bru made straight for her.

Miss Tibbs gave Bru a sour old maid's smile. "What do you want?" she asked, her nose going like a rabbit. Bru could see she could hardly wait to report his presence on campus.

"To do some research on the citrus canker."

Miss Tibbs sniffed. "We are a liberal arts library."

Bru checked out Miss Tibbs' partner on the reference desk. She was tatting away on a keyboard. She was absolutely outrageous--a Texan, tall and lanky with blonde hair that shot out everywhere. She wore blue jeans that looked as though they'd been painted on her body.

Melba T. Appleyard didn't fit in at Lawson College, a school that prided itself on the fact that most of its student body, which was about 65% female, had been rejected by Seven Sister colleges up East. For this reason alone Bru would have liked Melba. But he had an even better reason for liking her. She was the only librarian he'd ever known that had the nerve to break a rule. He wondered why she didn't look up and said hi. One of Melba's long, strong Texas fingers hit a key and the printer attached to her computer began to grind to work. A sheet of paper scrolled out the top. Once it stopped, she ripped it off and shot out of her chair and marched off toward the microfilm machines.

"Sorry, Dr. Bruton, I don't think we can help you. But if you want I'll ask the library director if you can have library privileges."

"That's all right, Miss Tibbs. I'll just go find myself a library carrel and work on my notes."

"If you think that's appropriate."

Bru wrinkled his nose at Miss Tibbs and stalked to the stacks. He found a carrel and opened up folder number one. Bru had disposed of about an inch of the stack of folders, finding nothing of interest, when a head of teased blonde hair thrust above the carrel. "Psst, Bru," Melba said in a stage whisper, "I have something for you." She offered a sheaf of papers. "These are the Newsbank articles on citrus canker we have on hand."

"Why didn't you say hi to me at the desk?"

"I didn't want to give Miss Tibbs the pleasure."

Melba had served on a committee Bru had chaired the past semester and they had gotten on very chummily. But Bru had been married and Melba had some boyfriend out in Texas. Talking with Melba brought an odd feeling over Bru. He'd thought he'd come to Lawson to stir things up. But he realized he'd come to campus--just as much--to seek out Melba's company. Beating a path to Melba's doorstep the day after he learned of Leta's defection made Bru feel cheap. After all, so far as he was concerned, he was still married, wasn't he?

"Is there anything I can do for you, Bru?"

"As a matter of fact there is," Bru said. He told her the things he'd liked researched, Goins, Arbuthnot, 1-2 DCA.

"Is there anything else I can do for you, Bru. I'm talking outside the research realm." Her breasts thrust over the top of the three-quarter partition. Her narrowed but square cowboy-booted toes poked under the bottom.

Bru supposed he'd have to break the tie binding him to Leta sooner or later. Should he ask Melba to help him with that? *What was he saying?* He didn't even like Melba's looks, not really. She was too tall, way over five-ten and too big--almost too threatening as a woman. He thought of her as just a friend. Bru needed someone small and comforting like Leta.

"I clipped my business card to the top of the stack-- in case you need any more help," Melba offered.

"I'm married," Bru said instinctively.

"I'm not," Melba said and laughed and turned and sauntered away. The carrel wall blocked the view of her hips twitching in the skin-tight jeans. Bru sprang bolt upright and, sure enough, before she disappeared around a corner of the stacks of books, he saw her rear end--high riding and sharply cut as though by tin snips--flexing, twitching one way then the other, straining against the heavy denim. Now Bru understood why she favored jeans. A less durable fabric would not have been able to rein in those enormous sensual hips of hers.

9

A head looming over the carrel intruded into Bru's thoughts. Bru looked up and saw a round Irish face with a drinker's stoplight nose. A baseball cap covered the head. A white shirt with the patches like scout badges were sewed to the shoulders. Hidden behind the carrel wall was the enormous paunch that shirt was constrained to hide. It was Chief Cronin, head of Lawson security. "What's up, chief?" Bru asked.

"You are wanted by Prince Charming. Pronto. Get your shit together and let's skedaddle."

Prince Charming was the chief's code name for President Newcombe. "I'm glad to see you," the chief said as they trudged across the Lawson campus. The chief carried Bru's files. He'd insisted. "We miss you around here, Bru."

There was no waiting to get into the president's office. As soon as the chief and Bru appeared, Eva, his personal secretary, picked up the phone and the heavy oak executive model door blasted open. There stood, Dr. Wilmer Newcombe in all his five-feet-nine-inch splendor.

Newcombe was a sallow-complexioned man of middling height who appeared tall because of his cadaverous build. In keeping with his funeral manner he had washed-out blond or gray hair--it was hard to tell which--combed into a pompadour. A birthmark, like the thumbprint of Cain, streaked in an angry whorl under his right eye and bled into the dark sunken patches that halfmooned each eye. His manner was suave in a smarmy, folksy way that presidents of rural colleges cultivate. Strangers and those any way above him universally regarded him as a very nice man but perhaps not stout enough for a job as demanding as his. To his subordinates, he was an absolute tyrant. In short, he had the perfect asskisser's temperament.

President Newcombe rushed across the plush carpeting to Bru. "Rupert, it's so good to see you," he said, grabbing Bru's hand and pumping. He wrapped his arm around Bru's shoulders and escorted him into the inner sanctum.

Newcombe led Bru to the leather divan. "Would you like something to drink? A cup of coffee? Or a coke?"

Bru deferred. Newcombe insisted. He pressed a lever on the desk. "Eva, bring us two cappuchinos, please. Decaf, of course." Newcombe was the only guy Bru knew who still used an intercom. He suspected he did it because pushing a button and barking orders made him feel like he was in command.

"How's the wife--Leta?" Bru could see Newcombe was pleased with himself for remembering Leta's name.

"She's fine, just fine." Which was true, Bru thought, she was fine. It just happened she wasn't with Bru anymore.

"And the daughter, Amber--oh, how could I have made such a blunder?"

Bru could see that Newcombe really had stumbled and that he felt remorse. Bru saw it flicker across his face-- for about the duration of a lightning bolt, a very small lightning bolt. Bru shrugged. "It's all right. That happens all the time."

"I'm sorry, Bru. That was very insensitive of me. I couldn't make the funeral, of course. I was out of town, but my wife was there," he said, then added, "I believe."

Bru remembered the deans coming, and all the members of the faculty, and Chief Cronin and most of the security people and the janitorial staff. All the librarians were there including Melba T. Appleyard, a woman he hadn't even met at the time, but he didn't remember any Newcombe, male or female.

"Oh, that's okay too. It happened a long time ago." This time, however, Bru's voice had a flat tone that indicated it wasn't all right. There are some things that can never be swept under the rug and forgotten. Turning Bru out of his job--that was, comparatively, no big deal. But missing his daughter's funeral was unforgivable, whatever the reason.

Eva showed up with the cappuchinos in styrofoam cups, and Eva and Newcombe got into a dance about whether Bru wanted to add some sugar. Eva left. The president strutted around the coffee table and sat down on the couch next to Bru. "Rupert, I'm sorry things worked out the way they did. It really had nothing to do with you and everything to do with demographics--we just don't have enough tuition-paying students."

Newcombe saying words that sounded apologetic didn't compute. Bru wondered if he was dreaming.

"I understand you are doing very well with Jerry Wiley's firm. That didn't surprise me. I always figured you for a fast burner and I was very sorry we didn't have a place for you." Newcombe stopped and looked at Bru.

Bru just looked back at him. Bru wondered how he'd heard that he'd been doing well with Jerry Wiley's firm.

"I know, Rupert, you don't need the money now, but it would make me feel better if you would accept our separation package."

Since there was nothing for Bru to say, he said nothing.

"The other two faculty we let go received three months salary. In your case we offered more because losing you was such a tragedy. If you like, we could add the standard severance pay to the nine months we offered you.

That'd give you a full year's salary. What do you say?"

What did he say? A full year's pay for signing on the dotted line--his signature waiving the right to appeal or sue. This money plus what he might gain from the Goins contract would give Bru more money than he'd ever had in his life in a lump sum.

"You must really be rolling in it," Newcombe joked. "It wouldn't take me a second to consider this if the shoe were on the other foot."

What if the Goins deal fell through? So far all he had from it was a bottle of champagne and a ruptured marriage. Bru couldn't rely on getting anything else from Jerry Wiley's firm. His current Lawson salary would terminate in a month, although it was set to pay in monthly increments until September. When he refused the separation package last Christmas, he'd been hot under the collar--and he'd had Jerry Wiley's offer. Now he didn't have that safety net down there. The only smart--the only adult--thing to do was take the money.

Bru shook his head. "Thank you, President Newcombe, for the offer but I'm still not interested."

"Why, for god's sake, Rupert?"

"Why should I take money I haven't earned?"

"That's a slightly outdated notion."

"I'm not going to do it. That's final."

President Newcombe gave a curt nod, a final nod. He jumped to his feet and instantly the friendly demeanor fled. He strutted to his desk--mahogany, naturally, and big enough to land an airplane on. He mashed down a lever on the squawk box. "Send Chief Cronin in here."

The chief appeared. "Chief," Newcombe shouted, "the next time this man shows his face I want you to arrest him for trespassing."

That was the lead Bru had been waiting for. "I always figured there was something fishy about my firing and now I know it, Newcombe. I'm going to find out what your nasty little secret is and before I'm through, you're going to have to issue me a contract for next year--with tenure."

Newcombe's face blanched white then abruptly it flushed red. Big fat blobs of sweat popped out on his forehead and dripped down his cheeks. His mouth opened and closed like a fish's. Finally, he said in a rather meek voice. "Did you hear that, chief? The man is stark raving mad."

"What I said scares hell out of you, Newcombe."

"Chief, get him out of here."

In the shade of a live oak before coming to the asphalt parking lot, the Chief said, "What do you expect to get out of Newcombe, Bru?"

"The truth, Chief."

"I'm telling you this as a friend, Bru. Let it alone."

"I can't do that."

The Chief took a deep breath and looked away. He gusted breath audibly. " Sometimes the only way to survive is to fight."

"You don't think this is one of those times," Bru said.

"I didn't say that. I put in my twenty years on the force in the Big Apple, fourteen of those as a detective. I know what a guilty man looks like. That guy is guilty. Do you really have anything on him?"

"I wish I could tell you different, but I don't, Chief. I'm willing to bet I'm smarter and meaner than Newcombe or anyone he's in cahoots with. If I'm not, I'm willing to pay the penalty."

"You will, Bru. Believe me you will. In the meantime try not to make it too obvious when you are sneaking around campus. And let me know if I can help you."

10

Deputy Hank Smith shot a dirty look at Old Man Goins in the booth opposite him. The old geezer was hunched forward so far that his nose hairs were practically hanging over Hank's plate of griddle cakes. The old boy's fist was wrapped around a fork.

"Bring him an order of griddle cakes," Deputy Hank told the flat-chested, piano-legged waitress.

"I don't want anything," Goins said.

"He says he doesn't want anything," Hazel, the waitress, said.

"Forget what he says and just bring a tall stack," Hank said.

Hazel bustled off and Hank looked away. He couldn't stand to eat when Goins's fuzzy eyebrows arched up and his beady little eyes zipped between Hank's face and his plate. Out of the corner of his eye, Hank saw a hand slash at his pancakes. The old fuck forked food into his mouth and stabbed again at the plate. All that money, and the old boy was too tight to order himself a pile of hotcakes.

Hank kept on looking away, as though unaware of the old man's petty filching. Hank owed Billy. Back after Deputy Hank had shot his second civilian and the media had got down on his back, Goins had staged a rally at the bandshell on the beach. The sheriff had been forced to come. There had been a band and a couple of thousand people were cheering and clapping. Hank had been presented with an award for gallantry by the Chamber of Commerce. Hank'd really been touched.

Hank thought back to his first recorded acquaintance with law enforcement. It occurred in April of 1975 when the American embassy in Saigon fell to the North Vietnamese. William Smith--the name he was christened with in the place of his birth, Long Island--staged his own one-man demonstration--trashing store windows and leading the local gendarmes on a two county high speed chase which ended in his incarceration in the local hoosegow. He had been pissed that the Vietnam War had ended before he was old enough to enlist in the Marines and "shoot a few gooks."

When Grenada was invaded, Hank was perfectly positioned. The Marines had rejected him as a pyscho--he had been too kill crazy--but he managed to slip by the Army shrinks and he was one of the first people off the plane in Grenada. He claimed the first two Cuban scalps. One was a woman and both were cleaning personnel. The Army was about to court martial Hank when some higher up in the Reagan administration intervened and insisted Hank be decorated and held up to the media as a hero.

In spite of that, his career in the armed forces didn't prosper and he was mustered out with a general discharge. He made his way south and found his true calling as Joe the Deputy, only he renamed himself Hank the Deputy.

A week earlier Billy Goins had called and asked they meet in a diner similar to the one Hank was in now--in an equally remote area, Bunnell, north of Daytona. After a fair amount of hemming and hawing on Billy's part about some fellow called Arbuthnot, Hank intervened and said, "You mean you want this guy offed." Billy had agreed that that was what he wanted. "I can do that for you," Hank had said, happy to oblige.

After polishing off the last of the pancakes, Billy Goins said, "So what did you learn yesterday?"

"Arbuthnot is toast," Hank said.

"I can read the papers. I'm talking about that

character that hangs around my daughter."

"Oh, that fellow. He circled your house most of the early afternoon until subject two, Dr. Bruton, exited your residence."

Billy Goins cursed. "That cut-rate Charley Manson was never supposed to have left California. That worthless booger once had Liz out peddling her muffin on the street."

Hank told Billy about Leroy's confrontation with Bruton.

"Hmm," Billy murmured. "You got anything else?"

"Later that evening your daughter disguised as a biker chick sneaked into Leroy's place."

"I wonder what in tarnation they're cooking up," Billy said.

"Yeah, I wonder too," the deputy parroted.

"Well, it ain't going to happen," Billy said. "Get rid of that sandhiller for me."

Hank was shoveling a load of hash browns into his mouth. As he chewed he buttered a slice of toast and peeled the foil top off a jam packet and knifed jam onto his bread. He took a bite of the toast and followed that by a sip of coffee. "I can oblige you," he said, "but it's going to cost you."

"How much?" Billy asked.

"Probably more than you can afford," Hank said, thinking fondly of his new assignment. "How about you pick up my breakfast tab?" He liked his affiliation with Mr. Goins. It was good and interesting work. He hoped it would continue for a long time.

11

In his Fiesta Bru located the paper on altering citrus diseases. He noticed something he'd missed the first go around. The penciled-in address also included a two-word phrase: "Canker Nursery." Bru wondered about his own sanity. He was considering following a lead that had been delivered to him by the agency of a tire-iron wielding biker. But how could he get to the heart of the artichoke if he didn't start peeling leaves away?

When Bru first started coming to Orlando to visit Leta on weekends the area now known as Daylando had been orange groves. On the way to the beach Leta and he had been treated to mile after mile of the trees--redolent of blossoms in the spring and ornamented with fruit like acres and acres of Christmas trees most of the rest of the year. Then the citrus canker struck. The state government sent crews with flamethrowers into all contaminated groves. Every tree, infected or not, was incinerated. A buffer zone of a quarter mile round was swept clear of any possible host tree as well.

More than a decade had gone by since the canker had been eradicated from the state. As Bru exited I-4 at Daylando, he saw nothing but roofs and a little grass and a few landscape trees. Bru took Camptown Road, an old grove road that abruptly passed from suburbs to a vast deserted stretch of pine-palmetto flatwoods.

Bru was vaguely aware that vast tracts of Florida were still owned by timber companies, which kept the region more pristine than any government agency could do, because the timber companies could keep everyone out. Black bears still roamed this region. Once, a man brought in the skin of an animal to one of Bru's colleagues in the Life Science department. The hide clearly showed the identifier cowlick and the kink in the tail--clear indications that it was a rare Florida panther. This big cat was killed by another panther. Two males fighting over territory.

At long last Camptown Spur Road appeared. No power or telephone lines stretched overhead. Could anyone live--or ever have lived--down this lonely reach? Then through the trees Bru saw an opening--like a pasture. A "No Trespassing" sign was nailed to the post. Another sign said, "Bad Dog." Bru turned into the tire tracks. A couple hundred feet distant, he saw a tin roofed, L-shaped house. The unpainted-board walls were peck cypress. A brick fireplace with a domed chimney--so the fire wouldn't be put out by a Florida downpour--provided the heating and cooking.

The tire-track ran through a gap by the house. The wire gate had been thrown carelessly aside. Bru kept on going. A largish outbuilding with new looking corrugated siding had collapsed--it looked as though it'd melted in the Florida sun. A storm window rested at an angle on its roof.

Bru drove past a couple of large fig trees and beyond them a banana grove. The pine forest pushed in close behind the bananas. Between the bananas and the trail stood a row of leafless trees in full bloom. Bru couldn't identify those deciduous trees; sand pears perhaps. Bru was looking for citrus, and everyone knew citrus trees were never deciduous. The track petered out after a couple hundred yards.

Bru turned the Fiesta around. An incredibly sweet smell drifted into the car. It reminded him of his dead daughter and wrecked marriage and lost job. Only citrus blossoms were that sweet and carried also such a dark undercurrent. But where was the citrus?

Bru braked the car. Leaving the door open and the Fiesta idling, he followed his nose to the row of deciduous trees. The twigs were curved into a vicious-looking crown of thorns pattern. The bark on the scaffold branches was streaked with green--like the grapefruit tree in Bru's backyard in Winter Park. Bru bent and collected leaves that had fallen to the ground. They were crucifix-like. The yellow golf-ball sized fruit lying on the ground looked like some kind of misbegotten orange.

Then Bru noticed the lesions. The twigs were loaded with large sunken sores. Yet the trees themselves seemed to be healthy enough--growing, producing a bumper crop of their strange fruit. He collected some of the fruits and leaves and hacked off green twigs ladened with the brown and sunken lesions. As he was depositing the bag onto the passenger seat through the open window, he heard a growl. Like a deep in the throat tiger's roar.

He looked up to see two dogs the size of horses charging at him. They were dark, short-haired, nearly tailless, with very small and very laid back ears. Bru made to run around the car. He was cut short by a shout. "Stay where you are, mister." The dogs bore down on him. He didn't think he could make it around to the driver side before they got him--but it looked like they would get him anyway.

Bru froze in place against the driver door. The voice said, "Butch, Whacko." The critters braked instantly, dirt flying. Foam flecked their jaws. Now relieved of the ardor of running, the dogs barked and yowled, begging to be allowed to set on Bru. Their paws dug at the turf. Grass flew. Bru gauged their distance as about fifty feet from him.

A figure in a black dress stumped toward Bru. She had a black hat and veil on. From her posture, which was crooked and misshapen, the woman seemed late sixties or more--and beat up. "Cain't you read, mister? The sign says no trespassing."

The woman quaked with rage. Foam flecked her mouth as it did her dogs. She had a rugged face. Her eyes were wet, red wounds. It was the face of a person who had suffered, but the suffering didn't seem to have redeemed her, only made her angrier. "What the hell are you doing back here in my grove?"

"Looking for citrus canker. I heard a man named Arbuthnot tended a canker nursery here."

That made her start. "Watch him, Butch," the woman said, to a dog that had nudged up to her ankles. She circled the car and reached through the open door and turned off the motor. She jerked the keys out of the ignition. She wound up like a fastball specialist and then she pitched Bru's key ring deep into the saw palmetto underbrush. Bru heard the two-key set hit a palm frond and make a hollow thud then drop to the forest floor. Fortunately Bru had a spare ring of keys stowed in the glove compartment.

"Whacko, go get my gun." Both of the dogs headed for the house.

Bru broke for his car. The woman shouted, "Butch! Whacko! Sic him."

Bru slammed open the passenger door and jumped in feet first. He rolled up the passenger window and banged the door lock down then fiddled in the glove compartment for his set of Lawson keys. The stick shift got caught on his pants leg. He tore it free and slapped his left foot down on the clutch. While fumbling with the keys, searching with his fingertips for the square-ended Ford ignition key, he kept an eye peeled on the dogs. Her command had made them tumble head over heels. Now the brutes were scrambling to get on their feet. Bru found the key. It slid into the ignition. The engine cranked, roared, well sputtered to life. He was home free.

Wrong. Bru'd lost track of the woman. A fist smashed through the plasticed-up driver window. It clipped his shoulder. Then her hand flew into the car and grabbed him around the throat. Bru let the clutch out. The car crept along. The woman was dragged alongside the Fiesta. She clung to Bru's throat. He took every bump in the throat. Bru drew his elbow up to smash at the woman--he couldn't make himself lash out. His vision began to blacken. The dogs were bearing down on him. Then, the Fiesta lurched into a rut. The woman's grip loosened. His throat was free. He could breathe. She clutched at his collar. The dogs weren't but a dozen paces from the car. He goosed the engine. She fell away tearing his collar.

The mutts snarled at Bru as he went by. They turned sharply and went down in a heap, Bru noted in the rear view mirror. At the house, he noticed the gate had been closed. The woman and the dogs were far behind him. He ran to the gate. A loop of heavy wire secured it to a post. The gate wouldn't budge. The dogs, barking and howling, pressed closer. The lead dog was within throwing distance. Bru gave it all he had. The gate pressed toward the fence post. Bru squeezed off the loop of wire and chucked the gate aside.

He leaped into the driver's seat, just as the closer dog lunged for him with a ferocious growl. The dog snapped its teeth and shook its head, saliva spattering Bru in the face. He could smell the mutt's breath, a combination of doggie odor and halitosis. But the car was moving. The dog appeared close to winded. Two hundred more feet and Bru'd be back to the road and safety.

Bru split his concentration between the sand track and the rear view mirror. The dogs's tongues were hanging out and they were coming on more slowly. The old lady was running up the road. Then there was a bend in the trail.

Bru lost sight of the enemy. He came to the road gate. It was up--and a chain was wrapped around the securing posts. The chain was padlocked. In the mirror, the dogs and woman emerged. Bru slammed his bumper against the middle post. He popped the clutch. The fence stretched. Bru stomped on the accelerator--nothing. He was stuck.

The mutts were bounding up the trail, tongues lolling, their barks snarling and angry. The woman carried a stick. A stick? Bru wondered. Then he understood. It was a rifle. He backed up, raced the engine and popped the clutch. There came a crack and the Fiesta stalled--but only momentarily--and then surged forward with all the power a ten year old four-cylinder engine with 150,000 miles could muster. Butch and Whacko were now neck and neck with the window. They were going for all they were worth. So was the Fiesta. It smashed into the gate and the posts broke loose.

Suddenly Bru heard another crack. His windshield starred. Another crack--the rear mirror smashed against the windshield--and a larger starburst--the size of the marksman's bullseye--appeared. Bru turned into the road, dragging fencing and posts. In the driveway one of the dogs lay, yelping and dripping blood. Bru hit the gas. At the junction with the trunk road he halted and pulled the fencing from the bumper and grill. He threw the debris into the ditch and shook his head. He wondered what had brought all that on. He supposed he'd pulled away a couple of leaves, but he was by no means sure he'd gotten any closer to the heart of the artichoke.

12

As Bru parked at his new digs, Salome, his landlady, hailed him from her porch, "Yoohoo, Dr. Bruton. A man came by to see you."

Bru thought about telling Salome to call him Bru, but decided against it as Salome leaped off the porch and dashed across the yard to him. Bru pressed back against the side of his Fiesta. Something about this woman disturbed Bru. She was short; even in her platform shoes she stood only five three or five four. From the way she'd torn across the yard he could tell she was in good shape. Hell, Bru's eyes could see she had great shape and she smelled seductive too, but not without a hint of original sin. Or maybe that was just the fragrance from the dooryard citrus trees, with their sweet but dark undercurrent, floating on the breeze. Her complexion was a lovely golden brown and her eyes were a lovelier shade of hazel. Maybe it was just the name, Salome, the woman who had asked for--and got-- John the Baptist's head. But Bru knew the real answer. She was a woman. Right now, women bothered him, after all one had just tried to kill him and one he'd been married to for almost two decades had dumped him on his head.

"What happened to your shirt? It looks like it went through a war."

Bru told her.

"You lead an interesting life, Dr. Bruton," she said. "Would you like a drink? I have some wine. And a pot roast on. It's not easy going from being married to becoming a bachelor in one day."

"Thanks no," Bru said.

"Maybe another time then," Salome said and grinned. "I know what you're going through. I've been through that wringer."

Bru sprung for the outside stairs and bounded up them. Salome smiled big and waved. Those white teeth against her so very attractive high-yellow complexion shot Bru a pang, a below the belt pang.

In the kitchen Bru dropped the bag of plant parts into a plastic trash sack then doubled the bag back on itself. Bru put that bag inside another garbage bag, and for good measure, put that bag in yet another one. You couldn't be too careful when dealing with the citrus canker. He secured all this with a twist-tie and put the bag in the cabinet under the sink and washed his hands. He felt like Typhoid Mary. He picked up the phone of Leta's fax/answering machine. A dial tone buzzed in his ear.

He moved the phone to the kitchen table and called information for the number of the extension service in Tangerine City. He tatted the number into the phone pad and asked if Harry Neilson still worked there. He was told yes but that Harry was out until the following morning. Bru left his name and number and said he'd be in touch. Next on the agenda was phoning Professor Khoury at the university in Gainesville. Calling Khoury was not a chore Bru looked forward to with any pleasure.

Bru didn't need directory assistance for the department number. The secretary picked up and he asked to be transferred to Professor Khoury. One ring and the phone answered, "Humbert Khoury speaking."

Bru always liked that "Humbert" part. Sounded a lot like humbug. It almost pained Bru to note the man sounded human, rather than the puffed up windbag Bru knew he was. "Dr. Khoury, it's Rupert Bruton. Remember me?"

"Certainly, I recollect you, Bru. How could I

forget?"

Indeed, how could he?

"I suppose you are still at Lawson College enlightening the masses to the first principles of life sciences," Professor Khoury said.

"Um-huh," Bru said.

"What kind of answer is that?" His tone was sharp-- that was more like it. The old Khoury was coming out.

Bru had no desire to explain his misfortunes to Khoury--mainly because the latter would be so delighted to hear them. "Actually, I'm doing a consulting job and your name came up in some of the research."

Khoury snorted with pleasure into the receiver. Bru could see him cocking his head from one side to the other-- and probably blowing on his fingernails and polishing them on his chest. The annoying thing about Khoury's massive ego was that his accomplishments justified it. "I see." His voice throbbed with self-satisfaction.

"What I mean is, it came up in an article by a guy named William Arbuthnot."

Suddenly, Khoury's voice broke. A high pitched squeak said, "Did he claim we were confederates, er I mean colleagues?"

"No, he only appended a note to a peculiar paper thanking you for your help. He claimed to be able to genetically alter a plant disease. This was back in the early eighties."

"I knew a William Arbuthnot then. Yes." His voice had recovered somewhat. It was flat and neutral.

"I need to talk to you about this guy and the work he was doing."

One large gulp of air was taken in. "Yes."

"Do you have a few minutes right now."

"I think tomorrow would be better, Bru. Can you come here?"

Bru would like to know what went on with this Arbuthnot right now. But he was by no means certain he'd get a full story without looking Khoury square in the eye. "Tomorrow's fine," Bru said. They made arrangements.

Bru dropped the phone into the cradle, his palm lingering on the handset. He heard a car in the shell drive and a car door open and slam close. Then presently the door framed his good buddy and former associate, Jerry Wiley.

"Is this thing locked?" Jerry asked as he tested the screen door. It pulled open. He walked in as though he were an old friend. Which was exactly what he was, with particular reference to old, as in former.

Jerry extracted an envelope from his inside jacket pocket and chucked it on top of the fax-answering machine.

"How'd you find me?"

"BellSouth. Something called directory assistance. If you don't know it, information also provides addresses these days. You indiscreetly allowed yours to be listed."

"I figure Leta will need to know where to find me late some lonely, unsatisfied night."

"*Touche*," Jerry said. "Aren't you going to ask me what's in the envelope?"

"I didn't figure I had to. I knew you'd tell me sooner rather than later." Not as good, Bru thought, as the unsatisfied night crack. But it would do.

"It's a check for twenty-five thousand dollars and a copy of a contract I drew up between you and Goins. Read the contract. Make sure it's acceptable and sign both copies and send one back to Goins. Goins agreed to pay one hundred thousand up front, twenty-five thousand now, another twenty-five next week and the remainder on receipt of the report. He still's talking about a one-hundred thousand dollar bonus, but between you and me, I wouldn't hold out much hope. That man is tight as a rain barrel."

Bru was disgusted by the gratitude that welled in his chest. He actually felt warm and fuzzy. Yuck. Beholden to Jerry Wiley. But the fact was Bru needed to keep an eye on money. He had cavalierly dismissed a whole year's salary today, and Jerry was certainly right about the unlikelihood of Goins's--a man who stole peanut butter sandwiches from his guest's plate--paying the bonus money. "What about your cut?" Bru asked.

"Under the circumstances we can forget the firm's cut." Jerry hung his head. Bru could see he wanted to say something more--something about how sorry he was about stealing Bru's wife. But what was there to say? "You know as far as I'm concerned our original agreement, so far as you and the firm goes, still stands."

The warm fuzzies died a quick death. Bile threatened to boil up. "Let's not be silly," Bru said. "I'll be down and clear my stuff out of that cubbyhole you gave me when I have a little time. Tell Leta I took her fax-answering machine. I'll be working out of here until I get an office. I needed a phone. I'm sorry I forgot to leave a note."

Jerry shrugged. "Don't sweat it. How'd your car get all beat up?"

"Doing something you don't want to hear about," Bru said.

Jerry's head perked up. "I guess that means you have to tell me."

"If you like. I went out to the address listed on that paper smuggled into my car by the biker."

"I told you not to do that, Bru."

"Seeing how an old lady tried to kill me I guess that was good advice."

"Hot damn!" Jerry exclaimed.

Bru drew Jerry a thumbnail sketch of his encounter on Camptown Spur Road.

"How do you explain all that?" Jerry asked. "I deal

with creeps who kill people all the time. They always have a reason, if frequently a very poor one."

Bru stopped and took a breath. He would much rather have this conversation with someone, anyone other than Jerry. But he needed this conversation to clear his head, to analyze what had happened to him and why.

"I found something that looks like citrus canker on her place."

"Holy moly, Bru. Citrus canker is supposed to be completely eliminated from this part of the state."

"I don't know that it is citrus canker, but I'm thinking of dropping in on a former student tomorrow, an agricultural extension agent. He can probably tell me what that stuff is. I called an old prof of mine who's name appeared in an article this Arbuthnot wrote. He didn't seem exactly thrilled to hear Arbuthnot's name."

Jerry looked at Bru's face intently then said, "You turned up something else today you aren't telling me."

"Nothing to do with this case."

"Hey, Arbuthnot has nothing to do with this case. Why does that name Arbuthnot seem familiar?" Jerry wondered.

Bru gave an all-right-you-asked-for-it look. "I had a little chat with President Newcombe. He offered me a full year's salary if I would give up my right to legal redress. Later the chief of security told me Newcombe looked guilty to him."

Jerry gave Bru a stern look and shook his head. "What do you think he thinks he's guilty of? You were an untenured faculty member on a year-to-year contract. He could dismiss you anytime he pleased--no questions asked. All he had to do was not renew your contract. That's what he did."

"The guy acted as if he was hiding something. Again I refer to Chief Cronin, who as a detective up north had to rely on his intuition."

"Isn't it customary to give a person turned down for tenure one terminal year? Do you suppose that's what Newcombe was acting guilty about? That he turned you out without the final year and which he is offering you now?"

Bru looked at Jerry hard, examining his face for a telltale sign of a hidden motive. "It seems to me that paying up because I had almost been denied tenure would fall under the heading of 'delicacy of feeling,'" Bru said. "I can't recall Newcombe ever being accused of that one before."

"That's right. It would. There is no legal obligation to give that terminal year when a person is dismissed for reasons having to do with student body attrition. Newcombe wouldn't give a hang about going against academic tradition." Jerry's hand went inside his coat to his shirt pocket. "You mind if I smoke?"

Adultery wasn't sitting well with this Baptist. First, drinking and swearing and now smoking. Bru did mind that he smoked but he threw his hands in the air. Jerry extracted a pack of cigarettes and tapped one out, which he offered Bru, a bit too expertly for a rank amateur. In a petty way which annoyed Bru, he enjoyed the feeling of moral superiority that watching Jerry light up gave him.

"Look, Bru," Jerry said, gusting smoke, "do yourself a favor and quit trying to see a conspiracy in all this. It makes you sound like a crackpot." Jerry smoked his cigarette down without saying a word. Then he turned the tap on, stuck the coal under the gush of water, and flicked the butt in the trash. "I wish the hell you would have told me your intuitions about Newcombe being involved in all this last night. I wouldn't have called Goins today."

"You are going awfully fast from being the devil's advocate to completely agreeing that all the dots are connected."

"I don't believe they are," Jerry said choosing his

words carefully. "But just for a moment, say they are. That means you would be involved in a plot beyond your wildest imaginings, a scheme so fantastic--involving as it would Newcombe and Goins and god knows who else--that it would probably take us all out. There would be no way we could possibly stop it or do anything about it. The results of this line of thinking is easy--there can't be any conspiracy. That's all there is to it."

"What would you have me do?" Bru said. "Just take on the chin my job, my identity, my life. And then roll over and get fucked."

"That's what a thinking man would do," Jerry advised. "Cut your losses. If you really believe Goins and Newcombe are out to get you, run as far away from them as you can."

Bru admitted to himself that that was excellent advice. A cornered rat could have done better with the old lady that afternoon. Being nonviolent--as he'd been since his murder of Etienne--was one thing, but not having the nerve to stand up for yourself was something else.

Suddenly Bru felt rage fuming in his heart. Bru might not stand up for himself, but at least he didn't have to take Jerry's shit. "I've had enough advice from the man who stole my wife. It's time for you to go."

The phone buzzed. Jerry didn't budge. Shooting Jerry a dirty look, Bru picked up.

"Bru--er Dr. Bruton. This is Kimberly."

"Kimberly," Bru repeated, astonished.

"Yes, Kimberly Chapman, Grandpa Goins' granddaughter."

"Goins' granddaughter," Bru repeated stupidly.

"Leroy's disappeared. I don't know what to do."

"Who's Leroy?"

"My stepfather. My friend. My father." She sounded on the edge of hysteria.

61

"I'm sorry, Kim," Bru said. "Why are you calling me?"

"Because there's nobody else. Grandpa's too old and mother--well, mother isn't here. Come to the Boot Hill Saloon and help me find him. Can you get here in an hour?"

"The Boot Hill Saloon? I'm not sure. Why?"

"Because I need you." She seemed to be sobbing. The phone clicked in Bru's ear.

Bru looked at the handset, puzzled.

"How old is that girl?"

"In her teens."

"Don't go over there. That would be my advice, no matter her age. You can't let yourself get mixed up in Goins's family."

"Thank you, Mr. Attorney."

"Jesus, Bru, don't get yourself in another mess. Forget about Lawson. That's in the past," Jerry said. "Forget about Arbuthnot or whatever his name is. Stay away from Goins's family. Do the job Goins hired you for and forget all the rest of this stuff. I'm giving you this advice as an attorney and as a friend."

"Weren't you on your way out?" Jerry stared at Bru for a while. Then as though realizing there was nothing more to be said, Jerry looked at Bru with pity and slouched toward the door.

"Better yet," Jerry said going out the door, "tear up Goins' check and contract and forget about all this shit."

Bru went into the bathroom. Bru knew Jerry was right about one thing. He had no business fooling with Goins's granddaughter. She could spell nothing but trouble. That she was near hysterical was an even better reason for staying away from her. What he did instead was change into jeans and tee shirt. The best he could find by way of shoes was an old pair of jogging shoes. Those wouldn't look much at home where he was going but then neither would the white tee. He was going to meet Kimberly. There was no way he could do anything else. Just the thought of that young child in the most notorious biker bar on the east coast of Florida made his blood run cold.

13

Bru found a parking spot on a block of seedy stucco houses, built in the twenties of chicken wire and plaster and unpainted since the seventies. He was reluctant to leave his car there. Then he got out of the automobile. A quick glance at his rust-spackled vehicle with the visquine windows brought a smile of amusement to his lips. Nobody would bother his personal specimen of automotive excellence, in that or any neighborhood.

He was swallowed by the street carnival hubbub-- Florida's version of Mardi Gras, the only accepted costume, black leather and chrome chains. Pretty girls flounced about in fringed leather halters and bikini bottoms, and beer-bellied tee-shirted males waddled, often as couples. *How could that many ugly guys have so many attractive women?* Bru wondered. Anything that jiggled and was exposed bore a tattoo. To better fit in, Bru bought a black-tinted commemorative "I Survived Bike Week" tee-shirt and a black leather barracks style cap with metal studs. He put the black tee shirt on over the white one.

Kimberly was waiting for him near the bar. The bar reeked of sweat and perfume and motor oil. Not even her black leather jacket with fringed sleeves could conceal the basic modesty of the girl, which Bru had intuited yesterday. She had on a pair of white slacks and a cable knit sweater. Just witnessing the frown on her face brighten when she spotted Bru told him she was really troubled. He'd been right in coming.

She rushed to Bru and threw her arms around him and hugged him. He could feel her breasts against his chest. It made for a nice but painfully poignant feeling. Bru could not help but think of Amber who would hug him like this on occasions when Bru would be called on to make everything right again. Over Kim's shoulder Bru saw a woman open her leather top to display a pair of very handsome and no doubt surgically enhanced breasts. In a side room some big bruisers seemed to be sticking electric cords in their mouths then falling down and writhing on the floor. Bru had to get Kimberly out of this place. What was she doing here anyway?

"Thank you for coming, Bru. I didn't know who else to call. Leroy's gone missing. Something bad has happened to him. I know it."

Who was this Leroy exactly? Step-father, friend, father, she had said on the phone. Delving into that relationship seemed a bit deep for starters, so Bru said, "How could you know something was wrong?"

"Because he stood me up on a date. He never stands me up."

"You'd better explain that," Bru said.

"I mean he has a hard time getting away from mom. So when he has it fixed up that he can see me he never misses. He didn't show this afternoon."

What could she mean *hard time getting away from mom?* Her mother lived with her and her grandfather and there didn't seem to be evidence of any Leroy in the big house.

"Why don't we go someplace else?" Bru suggested. He took Kimberly by the arm and tried to lead her toward the door.

Kimberly pulled back. Her sleeve tore out of Bru's

hand. "Huh-uh. This is where Leroy said we'd meet. I'm not leaving."

Kim's sudden mood swing puzzled Bru, but not so much as the big biker he saw pushing through the crowd. One of the more interesting aspects of Bike Week, Bru had noticed, was its marked civility. A voice raised in anger was seldom heard and the number of *thanks yous* and *yes, sirs* stood in stark contrast to discourse the remainder of the year in Central Florida. But this big bruiser was rudely pushing bodies out of the way. He seemed to be making right for Bru. What was even stranger the guy seemed vaguely familiar to Bru. A bandana was tied, headband fashion, around his skull and he was well over six feet and carried a fair amount of weight. He sported a mole below his left eye. Could this be Leroy? There was no doubt he was aiming directly for Bru and Kim.

Bru asked Kimberly if he was Leroy.

Kim turned hopefully. "Daddy?" she shouted, as the bruiser took the last step to bring him to Bru and Kim. Bru watched in horror as the big guy's fist came up. His fist was big as a ham. He drew his fist back and the look on his face, which was already fierce, became diabolical. The fist hurtled at Bru, who had just had enough time to flick his head to the side. A glancing sledgehammer blow struck Bru's cheekbone. Suddenly Bru felt like a wobbling top. He stumbled. His feet danced to correct his position. He went down.

Bru could hear fine. Seeing was the problem. His vision was splotched and spotty. Nobody seemed to notice he was on the floor. He heard the big guy say, "That dude molesting you, miss?"

"No, you fool, he was trying to help me find Leroy." Suddenly the outrage went out of Kim's voice. "Do you know Leroy?"

"Why would you think I might?" Now the man's

voice was meek.

"Because he dressed like you sometimes and he's about as tall as you but he's skinnier, a lot skinnier. You might say he's frail."

"Does he have a red fu manchu mustache?"

"Yes, that's him. I knew you knew him."

Now the anger came back in the big guy's voice. "You sure that guy's not bothering you? Some guy like you described accused him of fooling with his girl--you?"

"I told you about that already. Tell me about Leroy."

"Maybe we better get your friend off the floor first." Next thing Bru was aware of was the big guy standing over him with a wheeled janitorial pail in his hands. He tilted the bucket and a cascade of dirty water streamed over Bru and the big guy was lugging Bru to his feet. "Hey, no offense, old buddy. I seen this young 'un and I remembered what that guy said yesterday about you fooling with his woman, and then you went and left Heidi stranded in that rain shower."

Bru told him everything was all right. Since his vision was still a little blurred and his ears were ringing that statement didn't seem entirely accurate, but under the circumstances it seemed the best thing to say.

"Leroy," Kim demanded. "Tell me about him."

"Last I seen him a deputy shuriff was talking to him. Seeing how he'd just busted out this here fellow's window. I reckon he got lugged off to jail."

Kim breathed a long, soulful gust. "At least he's alive."

"There's a temporary police station a couple of blocks away. They may be able to help you."

Kim led Bru outside. Now that it was starry dark it was cool, if not quite chilly. That Bru's two shirts were soaked made him feel even cooler. The leather cap, which had set Bru back twenty-five bucks, was no longer on his head.

The mobile police station looked like something out of MASH, the TV show. A fatigue green tent was pitched next to a dining fly. Electric bulbs were strung around a bank of phones--in a cordoned off area where the public wasn't permitted. Two-way radios squawked. Two large, disheveled but very pacific bikers, their tee shirts up exposing enormous hairy paunches, were shackled and cuffed awaiting transport. Four others, three men, one woman, were in the custody of police. It was a time before Bru could catch a cop's eye. He took down the information Kim gave him then he said, "It'll be awhile before I can get to this."

But in a surprisingly short time the cop came over to them. "Let's see your licenses."

"I can't drive," Kim said. "I'm old enough but grandpa won't let me. But I have a Florida identity card."

The cop made an impatient gesture with his finger, telling her to fork it over. He took down their names, ages and numbers and asked if the addresses were correct. Bru provided his new address. The cop gave the cards back. "Does the subject, this Leroy, have any identifying marks?" he asked.

"I told you about the red fu manchu mustache," Kim said.

"I mean any other marks."

Kim stared into the middle distance, her lips and brows knotted in thought. "He had a tattoo. A funny shaped tattoo. I never understood what it was of. It was right here." Her finger touched a spot just above her breast.

The cop nodded. "The sheriff requests you report to the substation just west of town." The cop gave directions. His manner was very brisk, very cop.

"What's this all about?" Kim wanted to know. "Is

daddy all right?"

"I can't tell you that because I don't know," the cop said, his eyes shifting evasively. "If you don't show up, someone will come looking for you."

14

Even though it was eight-thirty in the evening, the sheriff's department was bustling with activity. When Bru identified himself to the dispatcher behind the glass partition, he expected to be asked to take a seat. He was brusquely told to stand just where he was. A man in a slightly darker uniform with sheriff department shoulder patches came out from behind a steel door and said, "Follow me."

"Are you going to take me to Leroy?" Kim asked a plaintive note in her voice. "Please tell me he's all right."

The officer strode in front of them. They went down a long corridor. The air conditioning was cranked up. The temperature was near sixty. There was a room tone that Bru couldn't identify. Ventilating fans humming in the duct work, he supposed, but possibly the rumble of incarcerated men elsewhere in the building.

A sign indicated the morgue. The officer turned in that direction. Kim gasped. Bru supposed he should be of more help to the girl, but he was groggy--and too far out of the picture. Kim hadn't seemed the least surprised to learn that her friend Leroy had assaulted Bru the day before, and what was she doing hanging out with characters, biker-types, like him anyway? These questions had been thwarted with a combination of non sequiturs--"He's a nice guy, really," and near hysterical ravings on the drive to the hoosegow.

The officer tatted a code into the lockbox on the

door labeled, "Morgue." The room itself was surprisingly small and much colder than the very chilly hallway. Along three walls were stainless steel face plates with handles. It reminded Bru of the freezer plant where Leta and he kept meat early in their marriage. Two cops, one a heavy-set female with very hard eyes and a tightly pursed mouth, were standing in the middle of the room. The officer in the dark uniform went to the wall and pulled on a handle. The face plate dropped and a gurney slid out. The corpse was concealed by a space-blanketlike sheet. The cop jerked on the cover. A head, almost bald on top, with a dull red fu manchu, was revealed. The body looked like a famine victim--skin stretched across a skeletal frame.

"That your fellow Leroy?" the cop asked.

"It doesn't look much like him," Kim sobbed.

Bru had to agree with that. This man looked smaller than the six two or so of his assailant. And his mustache wasn't as red, and he looked older, much older. But that was probably just the effect of death. From the anguished grimace on his face dying hadn't appeared to be much fun.

The cop pulled the sheet farther down. He pointed at a peculiar tattoo above the left nipple. "Does that look familiar to you? What about the needle tracks up and down his arm? Do they help?"

"Sort of," Kimberly said. Her eyes widened. She was looking at the gaping, blood rimed holes--two of them-- in the middle of his chest.

"Would there be any other identifying features?"

"The real Leroy has a kink in his dick," Kim said.

The three cops exchanged a glance, a very significant glance. Bru rather wanted to get in on that exchange of looks. He was pointedly ignored.

"But you can only see it if he has a hard-on."

The cop in the dark uniform lifted the corner of the sheet for a discreet peek at the crotch. "Sure enough, this guy has a regular L-shaped pud," he said. "I never heard of anything like that before." Raising the sheet exposed even more of Leroy's torso. Two gaping wounds in the abdomen were visible. His internal organs showed. Kim began to blubber, then she started to shriek. The woman cop said, "Let's get you out of here, dearie." Bru made to follow. The third cop, an Hispanic with very cold Apache eyes, said, "Not you. You come with me."

Another interminable hallway, only this time they passed through electronic sensors with a sign "Secure Area." Bru was made to go first. The cop followed. After a while, the cop told Bru to put his hands against the wall and spread his feet. He frisked Bru. His hands were very efficient and the physical violation could hardly give rise to the sense of howling outrage Bru felt at being patted down. The cop then tatted a code into a button-box and swung a steel door, which gave onto a room filled with desks. The officer opened what looked to be a closet and pointed with his finger to a chair. Bru sat down in the chair. The cop turned on a light. It was a closet. The cop said, "The sheriff wants to talk with you."

The best part of an hour later the door swung open and a rather attractive woman entered the room and closed the door. She was about Bru's age, of middling height with blond hair in a French braid. The sheriff's uniform didn't do much for her figure but her face was very pleasant. Bru looked at the patch above her breast. It read, "Buckett."

Okeelanta County was an outlying area. Normally Bru wouldn't even have heard the name of the sheriff, but Sheriff Buckett was notorious throughout Central Florida, hearkening back to the bad old days of the Deep South. This sheriff's department, though, was an equal opportunity abuser. Blacks, Hispanics or poor whites were equally likely to get thumped by Buckett's constabulary. Any cash the department's deputies came across was seized on the assumption it was drug money--this was accomplished mainly on the interstates where Buckett's cars would pull over and search drivers. All told, the department had a kitty totaling ten million dollars, which the sheriff used to buy expensive toys. During the last reelection campaign her deputies made a practice of intimidating the easily intimiditable, immigrants mostly, forcing campaign contributions, tearing down signs of the opposing candidate and making them put up the sheriff's posters. Then there was Deputy Smith and his homicides. Thinking back to the picture Bru'd seen of the sheriff and the notorious Hank in the paper, he did seem to remember the sheriff had been female.

The sheriff faced Bru. Her attractive features melted away. Her eyes looked like twin gun barrels. Before she ran for sheriff, she'd been a highway patrolwoman. She'd made a reputation busting drug runners. It was said, Bru recalled dimly because of Advocates of the First Amendment scrutiny, that Patrolman Buckett could look at a man and know if he was guilty. It was apparent to Bru now how she did that. She knew everyone was guilty. The question was simply of what.

A goose walked across Bru's grave. The flesh on the back of his neck crawled. Had she discovered the link to Etienne? Bru's heart palpitated in his chest. Those speculations were all nonsense, he supposed, but blurting out a confession wouldn't be. He blinked his eyes and made himself smile. "Yes, I'm Rupert Bruton."

"Formerly of Lawson College in Orlando."

"Currently of Lawson College," Bru said. "I'm still on the payroll."

"Our information says you have been terminated."

"My contract will not be renewed next year," Bru said, "but I haven't been terminated."

The sheriff smiled with satisfaction--and no warmth.

71

Bru could see he lost some points on that exchange. "So what are you doing with a sixteen year old girl--identifying the corpse of a fifty-year old murder victim?"

That was a good question. For the moment Bru didn't have an answer.

"Do you know who is the grandfather of that girl?

"She called me and asked me to help her find this Leroy," Bru said. He'd have to admit it didn't sound like much of an answer.

"And who is this Leroy?"

"I'm not sure exactly. She told me at different times that he was her friend, her father and her stepfather."

"Her father?"

"Or stepfather. That's what she said."

"That's all you know about him?" Buckett's eyes took Bru in. They seemed the peepers of some predatory nocturnal creature. She leaned forward. Her pupils grew larger and darker and more menacing.

"That plus the fact that he stopped me on the road yesterday and broke my window out with a tire iron."

That threw a monkey wrench at her. Bru almost smiled at the surprise that momentarily flickered across her face. Then immediately she was back to the same hard-ass tone. "You'd better explain that."

"I was going back to Orlando on 415 south of Osteen."

"On the flood plain of the Saint Johns," the sheriff put in.

"That's it. Right. This biker came around me and pointed at my tire. I thought I had a flat. I stopped and he smashed my car with a tire iron."

"He assaulted your car and not you?" Buckett said busily taking notes.

"Later we mixed it up a little bit."

"Did you report this incident?"

"I didn't have to," Bru said. "A deputy came on the scene."

"A deputy? From my department?"

"He's the most famous man in your department, Hank Smith," Bru smarted off. He told himself to cool it. But being dragged into this little room as though he were a criminal riled Bru--and those insinuations about something ulterior in his relations with Kim rankled too.

Why? Didn't Deputy Smith report this incident?"

"That comes under a confidential heading--police business," the sheriff said. But her tone of voice was subdued, feminine.

Bru continued: "Your deputy acted mighty peculiar. He pulled up behind me with his lights going and pretended to interrogate me about the incident, but he never took down my name or number. Then he got in his car and turned around and roared off after this Leroy. It was a remarkably half ass kind of interview. And according to the biker we talked to in Daytona, your Smith caught up to Leroy and was last seen with him."

"When was this?"

"Yesterday."

"Leroy's body was discovered this afternoon. He'd been dead only a couple of hours."

That too sounded like information covered by the heading police business to Bru--but he wasn't a big enough wiseass to say so. Still, he enjoyed the shock and little girl tone of the sheriff's voice. Unhappily, the sheriff caught that smug look on his face, and suddenly she was the butt-kicking Bull Conners type again.

"How did it happen that this Leroy broke your window out?"

Bru thought about that one for a while and shrugged. "I haven't a clue."

"Some guy busts up your car in a lonely spot on a

lonely road--come on, he didn't pick you at random?"

"He may have," Bru said and remembered for the first time--the past thirty-six hours had been a busy time and he hadn't much time for idle reflection--that he'd seen a guy with a red mustache on a motorcycle on the beach while he was talking with Goins. Bru forced a poker-playing look on his face. The sheriff would probably like that information, but Bru wasn't going to volunteer it unless asked.

"When did this incident occur?"

"You mean when the biker broke my window out?"

"Of course."

"Three-thirty, four o'clock in the afternoon."

The sheriff wrote something on her notepad. "And then you turn up with the granddaughter of one of the richest men in the world looking for him. What's your scam? How about you and this Leroy were trying to shake Mr. Goins down and you are using the granddaughter as your pawn. Then say Leroy gets greedy and you bump him off."

"Hey, come on. I'm a college professor. We don't bump people off."

"All right. So you erase him, like a mistake. So you can make off with all the plunder."

Bru said, "It's a theory. I like it. Maybe you should go into writing scripts for high-concept adventure movies. They need stuff like that."

"You haven't explained your relationship to that kid yet. You are not leaving here until you do."

Bru thought about that for a while. Billy Goins wasn't exactly going to be pleased with his performance tonight. Dragging his granddaughter to the sheriff's morgue, looking for some friend-father-stepfather. But Bru intuited that Billy would be a great deal more pissed about divulging his business dealings.

"Look, mister, when I was a bit younger than that

child, a slick-talking chicken fucker that you remind me a lot of molested me. If I get a glimmering that something like that is going on between you and her, your ass has had it. Now if you have a legitimate reason to be hanging around her, cough it up."

"I work for her grandfather."

"So what do you do?"

"I don't think he'd like my telling you his business."

"Do you have some documentation for that assertion?"

"You mean can I prove I work for him?"

"Isn't that what I said?"

Bru had left both copies of the contract on the kitchen table. No matter. He couldn't show her that contract. Goins would have his head for that. But he had the check. That would do. Bru extracted his wallet from his back pocket and unfolded the check. He handed it to Buckett."

A skeptical frown burred her eyebrows. "A personal check for twenty-five thousand dollars. What's this for?"

Bru shook his head.

"A ransom payment, maybe."

"Sure," Bru said. "That makes sense. Pay off your blackmailers and kidnappers by personal check. We also accept Visa and Mastercard."

"Generally salary is tendered by payroll check. You care to explain why he wrote you a personal one?"

"That's a question I must defer to Mr. Goins."

"You wouldn't mind if I called him and asked him about this?"

"I'd be delighted," Bru said. "As I'm sure he'd be pleased to tender your call."

"You have an attitude, mister, and I don't like it." To make certain Bru knew she was a cop she placed the check on the table built into the wall--instead of simply giving it back to him. Bru picked the check up and folded and put it back in his wallet. "I don't know what kind of trouble you got into at Lawson. But don't try to pull anything in my county, buddy. And don't get cute with that girl or Goins. I'll pin your ass to the wall." With that she up and left the room. Not knowing what else to do, Bru sat tight. After a few minutes the cop with the Apache eyes showed up and looked at Bru and broke into a grin. When he saw Bru wanted to share in his humor, he scowled, cop fashion, and threw his head toward the door.

He led Bru to a different waiting area. He nodded at a chair. "Take a load off," he said. After a while, Kim was brought in by a different female cop. When she saw Bru, he popped up and she ran to him and threw her arms around him. Her eyes were full of tears. "Oh, Bru," she gushed. "It was awful. That fat woman policeman felt me up and asked me all kinds of questions." She started to cry.

"Let's get out of here," he said.

"Oh, yes. Let's," Kim agreed.

Once, on asphalt and away from the eyes of the cops, Kim began to blubber. Bru led her by the hand around the building. She went to the driver's side of his car. "Leroy always used to let me in by the driver door. It would drive mom crazy," she said.

"Not tonight," Bru said. He opened the passenger door and installed her on that side.

They drove in silence. The tall pines on the side of the road were silhouetted by moonlight. "Who is this guy Leroy anyway?" Bru asked. The question he would have liked to ask was what she was doing hanging around a whacked-out junkee.

"That's what the cops wanted to know too."

"What did you tell them?"

"That it was none of their business."

"Do you think it's none of my business?"

"They told me never to talk about him."

"They?" Who could they be? Her grandfather? Her mother? That didn't seem likely. Who?

"I wish you wouldn't do this, Bru. I like you."

"Were the cops really tough on you?"

"Just the woman who touched me."

"That's her job. They patted me down too."

"Not the way she touched me. She felt me."

"I'm sorry," Bru said, feeling an unspeakable sorrow at not having protected her from that ugliness.

"There was nothing you could do about that, Bru," she said with a world weariness that didn't become her sixteen years. "They're always after me for sex."

"Who's that?" Bru asked. An ice tumor had grown in his gut.

"Everybody, it seems. To get out at night, I have to give the guard a hand job. He wants me to blow him, but I won't do that. He added a new wrinkle last week. Now he'll only let me out for a hand job. To call a cab, I have to blow him so I have been hitching. Grandpa put that guard box in and laid down the concertina wire to protect me from Leroy. That ugly wire on the beach costs him a thousand dollars a day in code violations, but it is his guards and the cops who are the real threat." She started to cry very quietly and very softly.

By the time they arrived at the beachside mansion, she'd fallen asleep. Because of the plasticed window, Bru had to open the door to speak with the guard, a snappily dressed young man in a spit-polished Sam Browne belt. "Call Kimberly's mother, please," he said.

"She's out," the guard said with an impudent glint in his eye.

"Call the Latin maid then. What's her name?"

"You can drop her off here. I'll see she's properly taken care of. On the q.t., buddy, I do this for her all the time."

"It is necessary to call the maid," Bru said. "And you won't be doing this for her much longer."

The impertinent glare went out of his eye. "Yes, sir," he said. The gate receded and Bru drove up the winding drive to the big house on the beach.

15

"Bru, open up. I know you're in there because your car's here."

He threw the sheet off and pulled on the jeans he'd peeled off the night before. He swung the door open--the person on the other side was a tall blonde--in jeans and shitkickers and a western-cut Joseph's Coat of a shirt. That shirt was so bright it made him yearn for an Alka Seltzer. And a couple of ibuprofen and an extra strength Tylenol to boot. And maybe a Goody's Extra Strength Headache Powder for good measure. Out of context, like this, it took Bru a moment to realize the person at the door was Melba, the reference librarian from Lawson.

"Hey, Bru," she said, "I brought you some breakfast."

Bru was famished. Still, it wouldn't do to let on that he was too anxious. Actually, he was by no means eager to get very chummy with this woman--what gave? Yesterday, he'd gone to Lawson in part to seek out Melba. Now that she was on his doorstep--with vittles in hand--he was playing hard to get.

Melba opened the screen door and pushed her way in. Bru took backward steps and the mattress, which he put on the floor for better back support, tripped him. He toppled onto the mattress. Melba settled on a straight back chair and smiled at Bru's predicament. He found a shoe and pulled the sock on and fumbled to get the shoe over his foot. Like a good Texas cowgirl, Melba was sitting the chair with her elbows and knees spread. Bru found himself on an eye level with her pussy, which his eyes locked on. It didn't help matters any that a perfect impression of her lips was visible through the jeans. Like everything else about Melba, that oval was frighteningly, if intriguingly, large. Melba caught on that Bru was looking.

Way to go, Bru.

But she just laughed and crossed her legs and said, "Now for breakfast. I figured you for herb tea or decaffeinated coffee. So I brought one of each. What will you have?"

"Either one's fine," Bru said. He was afraid his face was red. Well, maybe he wasn't so off females after all. It had been a long time since he'd had made satisfactory love. There was no doubt about that. He could feel his masculinity stirring. What if she peeled her clothes off instead of the lid to that coffee cup?

"I got a bagel and some yogurt and a bean burrito and two glasses of orange juice--fresh squeezed. After reading an article about the 1,2--DCA content in those new juice cans, I don't drink concentrate anymore."

"Where'd you hear about that?"

"Something I came across on line."

"Did I explain to you yesterday that I'm doing research in that topic?"

"No, you said citrus canker and you wanted information on a couple of people. What did you think of the bombshells I left on your answering machine?"

Bru blew on the cup of coffee until it was cool enough to drink. Then he took a sip. "I got in late and collapsed in the sack and didn't check my calls. What's bombshell number one?"

"That guy Arbuthnot you asked me to look up for you, he's dead. He was murdered in a home invasion style situation in broad daylight the day before yesterday. He lived in a tiny subdivision town out in the swamp somewhere on the way to the beach."

This news electrified Bru. "When did this happen? Day or night?"

"In the afternoon, I think. It was in yesterday morning's paper in the local section. I got a copy of the article here someplace."

The newspaper copy danced before Bru's eyes. The time of death was estimated at five p. m. The hair on the back of Bru's arms shot up. He had passed within a few miles of Arbuthnot's house, not many minutes before the man was killed. The article characterized Arbuthnot as an independently wealthy scientist who specialized in citrus research.

"Did you see my car?"

"Yeah, did you go through a war zone or something? As far as that goes, what's with your eye?" Melba set her styrofoam tea cup on the floor and swooped off the chair to Bru. She put her finger against the corner of his eye.

Bru took a sip of coffee. Melba's pushing up close to him made him edgy. He liked the way he felt. "Oh, that's nothing," Bru said.

"Looks like the beginnings of a hell of a shiner to me," she said.

"Maybe so. Some big biker took a poke at me."

"Where was this?"

"The Boot Hill Saloon."

"Egad, Bru, and here I used to think you were the original Clark Kent. And you hang out in places like the Boot Hill Saloon."

"I don't hang out there exactly."

She settled back on the chair. The sexual tension Bru felt dissipated some--but not much.

"I visited a farm run by an old lady who I think might have been Arbuthnot's mother. I found indication of citrus canker there. She took the shots at me."

"What you're doing, Bru, sounds so much more interesting than what you used to do," Melba observed.

That's what you call a cool response, Bru thought. "Did you say bombshells, plural?"

"Yes, the other one has to do with your friend Goins, the billionaire. I got you a lot of stuff on him." She tapped a leather bag which rested against her chair. "The bombshell is that he has a secret computer file at Lawson. Get this. I was able to access the directory name--Goins-- but I couldn't crack the special security code, which is usually pretty easy."

"Where is this file located?"

"In the registers controlled by the president and his endowment authority."

Bru's heart raced. Could this be the hard evidence he sought? Bru slowed down. He was getting far ahead of the data. "I suppose this file could simply say that Goins had been approached to give money and he said no."

"That's a possibility," Melba said. "But it is a directory, not a file, and it's of substantial size. The size of a small book."

"It's very important to me to find out what's in that file, Melba."

The phone rang. Sitting in the chair opposite him, Bru could smell Melba. He was snuffling her real scent--not some manufactured odor. She smelled of a fruit he couldn't place. Amber too had smelled like a fruit--the sprightly, spicy Surinam cherry. As he lifted the phone, Bru savored the thought of Amber and even enjoyed lingering over the pain of losing her; at least in his grief she still existed; she hadn't entirely vanished. "Hello," he said.

"Good morning, Rupert. It's President Newcombe, I mean Wilmer. How are you this morning?"

"Fantastic," Bru said. "I mean fantastic, Wilmer." Bru was pleased with the excited squeal Melba gave at hearing the name. He also liked calling Newcombe by his first name. Theoretically all faculty right up to and including the president were on a first-name basis at Lawson. In fact, anyone who wasn't a tenured full professor, never addressed Nuke'em as anything but "Dr. Newcombe Sir," or "President Newcombe," preferably with a genuflection. "I'm just enjoying the leisure you so thoughtfully provided for me."

"Now, now, Bru. Don't try to fool me. I know you are busily engaged in a very important research project for a very important man."

"How do you happen to know that, Wilmer?" Bru said.

"Er, a, well, er a. . . ." Newcombe sputtered. Certainly Newcombe and Goins were connected because the billionaire didn't just let out information about his business. Bru motioned for Melba to come and listen with him. She sidled up close to him and Bru put the receiver between their ears. Up close, her smell was overwhelming and delicious--something blonde and suggestive of the color of pink and Bru wished he could think of the fruit she smelled like. Something tropical and rich and fertile.

"Actually, Bru," Newcombe said, "you told me that when you stopped by yesterday."

"No, I didn't, Wilmer. My client specifically told me not to divulge his identity and I certainly haven't."

"Well, where I heard that is not important. You know how the old academic bush telegraph is. What is important is that we mend the rather bad way our meeting ended yesterday. I have sent Chief Cronin an e-mail telling him that of course you are welcome on campus at any time."

Melba was straining to keep from bursting out in a hoot. Bru could see her muscles tensing and her mouth was open and lopsided in a grin.

"That's mighty white of you, Wilmer," Bru said. He could feel Melba's muscles convulsing next to him.

"Let me get down to cases, Bru. In order to make up for my rudeness yesterday, I want to offer you a severance grant of eighteen months at full pay and benefits. I've got to run, Bru, so I can't discuss this offer in detail. But let me say it's yours when you want it." The phone clicked in his ear.

"He wasn't going to give you the chance to tell him to stuff it again," Melba said.

"How'd you hear of that?"

"The story is all over campus. You're sort of a folk hero, Bru."

"I'm glad he hung up in that case," Bru said, "before I accepted the offer."

"You weren't going to take him up," Melba said.

"I might have," Bru said.

"In that case you should be congratulated for showing good sense."

"You're easy to please," Bru said.

"I'm just easy, period," Melba said, wrinkling her nose at him.

"You are the most provocative woman," Bru said, still bumping butts with Melba even though he'd hung up the receiver. "Say, speaking of how my whereabouts became known, how did you find me? You left me your number. I didn't give you anything."

"You don't want to know."

"My wife gave it to you?"

Melba nodded. "Bringing the food was her idea too."

Bru had been thinking of the advisability of trying to bed Melba. That crack about being easy had gotten him going again. Mention of his wife snuffed that idea. It was almost as though he wilted. "I got to hit the shower. I have two appointments in north Florida today."

"You are not going to drive your busted up car out of the area, are you? Take my truck. I'm afraid your old clunker might not make it."

"My car's just a little breezy is all."

"Do you think you need a gun? If you want to zip by my apartment and get mine, we'll have to hustle. I have to make it to work."

The prospect of driving his car, beat up as it'd gotten in the past two days, was not thrilling. But there was no way Bru could take Melba's vehicle. He didn't know her well enough. He shook his head no, and suppressed a giggle on account of the offer of the gun. "I just need to take a shower."

"Well, all right." Melba kissed Bru on the cheek. "I'll crack that Goins's directory today and get back to you by time I get off work, which today is about seven in the evening." With that Melba made an exit, hair flying and bag trailing after her.

Dressing after showering to the tune of the fax's scratchy dot-matrix printer, Bru noticed the keys on the bureau top had an unmistakably Texas-looking key ring, a pair of very widely spread horns. Bru retrieved the bag of plant parts stowed under the sink and tore the fax off the machine and stuffed it, along with the research material and food Melba had left, into a backpack and ran out on the deck by the upstairs door. Sure enough, his clunker was gone. But a gleaming new pickup truck, a full-sized Ford F-250, sat in the parking spot. It had a crew cab, a snappy-looking black naugahyde cover stretched over the bed and, according to the writing on the side, was four wheel drive.

84

A yardstick could fit under the running boards. Bru hoped, a bit sheepishly, that Melba's truck had an automatic transmission because it had been a long time since he'd driven a stick.

No such luck. The truck stuttered and stammered as he negotiated the clutch and tried to coax the huge beast down the drive and onto the city street. The first stop on the day's itinerary was the bank. The closest facility was in the heart of downtown traffic, where Bru wanted to deposit Goins's check. He directed the snuffling and starting vehicle to a Suntrust branch where he deposited the twenty-five thousand. Then, after a fair bit of hassle, he drew a cashier's check for the amount and walked over to a nearby Barnett bank where, in the interest of saving time, he deposited the twenty-five thousand in a joint account he shared with Leta. Then he babied the huge truck up on I-4 which he took to the exchange for Florida's Turnpike, which he took to I-75 north and Tangerine County.

16

The monthly chiefs breakfast was something Shelby Buckett ducked as often as she could. This morning Shelby was late and trying to sneak to her seat at the head table when a cop spotted her. He popped to his feet. That was a sign for all the rest of them. Each of the twenty-odd chiefs sprung erect. The fattish, hair-thinning man at the podium took no notice. He continued to monotone the words his secretary had probably spent several sleepless nights on. Shelby motioned the cops to sit as she herself took her seat. That they sprung to attention every time she appeared annoyed the hell out of her. Had they done that because she was sheriff she wouldn't have minded. But they did it because she was a woman, and that pissed her royally.

The cop seated next to her poured her a cup of coffee. He was the chief from the tiny village called Palmdale, a nowhere place that had incorporated to keep from being swallowed up by neighboring Daylando. The speaker quit talking. There was modest applause. Shelby was about to sneak out when the guy next to her--she had to look at his nameplate to remember who he was, oh yeah the chief of Palmdale--said, "Shuriff, remember that homicide we had day before yesterday? Guy by the name of Arbuthnot?"

In a county with only fifty to sixty suspicious deaths a year, about half of which were homicides, of course Shelby remembered it. She told the chief as much.

"Well, sumpin kind of funny happened during the initial investigation. The complaint affidavit was filed by one of my boys, the cop on the beat."

"He responded to a call from a burglar alarm company, if memory serves," Shelby put in.

"True, but when he got there, one of your men was already there."

"So?" Shelby couldn't see anything strange in that. Her men beating the local cops. That sounded about right to her.

"Your guy didn't stick around."

"Why should he? A murder investigation is a FDLE matter, mainly."

"My guy thinks your guy took something from the house and put it in the trunk of his car just before our patrol car arrived."

"Oh," Shelby said. "What was the something?"

"The guy didn't get a good look. It was wrapped up in plastic and looked pretty bulky."

"Who was the officer?" Now Shelby switched into

her cop mode. Her eyes glazed and her face took on a cigar store Indian look.

"Hank Smith."

"Absolutely positive I.D.?"

"One hundred percent."

"Did any of this make its way onto the Complaint Affidavit or an Incident Report?"

"No, ma'am, it didn't."

"How long have you been sitting on this, chief?"

"The patrolman was a green kid. He completely let it pass at first, then got to thinking."

"Sloppy work, chief."

"I know, ma'am. What do you want me to do?"

"If you believe a violation of the law has occurred, file charges. If not, don't come to me with this halfway bullshit."

Shelby's car was idling near a bird of paradise plant and a couple of hibiscus bushes, standard landscaping fare for beachside hotels. She motioned to Al, the deputy who was driving. He pulled forward. Shelby took her laptop computer from the front seat and motioned for Al to buzz open the rear prisoner compartment. She got in and booted up the computer and hooked her cell phone into the telephone port. The laptop was powered by a super pentium c.p.u. with a speed of hundreds of megahertzs, bought by the money her troopers had confiscated on the interstate. She clicked on some very expensive software that had been developed in Australia. She typed in the name Hank Smith and added Arbuthnot. Then she added the names of Rupert Bruton, Leroy Wisnewski and, as an afterthought, Kimberly Chapman and Billy Goins.

She clicked the conclusion button. The machine groaned and churned in her lap for a time, then coughed up the following.

"Arbuthnot--independently wealthy researcher,

87

believed to have made most of his money in citrus research. Substantial criminal activity reported as a juvenile. During Vietnam War was listed as missing in action then later considered a prisoner of war. When he didn't voluntarily return with the prisoner exchange in 1973, he was deemed an enemy collaborator. He is believed to have spent part of his time under communist control in Red China during the Cultural Revolution. The attorney general under President Ford was preparing a case of criminal treason but this case was dismissed when the Carter administration came to power. Deceased--March 21, present year. Estimated time of death, 1600 to 1700 hours."

Shelby read all this and snorted. She added: "Body discovered by Deputy Hank Smith." She wondered, *When did Smith arrive on the scene?* She would have to check that out.

She continued reading: "Rupert Bruton, Ph.D. microbiology. Assistant Professor at Lawson College, which he left under a cloud. Research areas of note: eclectic. No arrests, no warrants. Past president of Advocates of the First Amendment." On reading of Bruton's affiliation with the AFA group, the sheriff snorted. Didn't surprise her at all that that Bruton would be associated with a commie organization like that. She clicked on the add button and typed, "Stopped by Deputy Smith on SR 415 on March 21 at approximately 1600 hours."

Shelby thought about the time of Smith's unreported interview with Bruton and the death of Arbuthnot and snorted again. Palmdale wasn't that far from the spot where Bruton had been attacked, less than ten miles. But how did it happen Smith went from bracing Wisnewski--unreported mind you--to Arbuthnot's place, also unreported, in just a few minutes? Or better yet, why did he go from Wisnewski to Arbuthnot's house in Palmdale--a place so obscure that Shelby had never been there, all this within minutes? Did

88

that fall under routine patrolling? Obviously a word with Smith's sergeant was in order.

The next entry that popped up was, "Leroy Wisnewski. Believed to have been a minor acolyte in the Charles Manson family in California in the late 1960s." Shelby's eyes registered shock at that news--Manson. "Continued after the incarceration of the major members of the family operating a string of girls, which he called the Jammin Family because of musical ambitions. Hardcore members of the group can be identified by a tattoo resembling a grandmother in the shape of a jam pot, believed to suggest Family Jams, a long-time Manson m.o. Multiple arrests for conspiracy to break and enter, bunko rackets, conspiracy of prostitution. Suspected in several contract murders, unproven. Has spent approximately five of the last twenty-five years in prison." Shelby added, "Exhibits interest in underage female juvenile, Kimberly Chapman, who reciprocates the same. Possibly felonious activity."

The next entry was: "William "Billy" Goins, listed as the world's 199th richest man by *Fortune* magazine. He has a net worth of approximately three billion dollars with considerable local assets in real estate, especially old citrus groves that have been developed into suburban subdivisions. His out-of-state and international holdings are varied and significant ranging to Latin America, particularly Brazil, and various corporations and holding companies. No arrests or convictions but, the Securities and Exchange Commission, the Federal Trade Commission and other oversight bodies have investigated him and his enterprises for suspicious business practices numerous times. Goins's firms pulled out of New York state after a exhaustive but inconclusive lawsuit by the Manhattan district attorney's office. He seems to have moved his private residence from Georgia after similar accusations were raised there--accusations which subsequently were settled in undisclosed ways.

Kimberly Chapman--granddaughter of one of the world's wealthiest men. Otherwise nothing. Recommend research-- citrus research and con scams and prostitution."

Sheriff Buckett looked at the computer screen and shook her head. What possible connection could there be between that rogue's gallery of characters--a communist collaborator from the Vietnam War era, an ex-Mansonite, a defrocked college professor and one of the world's richest men--and Deputy Hank Smith, for whom she had stuck her neck out more than once? She didn't know, but she was damn sure going to find out.

17

When the receptionist showed Bru into the master office at the Tangerine County Extension Service, Harry Neilson was sitting at his desk worrying some papers. On seeing Bru, Harry jumped to his feet and came around the desk and pumped Bru's hand.

Harry had been a student of Bru's at the university, while Bru taught part-time while finishing his PhD degree. Harry'd commuted from Tangerine, taking a few classes while working at the extension service. It had never seemed likely to Bru that Harry would actually complete a bachelor's degree. He was just too laid back, not to mention that he had early taken on the responsibility of a wife and three kids, who at that time were pretty far on their way to becoming college students themselves.

Bru had been wrong in a major way in his assessment of Harry. He had to have completed that bachelor's and a master's degree to be the head honcho in an extension office in a county of the agricultural importance of Tangerine. All this meant that Harry, as all extension agents, was ranked as an associate professor of the University of Florida. In a sense he outranked Bru, who would become an associate professor only if he were granted tenure at Lawson, a very bleak and remote prospect indeed. Now Harry looked the part of a senior professional. His hair was graying at the temples. Age and his natural slowness of manner, which had made him seem dull at the university, gave him a natural dignity now that he was pushing fifty.

"What brings you to my neck of the woods, Bru?" Harry asked.

"I'm working up a report on the citrus canker," Bru said. "I thought you'd be the guy to give me the background on it."

Through the thick lenses, Bru could see Harry's eyes narrowing in his plain, horsey face. Bru wondered if he had overstepped himself--obviously the citrus canker was still an emotional topic in the orange belt.

"Why don't I give you the nickel tour, Bru? Show you my demonstration grove and tell you how a citrus tree is made and all."

"Sure, Harry," Bru said. What else was there to say?

Harry led Bru across the Saint Augustine lawn to the citrus trees that surrounded the extension building on three sides. Rows of citrus trees ran down a slope to a perfectly circular lake. The earthy, swampy smell of the cattails and water lilies mingled with the overpowering scent of orange blossoms. Ranks of dark green trees, spangled with white blooms, undulated as far as Bru could see.

"I suppose you know why we plant on slopes?"

Bru wished Harry would come flat out and say he didn't want to discuss the canker so he could get about his business. He said, "Not really, Harry."

"For cold protection. Many people think the water

in the lakes at the bottom of the hills provides the cold protection. It's the elevation that makes the difference. The coldest air drops right down the slopes on top of the lake and leaves the hilltops and slopes relatively toasty. Those trees yonder loaded up with fruit are Valencias, which a real Florida citrus man invariably pronounces 'Valenchia.' You've probably heard of them."

"Bing Crosby used to pitch them in the o.j. commercials."

"Well, Bing was right about the Valencia being the world's most popular and best juicing orange, just about everywhere oranges are grown except for two places. The first place they are seldom grown, I'm told, is the Valencia district of Spain. The second place is right here at the northern end of the citrus belt in Florida. The Valencia is a late-season fruit. We don't pick them until April and they can hang on the tree until June or later. All that hang time makes for better development of sugar and flavor and a good deep color. Unfortunately it also makes them vulnerable to freeze damage. Since concentrate plants pay a premium for Valencias, you used to see a lot of this variety up here in the northern end of the citrus belt. Local growers seldom plant them now. Losing your trees productivity the following year to a freeze was bad enough without also losing this year's income, which is what happened when the Valencia crop was frozen.

"Nowadays we grow almost exclusively a variety called Hamlin. It's a very early fruit, ripening in October or November. The color's not good and the sugar content is nothing to write mom about, but it bears heavily and the crop is never threatened by frost. We also grow some Parson Browns and a few Washington Navels. The latter are shy bearers here and tremendously fickle and best left alone, but their reputation lure growers to taking the plunge. The variety I want to show you now is nothing like these

92

round oranges." Harry waded between a double row of trees with branches conspicuously bare of fruit.

As soon as the row of trees swallowed Bru up, Bru became aware of the heat. He began to sweat. Harry waded past four or five trees until he came to one with triangular shaped fruits. The oranges were a deep cadmium. Harry pulled a fruit from the tree with a twisting motion. An incredibly brilliant fragrance of citrus drifted to Bru's nostrils.

The skin peeled easily. "If the Temple ain't the world's tastiest citrus fruit, you're going to have to show me what's better," Harry said. "We call it an orange but really it's a tangor, a natural cross between a tangerine and an orange. I would tell you who discovered this variety-- properly called a cultivar--but there are too many proud fathers to say for sure. Everyone agrees this fruit is a native hybrid of the Sunshine State.

"Most years I believe this is the best fruit that grows, if not in the world, at least in Florida. But there are seasons when the Minneola or the Orlando, which are manmade crosses of the tangerine with the grapefruit are tastier. I can't tell you what determines which will be better. I can't even tell you which of the two fruits we just peeled will be tastier. It varies a lot from fruit to fruit and position on the tree, amount of sun exposure and so on.

"When you talk citrus in Florida you are talking juice. That's what most oranges are grown for in this state. And do we ever grow oranges here. This little state, or rather this little section of the state called Central Florida, grows more citrus than any other region of the world."

"Wait up there a minute, Harry. I thought Brazil surpassed Florida as the largest producer of citrus in the world some years ago."

"Yes and no, Bru. Back after the canker problem and a significant freeze or two, Brazil's citrus output ran three, maybe four times that of Florida's. But Florida is back on line now. True, Brazil still produces a bit more citrus, about 1.8 million tons of juice a year to 1.5 for us, but we are a much smaller region. From the land/yield ratio, Florida is easily the most productive citrus region on the globe."

"Is it really true Florida's oranges have better quality than those grown any other place?"

"Of course, that's true. But then my wife is the best looking woman in Tangerine City too. Californians like to brag their fruit is better because it is sold fresh around the country. The reason for that is that California fruit doesn't have a rind. It has armor plating because of the less beneficial climate they have out there. Also, their fruits aren't nearly as sweet as the Florida ones. That can be and is measured in degrees Brix, just like sugar is measured in grape juice for wine. What I'm saying, Bru, is that while yes, I believe Florida oranges are superior to those grown anywhere in the world, it doesn't make a damn bit of difference because a team of researchers working for the state of Florida just after the second world war invented frozen concentrated orange juice."

"Why would that make any difference?" Bru asked, as he helped himself to another section of the Temple orange, which tasted as sweet as candy.

"Because concentrated orange juice bears about the same resemblance to that fruit in your hand as kool-aid. The only thing that survives the concentrating process is the sugar. The orange flavors are all destroyed so those have to be reintroduced into concentrate. You can get that kind of information from your local home ec teacher. What I brought you out there for was to show you how a citrus tree is made, and that's important to know if you want to understand about the citrus canker. If you bend your hinges and look at this Temple's trunk down close to the ground, you will notice a line that goes around it."

"Sure," Bru agreed. "The texture of the trunk above is different from that below."

"And for a good reason," Harry said. "Two completely different kinds of citrus trees are represented right here. The top is obviously a Temple orange. It's apparent why we want a Temple on top. It is one of the finest fruits in the world. But why not plant the tree on it own roots? It would take one of those seeds we spit out, grown into a tree, seven or ten years to fruit. The tree would be leggy--tall and hard to pick--and also very thorny. But worst of all, the Temple on its own roots doesn't do well in the deep sand of the ridge country. But, fortunately, there are kinds of citrus that grow very well here. As it happens those trees don't produce useful fruits, but they can act as host plants for a graft of useful varieties.

"In days gone by we planted almost exclusively on rough lemon. But a disease made us start looking for something else about twenty years ago. We settled on hybrids made by the same guy that produced the tangelos. I can see you are getting a bit drifty, Bru, but bear with me. These hybrids had as one of their parents a deciduous citrus called the trifoliate orange. The trifoliate is hardy--actually I've heard the thing will live outside as far north as Boston. Its homeland is in central China, just north of Indochina where the edible citrus cultivars developed. Of course to live as far poleward as it does, it has to lose its leaves, which it does. So far as I know it is the only one of the so-called true citrus fruits that does."

Suddenly Harry had Bru's attention. A deciduous orange tree called trifoliate--three leaves. "Harry, what do the leaves of these trifoliate oranges look like?"

"They have what we call a leaflet, which means a leaf that's broken into several parts."

"Is the leaflet cross shaped?" Bru asked.

"Exactly. It sounds like you've seen one of those leaves before. By the eighties they were used as rootstocks to the tune of several million trees. It was to trees on Swingle stock that what you call the citrus canker struck most harshly."

"What do you mean by 'what you call citrus canker'?" Bru asked.

"Because the real name for it is the E strain or "Citrus Bacterial Spot," or CBS for short."

"Was that or was that not canker?" Bru wanted to know.

"It was canker-related but it wasn't the A strain or Asiatic canker. It's like chickenpox and smallpox. There are diseases you can live with and diseases that kill you. CBS can be lived with but Asiatic canker will destroy your crop--only we got it turned around and destroyed our crops ourselves for a disease that was practically harmless."

Bru was certain he had just learned something significant. "The canker doesn't seem to have done much damage to the grove land I see around us," Bru said.

"It's worse than it looks, Bru," Harry said, shaking his head. "Much worse. All the trees you are looking at here were replanted afterward. The canker turned this whole area into a desert. Beforehand, all this territory was owned in small lots, by little guys. The trees had been planted and tended by hand by pop and his boys and sometimes the mother and daughters even. Once the grove got up to producing size, generally the groves were taken care of by management outfits that fertilized the trees and picked and sold the crop. By now mom and pop were getting on in years and the money they got from their groves counted a lot toward their well being. Generally, one acre of grove land could be counted on to return one thousand dollars a year. If you had five acres, you had a small supplement to your income. If you had a hundred acres, which hardly anybody did up here, you were in deep clover. Then came the so-called citrus canker.

"See, no matter how well you take care of your trees, a few die every year--natural attrition. These trees were replaced with what we call resets, small trees on Swingle rootstock. Most of the resets were infected with the canker, which meant every citrus tree within eyeshot was destroyed by state crews with flamethrowers. Sure, the state indemnified the owner, but that payment was token. Taxes were still due and the price of replanting a grove had gone up. You couldn't just stick the trees in the ground and wait seven or more years for the grove to come into production. You had to irrigate and freeze-proof it. And all that took money, which the little guys didn't have, so they started selling out to the big boys. Around here the big boys were growers but elsewhere they were real estate developers." Harry hawked up a gob of phlegm and spit. "That's what I think of your citrus canker, Bru."

"So you mean to tell me that those five- and ten-acre grove owners sold out at rock bottom prices were hustled?"

"You're damn right they were hustled, Bru. The state said it made a mistake and that it was sorry--although it didn't say it very loudly. In the meantime the family farm was gone."

"Where did the disease come from, Harry?"

"Bru, last I checked, I was the only person in Tangerine county to believe that Lee Harvey Oswald shot John F. Kennedy. But I wouldn't bet you a quarter that that canker spontaneously developed in Florida."

"Why's that Harry?"

"Look at AIDS, Bru. Did it start full blown with a million cases a year? Of course not. It began with a few cases, the number of which doubled or tripled every year. With canker we had an epidemic the first year it was discovered, and the groves that were most infected were

97

those around cities where the land was most valuable. You probably know about Daylando, between Orlando and Daytona and similar areas were infected around Tampa and Sarasota and Fort Myers. It was a swindle of unbelievable proportions, Bru. And we just sat here like boobs and took it. The big guys down in the groves on the ridge south of Orlando hardly lost a tree, but the family grove owner, he was the one that was wiped out."

Harry's voice quavered. His jaw and neck was shaking with rage.

"Did you lose property?" Bru asked.

"Not me, Bru. I had this job. I was directing the crews that showed up like stormtroopers and incinerated peoples's groves. But friends and family did. It was a nightmare. I suppose it is too much to ask that the son of a bitch that was responsible for this pays one day. I'm not a vengeful person, Bru. I don't ask it to make me feel better. I want it so some sense of proportion and justice be reestablished in the world."

"Harry, I have something to show you," Bru said. "Let me get this bag and we'll open it in your office."

Bru put the bulky bag on Harry's desk. He untwisted the tie and removed the various plastic bags. Harry took a quick look at the lesions on the twigs and jumped back. "Jesus, Bru, you know what that is--" His voice trailed off. His eyes narrowed and he brought his head closer to the twigs. He felt the branchlets and his nose wrinkled as though he was sniffing. Then he opened the tray drawer of his desk and took out a magnifying glass and turned on a desk lamp and made a very close examination of the plant material. He went over each leaf and branch.

After two minutes of silence, he shook his head. "I'm not a plant pathologist, Bru. So I can't tell you what this disease is, but I can tell you what it is not. It's not Citrus Bacterial Spot, the disease we thought was the canker."

"So what is it?"

"Like I said, I don't know," Harry said. "My training in this field is limited to recognizing major citrus diseases. I can tell the difference between greasy spot and sooty mold and tristesta. I can tell what is and what is not CBS. What you have here is definitely some kind of disease--or more likely several different diseases. Each branch seems to exhibit different symptoms. This one has lesions. That one sunmarks. That one there looks waterstained."

Bru examined the twigs and noticed today what he'd missed the day before, that the symptoms were widely divergent.

"To my eye," Harry went on, "the symptoms appear to be bacterial and they could be related to the canker family. It may even be the real canker, that is the Asian canker. But what it isn't is the disease that played such havoc with our groves back in the eighties. I can tell that for a dead certainty." Harry looked at Bru's face and then added, "Sorry to have disappointed you, Bru."

"I think puzzled me is the better term."

"You have a perfect right to be puzzled. The disease is on a trifolitata twig. That citrus species was outlawed in this state twelve, fourteen years ago. Before they figured out CBS was not that threatening a disease, you would go to jail for growing a trifoliate orange tree."

"I found an entire grove of the things--big mature trees. They date back into the eighties or before, and they were loaded up with this disease."

Harry shook his head.

Bru considered taking Harry into his confidence, about telling him about the possible link of his case to the so-called KiDS epidemic. He didn't. It all seemed so very fantastic, especially now that the disease turned out not to be the canker. He simply said, "Thanks for your help, Harry."

"Anytime, Bru," Harry said. "And Bru keep an eye on your backside. The people who perpetrated that canker scam are greedy, ruthless bastards. Don't ever forget that, Bru."

18

Bru was fifteen minutes late for his appointment with Professor Khoury when he left Harry so he stopped at a convenience store and called. Then Bru remembered he hadn't gotten back to Michaelson Labs in Minneapolis. He found that number and dialed it wishing he'd stolen Leta's cell phone along with her answering machine. He got on the line at Michaelson and told the agent to go ahead with the 1,2--DCA tests on the plastic citrus juice cans. She said she'd draw up a contract and fax it to Bru for approval.

University professors usually have modest, even ratty, offices. As a Nobel laureate and an endowed chair not to mention an egomaniac, Bru expected Khoury would have promoted himself something lavish. Pushing out of a corridor of mixed labs and offices smelling of strong chemicals and into Khoury's office, Bru entered an inner sanctum set up with a TV and a couch and one of those easy chairs that makes the sitter seem as though he's in traction. There was also a wet bar and microwave and a refrigerator. Bru heard water running. A door opened and Prof. Humbert Khoury shuffled into the room. The old man in carpet slippers bore only a shadow of a resemblance to the fellow Bru had known--and hated. He still wore the same scruffy gray goatlike beard, but vast amounts of lard had melted away. His brown eyes were rheumy and old-man looking and his complexion had a pasty unhealthy pallor.

"You're looking fit," Bru lied.

"So are you," Khoury returned in a false tone.

"I'm not," Bru said. "I was turned out by Lawson." Bru had to get that out before Khoury extracted it on his own.

Dr. Khoury was extending his hand to Bru. Suddenly he stopped as though stricken, his hand frozen at about one-quarter extension. "I'm sorry to hear that, Bru. Very sorry. How are Leta and that young one of yours bearing up?"

Bru explained about his daughter's death and his wife's defection.

"God, Bru," the old man said, "that's more than a man should have to bear." That hand extended to shake went around Bru's shoulder and suddenly Bru found the old man embracing him. Bru doubted if this guy, who had caused Bru and his family more grief than any person he could think of, had ever shook his hand before. Now here he was hugging him. Bru could feel his shrunken flesh and smell his old man's b.o. But none of that was distasteful. Just the opposite. Bru drew strength from his condolences while, paradoxically, for a moment Bru thought he might break down and cry. So much had happened to Bru so fast that he hadn't had time to stop and let himself react emotionally. For sure, he hadn't had time to process Leta's disappearance yet. He couldn't possibly take it as stoically as he appeared to--or could he?

The old man stepped back. His face now looked even older and sadder and more drawn. "Your wife, that nice Czech," he pronounced the word *Zheck*, "girl from Cleveland. She took off on you just because you suffered a little misfortune."

Bru was impressed that his old nemesis remembered

so much about his family life. "Don't think harshly of her," Bru said. "After Amber died, we only went through the motions of pretending we were a couple. When she was here we met each other's needs. When she wasn't we didn't. It was about as simple as that."

"I hope you can hang onto that vision when times get tough."

"I hope I can too. She went back to Jerry Wiley. You probably don't remember him--"

"Of course, I remember Jerry Wiley. He was one of those young political nerds. Ran around in a coat and tie back in the seventies when practically everyone else was going around nude. He'd figured out there was a lot of money in the student activity fund and was milking that."

"In a way I'm rather glad she's with Jerry. I don't have to worry about her. I know she will be looked after."

Khoury took a step back from Bru and looked at him full for a moment then shook his head. "You're a decent man, Bru. I always remembered that about you. You were honest and reliable to a fault--like that time you corrected my transference-translation mistake to your lab classes. You must have known, given my ego, that I would rage at you on account of it. But you straightened the students out. Only your lab sections got it right on the exam and I got even with you for it."

"I think I was probably just naive," Bru said. "I'd heard stories about departmental politics and jealous professors taking their grudges against their colleagues out on the other's grad students and the like, but I didn't believe that such things happened."

"Well, I taught you different, didn't I, Bru?" Khoury said, "How about a drink, Bru?"

Bru couldn't imagine himself having a drink in the middle of the day in a university office. He heard himself say, "That's a swell idea." He noticed Khoury had taken a step back and tears were flowing down his face. The old man stooped over a credenza and slid open a door and brought up a bottle of Early Times and two large glasses. Bru watched him pour five fingers into each glass. "You want some ice or water?"

Bru shook his head no. The old man pushed the glass into Bru's fingers and said, "Sometimes life can really be shit."

Bru slumped to the couch. He took a tentative sip of the bourbon. Then he took a slug of it. It tasted very good. Maybe he didn't feel so stoic about Leta's going away after all. Khoury, who'd sat down next to him, shook Bru's arm.

"I was turned out from the first position I held--a post doc research professorship that would supposedly end up as a cushy tenured spot at a fancy ivy think tank. At the time--and I was no spring chicken--I thought my career was through. The only job I could find was down here in the Deep South. They didn't call the place the sunbelt yet and my colleagues would have fallen on the floor if anyone had suggested Florida would become as large and important a state as it is. I had to make myself over to do work in genetics--a field I really knew little about and wasn't very fond of. And guess what, I ended a Nobel Laureate. I hope you can do as well with your crisis, Bru."

"Thank you, sir. Now about this Arbuthnot."

"He was a strange bird, Bru, one of those self-educated hangers-on. He built lab experiments. You have to have something on the ball to do that. A good lab man frequently knows more chemistry than the graduate students who are teaching the lab classes. He was a tall gangly guy. Maybe you remember him from that description. As I recall he worked here about the time you were in grad school."

"None of that rings a bell, but I was scrambling hard to get through as fast as possible and then later to start and rear a family."

"Arbuthnot's gangliness was due in part from his internment by the communists during the Vietnam War."

"If I ever knew this guy, I wouldn't forget something like that."

"Probably not," Khoury agreed. "He was one of those who kept his own company. There were those I learned later who claimed he was actually an American deserter who had gone over to the communists."

"Those were some pretty weird times," Bru said. "I was just a little too young for the draft but my dad was career army. According to him I wouldn't have needed any draft to sign up because he personally would have hunted me down and shot me had I tried to run off to Canada instead of going into the service."

"Personally, I think there may have been something in the claim this Arbuthnot was a collaborator because he came to me with this citrus disease. He claimed he'd started with the A strain of canker, that is the virulent Asian canker, and transformed it through a secret process to a milder version. He believed he was in the way to making a fortune by selling his milder version to grove owners to innoculate their citrus trees in the field against the deadly strain. I considered him a crank right from the start. I said before that some of our lab technicians know more than the graduate students. What I meant was the technicians hang around and absorb requisite knowledge about a certain complex of experiments. Their knowledge, while impressive, is empirical and has no depth or theory to back it up."

"They talk the talk," Bru said, "but they don't walk the walk."

"That's it exactly," Dr. Khoury said. "This fellow was a little brighter than the general run but it didn't take long for me to determine he had not genetically engineered that bacterial disease. He'd found it someplace. Later we learned the preferred host plant for the canker outbreak in Florida was the trifoliate orange, native to the temperate regions of China. I wouldn't be surprised if he acquired it in China and brought it back. I think his plan was to develop a sort of protection racket among the citrus growers. They'd pay off or he'd infect their groves, and of course they didn't know his strain was not the virulent one. Clearly, he wanted to make money out of his discovery, but he wanted intellectual fame too. That's why he hung around the university and ultimately came to me. He thought he could graft into my budding glory in those years."

"What happened to him?"

"I don't know. Like you I was pretty busy myself at the time. Once I determined to my satisfaction he was a crank, I forgot about him and I presume he drifted away from the university community. Those were the very years when it was bruited about that I was being nominated for the Nobel."

"So?" Bru said.

"So I kept mum about Arbuthnot's possible role in all this because I didn't want any scandal. It would be sure to stop the Nobel committee from awarding me the prize. Then afterward I guess I felt I sat on that information too long to go public with it. In any case, I've never told anyone about Arbuthnot before. I'm glad to get it off my chest. You've figured out I'm dying, haven't you, Bru?"

Bru nodded, and the truth of that assertion just then struck Bru. "Cancer?"

"Yes. I have the Big C. It doesn't greatly matter. I haven't done a lick of work since I got that damn prize. I was so fucking vainglorious about it. I was the only person who was awarded a prize by himself in science that year. I made a career out of gloating and chest thumping afterward. Of course, I wouldn't turn Arbuthnot's name over to the authorities. What did I care if thousands of acres of citrus were needlessly destroyed? What did the shattered lives of the people whose livelihood depended on those trees matter to a Nobel Laureate? I was an ass, Bru. I'm glad you've come here and given me the chance to get that Arbuthnot thing off my chest--and an opportunity to make things right with you. I fucked you over. Your prelim was marginal but could have passed, but I flunked you because I was pissed. I'm sorry about that."

Bru put the pad he'd been furiously scribbling notes into onto his lap and picked up the glass of bourbon.

"I only have one other thing to tell you about this guy, Bru. Some months ago--not many but not just recently either--he stopped by to see me again. He'd heard somehow that my health wasn't of the best, he said, and wanted to pay his respects. He hadn't changed much. He was tall and thin and a little gray now with a professorial air, but he was wearing overalls like a factory worker. I thought that was odd. He seemed to be proud of his overalls, as though they were a badge of office. Our discussion was really strange. Naturally, neither of us alluded to the canker episode and his role in it, although it had to be at the front of his mind as well as my own. He didn't act smug but somehow it was apparent he thought he'd made good in the world and he wanted me to celebrate his triumph with him. All this was particularly odd with him in those overalls, still soiled from work. He advised me to get into the orange juice commodities market. He said there would be some big money to be made there--and very soon."

"I don't know much about the futures markets," Bru said, "but there must be some time line involved. Did he give you any indication of when to buy your contracts?"

"Yes, starting in the fall. He said orange juice prices would be going up--way up--by then."

About an inch of liquor filled the bottom of Bru's glass. He swished the liquor and watched the waves chase each other around the circle of the glass. Suddenly he upended the glass and chugged all the bourbon. What a bomb Khoury had just dropped.

Even stranger, Bru was overcome by an altogether different feeling. Here he was billing and cooing with an old man he couldn't stand. Sure, all this lovy-dovey, kiss-your-enemy shit was supposed to be touching. But why then did he feel deep anger, instead of cheek-turning Christian piety? He didn't know exactly what to say to the old fart--that he understood. That that year he'd taken Bru away from Amber was perfectly all right. He didn't mind.

Before Bru was able to get too worked up, Khoury said, "What kind of work led you to Arbuthnot--and me--anyway?"

"I was hired to write a report showing that there is no chemical contamination in frozen orange juice because of the new plastic orange juice containers."

"Jesus, Bru, it sounds like someone is trying to play you for the fool, given what I just told you about Arbuthnot."

"It would sort of seem that way," Bru said.

"What's the chemical contaminant you are supposed to give a clean bill of health?"

"1,2--DCA or 1,2 Di---"

"I know perfectly well what it stands for. When I was a young fellow, I pulled a hitch as a consultant doing a study on 1,2--DCA. We wanted to show it was toxic."

"Were you able to make your case?"

"No. The corporation we were doing the work for was trying to deflect liability from itself. The corporate lawyers thought that 'aldehyde' suffix would fly well with a jury of lay folks. The only problem was that its scientific team--us--couldn't turn up any results. The company spent a bundle too."

"My preliminary research shows 1,2--DCA is

completely harmless," Bru said.

"That's almost an understatement, Bru. You could drink a tumbler of the stuff. Nevertheless, it seems suspicious that anyone would hire you--a defrocked teaching professor at a liberal arts college--to carry out a study of this sort. If you don't mind my saying so, one would think a little more horsepower might be called for."

"Yes, that does look suspicious," Bru admitted. "It would certainly be easier to pull the wool over one guy, especially a nonspecialist in the field, than over the heads of a team of crack guys. I raised that question and was told the big national labs would take too long to produce a report. If your friend Arbuthnot's information is correct--and if they needed an erroneous report to help lull the market--it would obviously have to be ready soon. My time line was twenty-eight days, one lunar month."

"The question is who's 'they' and what is at stake anyway? I mean I can't imagine a little chemical contamination of o.j. making so much difference that the market would collapse."

"The guy that hired me said he wanted the report to cool the claims that 1,2--DCA--and by extension orange juice--causes that KiDS epidemic the media is harping about."

"Fear of KiDS might make the o.j. market collapse all right. Who hired you anyway? Anybody of stature?"

"Billy Goins," Bru said.

Khoury shook his head. "Never heard of him. Should I have?"

"He's just your garden-variety, self-made billionaire. Mean as a snake but a whole lot greedier."

"In short the kind of guy who might actually be behind some kind of orange juice swindle."

"Yes, actually, he may have teamed up with your friend Arbuthnot. Someone seems to have. A very level-headed country extension agent told me this afternoon that thousands and thousands of acres were grabbed up after groves contaminated by the canker were destroyed."

"I wish you'd quit calling Arbuthnot my friend, Bru. Do you know for a fact that Arbuthnot and your employer Goins are in cahoots?"

"No. Just supposition."

Khoury shook his head. "Supposition is not a good thing for a scientist. But, on the other hand, you have to follow your intuition. The scientific method requires you posit, that is develop, a hypothesis or theory so that you can then test it," Khoury lectured Bru like a college freshman.

"Yes, I know," Bru said.

"Of course you do, Bru, but never forget your intuition needs to be tested by scientific investigation. Don't let yourself hang out on a limb without the evidence to back you up. Jesus, the KiDS epidemic. That shit is vicious. It's hard to believe anyone could be evil enough to harm children just to make money."

"Especially a guy like Goins who couldn't possibly spend what he already has."

"How much you've got hasn't anything to do with what you want, Bru. You should have learned that by now."

"I suppose so," Bru said.

Khoury tilted his head, and looked at Bru out of half-lidded eyes. His dark, always-before-so-inscrutable orbs seemed to regard Bru with a combination of pity and puzzlement. "Bru, what would you do if your worst case scenario plays out?"

"Bust them, of course."

"How do you plan to do that?"

"By taking my evidence to the authorities."

"And what could that be, the voluminous studies showing 1,2--DCA to be perfectly harmless? How are the authorities going to be able to tell you are not some crank?"

"I don't know," Bru said, thinking of the reaction Jerry had yesterday when Bru intimated that President Newcombe was in collusion with Goins.

"If you get in too deep, you come to me, Bru. I'll throw the weight of my Nobel Laureate behind you. They'll have to pay attention to that. I owe you that."

"Thank you, sir," Bru said.

"Jesus, Bru, don't call me 'sir.' That sounds like sarcasm."

"It wasn't," Bru said.

"I know it. Now you'd better get me up to speed on what you have learned so far."

Bru obliged the old man, but he had hardly started the presentation of his evidence when Bru could see Khoury was fading. Bru could tell it was time for him to go, to let the old man rest. He wondered if the old guy would have the stamina to back him up, if it came to that. He said, "Dr. Khoury, can you tell me how to test for 1,2--DCA? I'm a little rusty on that procedure and I'd prefer not to have to look it up."

Khoury said, "No problem, Bru," and, tired as he was, he tatted out the steps that had to be followed. Bru tiptoed out of the room like a man leaving a hospital ward. In the corridor, Bru shook his head. This interview hadn't turned out like anything he expected. Nothing at all like it.

19

Al, the driver of the sheriff's cruiser, said, "Sheriff Buckett to see Mr. Goins." The guard in the spit-shined Sam Browne belt with a toothpick in his mouth picked up a clipboard and consulted it breezily. "Sorry, you're not on the list--" Suddenly the arrogant young man did a double take.

Sheriff Shelby Buckett leaned forward and said, "Just slide that gate open, please, and phone the big house that the sheriff is here to see Mr. Goins."

Al pressed the button. The window went up. The guard started talking but the gate was sliding open. Al drove. The car went up the drive. The house came into view. Shelby was disappointed. Goins was supposed to be one of the two hundred richest individuals in the world. Compared to the neighboring domiciles with their gleaming tile roofs and garish, modern colors and overbuilt--in relation to lot size--houses, his old, not-very-well-kept-up place looked like a dive. The grass needed mowing, and on driving closer to the house, Shelby could see the paint was peeling.

So this is how the 199th richest man in the world spends his money, Shelby thought. *Or rather how he doesn't spend his money.* But Shelby was very much aware that Goins had been more liberal with his funds last election season. Twenty-five thousand dollars had flowed from the old man to the sheriff's election coffers. That tidy little sum amounted to about a tenth of what it cost her to keep her job as sheriff. But not a dollar of his so very generous contributions made a bit of difference to Shelby now. She wasn't even bothered by the fact that those monies, given through five different individuals, came to ten times the legal limit for campaign contributions. Shelby Buckett's goal was to fight crime. Anyway she could. And she couldn't fight crime if she wasn't in office. She pushed the door bell-- once, twice, three times. The extra punches were to show she wasn't intimidated by Goins' vast fortune, or by the cash he'd funneled to her the year before, legal or not.

The heavy steel door--selected to withstand

111

hurricanes or sieges--swung open and a woman, with her hair in a gravity-defying winged do and dressed to the nines, said, "Why, sheriff, it is so nice of you to call." Her accent was incredibly southern. In Central Florida Shelby rarely met a person in the thirties who spoke with such a pronounced drawl. And her manner was very feminine.

"Right this way, sheriff."

Shelby was led through the foyer and into a ballroom that had the dusty, moldy smell of an old rug. The woman paused to unlock a door, then whisked Shelby into a closet sized room. Two fancy old-fashioned chairs were separated by an old table. A room air conditioner had the air chilled down to about the temperature of a frosted beer mug. The woman graciously installed Shelby in the first chair. She made a little curtsy. Shelby caught a whiff of the woman's fragrance--something flowery and southern and old-fashioned. Cape Jasmine. She also showed Shelby a generous portion of breast while managing to appear completely proper and chaste.

"I don't believe I got your name," Shelby said.

"It's Elizabeth," the belle said. "Elizabeth Chapman--why sheriff, don't tell me you forgot I contributed five thousand dollars to your campaign last year." This was delivered with direct and flirtatious eye contact. Then her eyes dropped into her lap. She seemed to study her hands "I know my puny gift wasn't very much, but it was all I could afford. My father is not a very generous man. He insists I act as his majordomo and chief of staff in order, he says, that I may know how to manage his concerns after he's gone. Alas, my position is unsalaried."

Elizabeth Chapman, Goins's daughter and mother of the girl at the substation last night. That made sense. Somehow Shelby had completely overlooked her. She seemed to remember that Elizabeth Chapman was one of the names Goins's money came in under.

112

"Sheriff, I cannot thank you enough for what you did for my daughter yesterday evening."

What exactly had Shelby done for the daughter that she should be thanked for? "The girl seemed in a bad way."

Elizabeth sat bolt upright in her chair. "Why, I should say so. The little vixen sneaked out of the house and called a stranger man. That's my idea of a very bad situation indeed."

"Tell me about this fellow Bruton she was out with."

"Bruton, oh, er, Dr. Bruton," she danced verbally. "I er don't think he, um, was trying to be anything but helpful."

"But what was he doing with your daughter?"

Elizabeth's eyes flashed and, for a moment, her gray-green eyes seemed those of an angry bird of prey. "Yes, what was the--my daughter doing with him?" Then she collapsed on herself and did the trick with her hands in her lap. "I was so distressed to learn my darling was out of the house it never occurred to me to ask how she became attached to Dr. Bruton. Can you tell me?"

"No, ma'am, I came here for that information in particular."

"Dr. Bruton works as a consultant for my father." Elizabeth's eyes seemed to light up with pleasure when she said Bruton's name. "You know he was my professor at the University of Florida."

Shelby didn't like what she'd just heard. And why was that? Because she had a hard-on for Bruton. She'd disliked him originally because she'd caught him out with an underage woman. But his sexist backsass last night didn't help matters any. Nor those commie pinko ideas of his.

"What does Bruton do for your father?"

"Tsk, tsk, sheriff. You don't really expect me to answer that one. I will reveal to you the secrets of my sex life, but I wouldn't dream to talk about business with a lawman who didn't have a warrant. My father would kill me." She stopped as though dumbstruck. Her face turned lobster red. "Oh, goodness, how could I have been so crude? What will you think of me?"

"So you don't think there is anything wrong with Bruton's relations with your daughter."

"Certainly not," she snapped. Then dropping her eyes she said in a pensive tone, "Well, I hope not. I have been disappointed by men many times in my life.

"I suppose the real question is why was your daughter so interested in this Wisnewski character."

Elizabeth's hand came to her temples. "I was afraid you'd bring that dreadful subject up. The doctors explain it as Stockholm syndrome. My husband and I settled in Southern California where this Wisnewski's gang kidnapped Kimberly and held her for ransom--on the installment plan. The man was simply awful. He had these girls who worked for him doing unspeakable things. During the time Kimberly was held she came to identify with Wisnewski. I'm told it is not uncommon for such things to happen, but this Leroy Wisnewski was not relying on chance. He was capable of what used to be called brainwashing. He could take a perfectly ordinary middle class girl and turn her into a prostitute or worse in a matter of days. We were able to get Kimberly away from him with the help of private detectives in a few weeks, but I'm afraid the damage was done. She sometimes claims Wisnewski was her father and at other times her lover, and I hope the latter claims are childish fantasy. The doctor wanted to check to see if she was still intact but I put my foot down. We are not that kind of family." The woman was sobbing, tears leaking out of her eyes and coursing across her cheeks. "You must excuse me, sheriff. I'm so weak."

"Did Wisnewski maintain contact with her?"

"We were deathly afraid he'd try to steal her away

again. That's the reason for the fierce display of protective devices around here."

"Well, I guess you don't have to worry about him anymore."

"Oh but we do," Elizabeth blubbered. "We don't know what his influence will make Kimberly want to do."

"Was any of this reported to the police in California?"

"No, I begged my father to go to the authorities but he insisted on handling it himself."

"Would you please ask your father if he would mind talking with me?"

Elizabeth sobbed for a few seconds then looked up and said, "Sorry, he's not here."

"Then would it be all right if I had a word with Kimberly?"

"It most certainly would be but she is under the influence of the sedatives the doctor administered."

"Well, then I think it best I go. Thank you for your help."

"Oh, sheriff, do you have to leave so soon? I haven't even had time to offer you tea or cucumber sandwiches." Now this Elizabeth was hovering over Shelby's chair, showing her tits and her tear-streaked face powder.

Shelby brusquely fought her way out of the chair and to the door. Elizabeth clung to her as for support and comfort. When Shelby made it back to the cruiser, she turned on her laptop and thought about entering Elizabeth's name into her Australian data base. Then she laughed and thought why bother. Anybody could see Elizabeth was a Suzi Creamcheese who hadn't had an independent thought in her life. There was no point wasting the time.

20

Bru exited I-4 at East Colonial and drove until he found a supermarket. He hadn't eaten a thing since gobbling up the food Melba left him on the way to Tangerine City, but the first aisle he sought out bore the legend "household goods." He put a large Pyrex measuring cup in his basket then found the detergent aisle and picked up a gallon of bleach. Then he went to the drink aisle. Across from the milk he found a gallon of distilled water. He helped himself to three different brands of frozen orange juice. A large iced tea jar with a plastic dispenser top was displayed at the end of an aisle. He tucked one of those jars between his elbow and his ribs and made for the check-out lane, where he picked up a disposable propane lighter while waiting for the cashier. After checking out, he went into the Eckerd's pharmacy next door and asked the druggist for iodine.

Once in the kitchen of his garage apartment, Bru realized he should have also gotten a pair of pliers--and not bothered with the propane lighter because the unit had a nice gas stove that would serve his purpose. He appreciated the opportunity presented to ask Salome for the use of a pair of pliers, but he was even happier on looking in a drawer to find a pair a previous tenant had left. He measured exactly one half liter of distilled water into the iced tea jar and that was followed by a quarter liter of bleach. Then he pulled the plastic tab from the orange juice carton and went to the bathroom and scooped the frozen orange pulp into the toilet. With his pocket knife, he cut a 12 centimeter square from the carton. This square he washed under the tap, then he dried it on his shirttail and, squeezing the piece of plastic in the jaws of the pliers, he fired up a burner on the stove with the aid of disposable propane lighter.

He held the pliers over the flame until the plastic was charred. The ash was deposited in the distilled water. The lid was screwed on the jar, and then Bru agitated the water until the ash went more or less into solution. He took the iodine bottle and sucked up exactly fifty milliliters, which he dribbled into the iced tea jar. He watched the face of his watch for sixty seconds then checked out the solution in the jar--no color change. No 1,2--DCA. Bru selected a second o.j. can and repeated the experiment. The results were the same. He took the third cylinder of o.j. and put it in the refrigerator and washed up the iced tea jar and turned it upside down on the enamel grooves of the sink top.

He had no idea what a positive test would have proved, after that discussion with Khoury about the relative harmlessness of the chemical. Bru went downstairs, booted up his computer, and ran an on-line search for KiDS. An article Bru turned up on a news service listed the possible KiDS death total nationwide at 100--double what it had been the last time he'd checked just a couple of days before.

Bru hiked up the stairs and called Sam Goldstein, who taught in Lawson's famed MBA program. The phone rang and rang. Bru left a detailed voicemail message asking Sam to check the orange futures market and to report any unusual activity especially for the fall months.

Weighed down with these thoughts Bru trudged up the shell drive toward Salome's house. He wondered if she had roast beef leftover from last night. Just as he made the walk, a stretch limo glided up to what would be the curb if Florida had curbs. The driver, a white guy in a shapeless black polyester suit, bustled around and opened the rear door and there emerged a black man not much shorter than the gantry they use to hoist up rockets over at the Cape.

His skull was shaved bare except for a goatee. He had on a tuxedo with a pink tie and cummerbund. A Mr. Clean earring gleamed in his left ear. As anybody who had been breathing in the city for the past year knew, it was Todd Tolson, the Orlando Magic's hope to replace Shaquille O'Neill and Penny Hardaway. The screen door slammed and Salome came running. She was dressed to kill in a lame dress that complimented her complexion. She looked positively gorgeous. Tolson caught her hands. Salome leaped from the pavement and delivered a kiss to his cheek.

In spite of these acrobatics, Salome noticed Bru. "Hey, Dr. Bruton," she called. "Are you doing better today? You didn't look so good yesterday."

"Yeah, lots better," Bru said.

"That's good," she said, flashing one of her very brilliant smiles at him. The driver somehow got between Salome and Bru, and she was shunted into the car. The last Bru saw of her was a hand waving between the two men, then she was inside the darkened windows of the limo and it was moving away.

Before Bru had time to cogitate on this scene, a two-door, snot-green Chevrolet of late eighties origin bounced over the sidewalk. It skidded to a wheel-locked stop. Bru heard a gravelly old man voice say, "Joo-an, get him in here. Then go complete your assignment." Goins's manservant, in starched madras shirt and matching shorts, circled the vehicle.

"Why doesn't he come inside my place?" Bru offered.

"Tell him to get his ass over here," the old man said.

Juan Robert pointed toward the car. Bru slid through the open door onto the Chevy's bench seat. "Close the door," the old man barked.

Bru obliged him and the old man said, "Where the hell have you been all day? We tracked your car down to the library at Lawson College, and then we had the Lawson security detail turn that place upside down and inside out. No Bruton was found. Are you trying to throw me off the scent?"

"You hired me to research a report, remember?" The heat in Bru's voice matched Goins's.

"I hired you to do a report. So why aren't you writing?"

"Because I have to get the facts straight first," Bru said. "And from what I've found so far the facts in this case are far from being straight."

"I didn't come here to talk about any nickel and dime report," Goins's said. I want to know what you were doing with my granddaughter last night." Like antennae, the old man's bushy eyebrows seemed to pop erect and track Bru. The old man's eyes were red and angry.

"I'd like to know the answer to that question myself. She called me and asked me to help her find some guy named Leroy who she described as her father and/or friend and/or stepfather. I found the guy for her all right, but he was on a slab of marble at the morgue in the county jail. Stranger yet, this same guy stopped me on a motorcycle the day before and broke out the driver side windows--all of them. So maybe you can tell me something about who this Leroy is and what the hell is going"

"That's none of your business."

"What?" Bru screeched. "That guy attacked me. Your granddaughter called me up to find him, and you tell me that's none of my business."

"Exactly right. Nothing having to do with my family is any of your business," Goins brayed at Bru. He looked away from Bru toward the garage apartment. Bru followed his line of sight and saw Juan Robert emerge from his upstairs door with the 1,2--DCA files. He carried the stack in both hands, straight down in front of him. The weight made him roll like a pregnant woman. "And as far as that goes nothing concerning me is any of your concern. As of this moment you are terminated as an employee of mine. I will thank you to return that twenty-five thousand dollars Jerry Wiley browbeat out of me and which you so craftily deposited in your account at Suntrust bank and removed to yet another account this morning."

The only thing Bru could think of was the two copies of the contract which he'd left lying on the kitchen table. No doubt Juan Robert had swept up both of them up, and so Bru would have no paper trail leading him back to Goins, to explain that twenty-five thousand dollar check the sheriff had thought so peculiar should that ever become necessary again. Bru told himself he was on the wrong tack here. He was being defensive, which he'd been ever since meeting Goins. The only person he'd shown any spine to was the sheriff--the sheriff, that was the ticket.

"You want your money back, I'll give it back to you. A check will be all right, won't it?"

"Why are you being a smart ass, Bruton? You know something, don't you? I knew I never should have let them talk me into getting involved with a dumb fuck Ph.D."

"That's my problem. I don't know a fucking thing. But everyone keeps thinking I do, such as the sheriff who insisted I divulge the nature of my business dealings with you last night. I of course refused then. Because I was working for you. But now that I'm not an employee and, once I give the money back, will never have been an employee, I suppose as a good citizen I'll have to mosey over to the sheriff's office and have a little chat with her."

Bru quit talking and looked Goins full in the face. The old duffer was an arm's length away. Dandruff dusted his shoulders and the vegetation in his ears and nostrils had seemed to have produced more of a bumper crop since Bru'd last checked. But his eyes were half-lidded. His pupils were very small and very dark and vertical, like a reptile's, a very dangerous reptile's.

"I'm sure the sheriff would like to learn about one William Arbuthnot," Bru said.

The reaction wasn't near what Bru expected. All he got was, "Arbuthnot? What the hell kind of name is that?"

"A very peculiar name. Or at least a very peculiar man. He seems to have brought the citrus canker to Florida from China by way of Southeast Asia, where he was a defector during the Vietnam War."

"Where did you ever get this outlandish nonsense from?"

"Those files you gave me," Bru said.

"You'd better explain that."

"There was a scientific paper in there with a note that said, 'Bruton, Check this out.' The paper was on altering the citrus canker. I did as I supposed you had bid me. I checked it out."

"And what did you find?" Goins asked.

"That this fellow Arbuthnot had brought the harmless strain of citrus canker from Asia. And that he'd gone around trying to figure some scheme to make money out of it."

"Did he succeed?" Goins said, not bothering with any of the intermediate questions that an unknowledgeable party might ask, such as what is citrus canker.

"He certainly did. I also have uncovered evidence that he was employed by a factory, probably a plastic works not many months ago, probably in north Florida."

"What do you suppose he was doing there?" Goins asked.

"I think you should probably answer that question yourself, Mr. Goins."

The old man broke eye lock with Bru. He snorted and scratched his head. "All this is more peculiar than I expected when I hired you." He cranked down the window and jerked his head at Juan. "Take those things back into his house. I'm going to leave this guy on the payroll for a while. He's producing results."

Juan turned at right angles and headed off toward the garage apartment. Bru bounded out of the car, catching Juan. He lifted the first file in the stack. Sure enough, Bru saw both copies of the contract Jerry Wiley had drawn up and Goins had signed. "This one is yours and I'll keep the other one," Bru said, handing the document to Goins through the driver window.

The old man's beetle brows went up as he scanned the sheet and fell when he recognized it. "I suppose you want more money," Goins said to Bru.

"No, I don't want any more money from you," Bru said. "I'll keep the twenty-five thousand because it's going to cost almost that much to get those 1,2--DCA tests run at the lab. They'll be back in less than two weeks."

"Take those files from Juan. Juan, you write him a check for the rest of the contract, what was it, seventy-five thousand dollars?"

"Didn't you hear me, Goins. I don't want any thing from you. I think you are a crook and a cheat on a monumental scale. I think it's likely you were behind that citrus canker scam in the eighties, and I think you are using that report you want me to write to somehow make some money out of citrus futures now."

"All right, I won't give you any money. But you are still working for me, whether you want to acknowledge it or not." Goins waved the contract at Bru. "The results you produce from your investigation are mine. If you give that information to anybody else, I'll sue your sorry ass."

Bru bent and brought his face to within inches of the old man. "Goins, if I find you are somehow behind this KiDS epidemic, you won't be suing anyone. Billionaire or not, vengeance will be mine."

Goins's eyes widened and the irises seemed to spin like little wheels. "And I would deserve whatever vengeance you would mete out," Goins said.

His response disconcerted Bru. Before he had a chance to wonder if the old man was just a good actor, the old man inched his finger at Bru. "Young man, come here. Here are your orders in plain English. Stay away from my family. I'm giving you this advice in a friendly spirit. People who fool with that shit-on-a-stick daughter of mine end up suckered by her, without exception. And those who bother my granddaughter always end up wishing they hadn't."

Goins' left hand cranked up the window. His right hand threw the Chevrolet into reverse. The car tore out of the drive shooting fragments of shell at Bru's knees and shoes. In the last light of the day he flipped through the file folders. He wanted to make sure the citrus canker paper with the notation was still there. The time might come when he'd need that as evidence. Indeed, there it was right on top, just where he left it. However, rather than getting a sense of relief from finding the paper, Bru thought about the threat Goins had tendered to those who bothered his family. Bru's considered opinion was that threat--considering the marble slab on which Leroy resided--was as genuine as the the folder in his hand. Was his threat against Goins as good?

21

It didn't surprise Elizabeth to see her father's chicken-shit green Chevy in the drive when she passed by the address

Jerry Wiley gave her for Bruton. She drove around until she found a store selling peekaboo lingerie and sex toys. She killed a half hour shoplifting a bottle of ginger-scented sex oil, a bubble-gum textured dildo and a pair of split-crotch panties. On impulse she went into the backroom and pulled up the mid-length skirt any proper southern matron would be wearing and rolled her panties down her legs and kicked them in the trash. She put on the split-crotch model.

What will Dr. Bruton think when he sticks his finger in these babies? she wondered with a wicked smile.

She wheedled thirty-five cents out of the clerk and went outside and called Bruton's number. He picked up after the fourth ring. "Hello, Dr. Bruton, Rupert, Bru. It's Elizabeth."

There was a pause at the other end of the line. "What can I do for you?" he asked.

"It's about Kimberly. You have to help me with her."

"Actually, I need to talk to you about her," he said.

"I'm in Orlando. Why don't I drop by?" Elizabeth asked. Elizabeth wanted to get laid. She badly needed to get laid. Leroy hadn't been much good to her in that way once the HIV turned into fullblown AIDS.

"No, I don't want you to come here."

On second thought it was probably best she not go to his place. The last reason she'd called Bruton for was sex.

"Do you know were Lake Eola is?"

Elizabeth said she didn't although she did. Bruton gave directions. In the car Elizabeth popped a couple of uppers, then fearing they would make her too hyper, swallowed a Valium. She drove around a bit to give her pharmaceuticals time to kick in. He was there when she came up the walk. He was leaning on his elbows on the railing watching a family of ducks swimming in the lily pads at the foot of the gazebo.

Elizabeth had always had the hots for Bru. Nothing serious. Just that she would have liked to have fucked him. She remembered doing all kinds of stuff to get him to do her in that course she took from him at the university. She shot him some great beaver in class, and she dropped around his office two or three times, and once she just flat out asked if he'd let her give him head. Or maybe that was some other teacher she had. She wasn't sure. The only thing she was sure of, given the drug-induced spin in her head, was that she couldn't let on that she knew President Wilmer Newcombe of Lawson. He was her main ally now that Leroy was gone. Leroy had made her befriend him for some mysterious reason. Newcombe had sent her to Bru. He wanted to know what Leroy had on Bruton, why Leroy had picked Bruton to be the guy to carry out the 1,2--DCA report.

"Oh, Dr. Bruton," she blubbered. "You have no idea how helpless a single mother with a wayward child feels."

Bruton looked at her skeptically. "I don't know that I would call Kimberly wayward," he said.

Elizabeth didn't like his body language. He stood tall and stiff.

"I misspoke myself," Elizabeth said thinking this guy needs some straightening out when it came to that little twot daughter of hers. "She's a darling child in her difficult years."

"Your daughter is sneaking out at night with the connivance of one of the gatekeepers," Bru said woodenly. "He's the guy who wears a Sam Browne belt and has a toothpick in his mouth most of the time."

"I know which one you mean," she said, thinking it was Paul, the same one that let her out. "He's insolent."

"He's worse than that. He's been demanding sexual favors of Kimberly."

Elizabeth burst out in a laugh then remembered to cover her face and pretend as though she was stifling a howl of rage. So her cub had to come across with some real sex while Elizabeth got by with just flashing a little tit. When she managed to straighten her face, Elizabeth asked, "What sort of sexual favor?"

"She called it a hand job," Bru said. "He's after her for oral sex though."

"The pig," Elizabeth said.

"Prosecute him," Bru urged.

Elizabeth took a step toward Bruton. He made a giant step away. "What's wrong?" she asked.

"Your father warned me to stay away from his family--and you in particular."

"Father is over protective. His concern turned me into a little old lady before my time, and now he's trying to do the same to Kimberly. But his heart is in the right place," Elizabeth said--with an inward smile. Bruton could have told her all of this on the phone. He was sniffing the bait.

With a deft move, Elizabeth closed the distance between them. She clutched his arm. "Your news has been quite a blow. Stay with me for a while, Bru. I implore you as a mother."

The trick was keeping her flesh pressed against his. She twined her arm around his and grasped his hand, her body pressing against him. She let out a sniffle to show how broken up she was about the news he brought of her daughter's escapades. They ambled along the broad sidewalk circling the lake. Street and building lights reflected in the water.

"The sheriff came to visit today," Elizabeth said. She felt Bruton's body stiffen. She wondered if Mr. Clean-looking professor had a troubled past. This pleased Elizabeth, but she said as prissy as she could, "She, the sheriff, told me what a fine thing you did for Kimberly."

127

"The sheriff didn't seem to think my motives were so noble last night. She didn't like Kim's involvement with me and the dead guy, Leroy. I kind of wonder about the dead guy myself."

"As indeed you should, sir. To look at her, you'd never expect Kimberly was--let me see if I can think of the term the courts use for her. 'An incorrigible runaway,' that's it. She's been taking off since before she became a teenager. One of the nice things about Father's money is that she's never been gone long before his operatives find her and bring her back. This Leroy was one of the johns she met on the street. I'm afraid he made free with her prepubescent charms and filled her head full of the wildest trash about his relations with her."

Elizabeth paused to check out Bruton. He dropped her arm--and his chin had dropped in astonishment too. He seemed almost in shock. Elizabeth was pleased with the effect of her lie. The only trouble was this story was different from the tale she'd fed the sheriff. Keeping your stories straight was important. Elizabeth wished she'd have dropped a second Valium.

"I had no idea about Kimberly," Bruton said.

"Nobody ever does," Elizabeth said.

"You never had anything to do with that Leroy?" Bru asked. "She indicated you and he were quite thick."

Shit! Fuck! "Would you mind if we sat for a moment on that park bench?" Elizabeth asked, faking a swoon. "This is all rather hard on me." Bruton led her to the park bench. He stood. *Screw it.* When in doubt, fuck their brains out. She patted the seat. Reluctantly he sat. All right, Elizabeth thought, now is the time to show him what she could give him that little Miss No Tits couldn't. The bench was encircled by tall, bushy Formosan azaleas. Their flaming blooms sheltered Elizabeth and this john from the eyes of passersby.

She pressed her knee against his. Her large breast gouged into his rib cage. Bruton squirmed as if uncomfortable. Elizabeth began to sob quietly. She put her head on his shoulder. Her arm reached across his chest. She could feel his body stiffening, from lack of interest.

"Be nice to me, Dr. Bruton, please," she begged.

That didn't help much. His body stayed frozen in the same old Duddly Do Right posture. "Touch me, please. I need the comfort of a human touch."

After a time, his hand came around and settled on her shoulder. Elizabeth had twisted around and was practically sitting in his lap--face to face--his hand didn't have far to go. It settled just about on top of her tattoo. When she got him back to his place she would have to remember to leave her camisole on. She couldn't let him get a glimpse of that tattoo. Good southern ladies didn't bear tattoos, especially Manson family trademarks. She shuttled her crotch on his leg. She moistened. She could smell herself, that meaty smell, like ham. The moisture let her glide back and forth. Her crotchless panties were leaving wetness on his trouser legs, she supposed. "Kiss me," she said but she didn't wait for Bruton. She pulled his head to her lips and just as soon as they met she pressed her tongue into his mouth. The idea was to get him thinking what that extraordinary organ could do to other parts of his anatomy. Her right knee, which was jammed between his legs, worked forward. Bingo, she hit his dick. It was hard.

Her hand wandered down his torso and ended up on top his rigid prick. Why not show old Professor Bruton what her extraordinary tongue could do right here. That way he couldn't discover the tattoo.

Elizabeth couldn't locate the zipper. She flailed at his crotch. Bruton's hands were tearing at her hand. "Elizabeth, stop," he said.

"I crave it," Elizabeth said, pushing her head into his

129

lap.

Bruton's strong arms forced her head away.

"I want it. I want you, Bru," she pleaded.

He stood. I'm taking you to your car."

Elizabeth was disheveled, hair mussed, clothes a mess. He was a perfect little gentleman, except for-- Elizabeth noted with glee--the bulge in his pants. That boded hope for him yet.

22

"I owe you an apology, Joo-an," the old man said as Juan securely fastened the bicyclist's helmet to his head. The helmet, Juan would agree, looked a touch eccentric but the old man was a crappy driver. Even he understood he was a lousy driver, but he was a control freak too. He couldn't give over to anyone command of anything, not even the car he was riding in. So when they rode together Juan strapped on the bicyclist's helmet. For the moment, the old duffer was headed back toward the beach on the slowest, most congested route, 17-92. It was Juan's fault. He suggested they take the freeway.

"I suspected you of trying to gouge me. I should have known better. I should have known it was that slut of a daughter of mine from the first moment we got wind that Wisnewski was in town. I must be slipping, Juan. In days gone by, I'd never have made a mistake like that."

Juan said, "The light's been green for ten seconds now."

Goins applied foot to accelerator. The car lurched forward. "I've bet my entire fortune on this deal, and I'm not going to let it be queered because some stupid Ph.D., a

Fud as they say, has his nose in the wrong hole, like my daughter's cunt. Frankly, I suspected you because I didn't think that Leroy or my daughter between them had the smarts to pull this deal off. And I couldn't figure how they got on to that citrus canker caper we pulled back in the eighties. Oh, shit," the old man said a rictus of pain came over his face. "Check the cubby hole for some Pepcid or Tagament."

Juan pushed the button. He saw some foil packets of both products. "Doesn't look like any are in here," he said.

The old man turned into the first gas station. He went into the station himself and came out with a plastic tumbler foaming over with a bromide. He trundled toward the restroom on the far property line. Just the opportunity Juan hoped for. He slipped out of the car, went to the pay phone and dropped thirty-five cents in the slot. After the sixth ring, the machine picked up. The recording was a woman's voice. She gave a number, not the one Juan had dialed. The voice went through the whole spiel including about how they weren't available right now but how important Juan's call was to them. Juan was about to piss in his pants. If the old fuck came back, while he was on the line, there would be hell to pay. Finally, the beep came and Juan said, "The fax. Why haven't you done anything with the fax? Get on it."

He slammed the phone onto the hook and beat it back to the Chevy. Goins exited the bathroom wiping his hands on his shirtfront. As Goins with his baggy clothes and hirsute nose and ears shambled across the asphalt toward the car, Juan thought with disgust, "One of the world's richest men and he looks like a street person."

23

The F 250's headlights spotted the Fiesta as Bru drove up the shell drive to his garage apartment. Melba opened the downstairs door. Bru grinned on seeing her. He was happy that she was there.

"Am I ever glad to see you, Bru." She smiled showing a Texas-sized mouthful of teeth. "I got this big pizza and I was about to starve waiting for you."

"What a woman," Bru said. "I'm nearly famished. I'm sorry that there's nothing to drink."

"That's okay. I brought a six pack of Lowenbrau."

"You go on and sit down," Bru said. "I'll be just a minute."

Bru went upstairs. He took off his trousers and shirt and put on a pair of shorts and a tee shirt. He could smell Elizabeth's pussy odor clinging to his pants. He removed his wallet and cash and opened the closet door and threw the trousers and shirt into the corner. He went into the bathroom. He turned on the tap. He washed his hands. Even though he never touched her cunt that rank odor clung to his fingers. He worked at the cuticles and smelled his fingers. That oh-so-penetrating smell was still there. He washed again then toweled dry and went downstairs.

Melba had set the table with paper plates and napkins. While Bru'd been in the bathroom, she'd retrieved two bottles of beer. "Come on, Bru, I'm starving. Somebody took the burrito I'd bought for lunch with him today."

"Jesus, that thing almost tore my head off. What did

you put on it?"

"Just a little Texas sweat," Melba said showering a pizza slice with drops of hot sauce from a bottle she had brought along with the pizza.

"Give me that stuff, will you?" Bru said.

Melba passed the bottle. "Take it easy with that joy juice," she warned. "That's not that sissy Louisiana style sauce."

"Not to worry. I'm not going to dose my food with it. 'Habanero peppers, vinegar, salt and Xanthan gum,'" Bru said as he read the label. Actually, Bru was making conversation. After his initial flush of pleasure at seeing Melba, he now felt uncomfortable. He could still smell Elizabeth on his fingers. And if the truth be known Bru regretted ungallantly abandoning her in the park. Elizabeth was an attractive woman, and not the least of her charms was a daughter who needed some help which Bru would be pleased to give. And then of course, not to be overlooked, was all that family money. Next to that, Melba didn't seem to have much to offer. Bru felt sad to be the recipient of Melba's unsolicited generosity while feeling so little loyalty to her.

"Are you ready for the big news?" Melba asked. "I cracked the Goins file. He gave a million dollars to Lawson's endowment fund--all on the q. t."

Suddenly Elizabeth didn't seem so attractive--by simple association with her father. "That son of bitch," Bru said. "Those sons of bitches--Goins and Newcombe."

"The first hundred thousand was paid December 1."

"A week before I received notice of termination. It's too much to consider that a coincidence. Was there anything in that file that indicated a tit-for-tat agreement?"

"Of course not. Goins and Nuke'em might be crooked but they aren't stupid," Melba said.

Bru shook his head. He didn't want to show the

emotion he felt surging through him. "Have I drawn the big picture for you on this thing, Melba?"

"Not really."

So Bru gave Melba a rundown of what he knew, starting with the attack by the now dead biker Leroy Wiesnewski. Bru wondered how Melba was going to receive his take on this. The way Jerry had yesterday, inferring Bru was a paranoid kook? Or more like Professor Khoury, who clearly agreed Bru's suspicions were plausible? But then Bru hadn't divulged to Khoury his belief in a Newcombe-Goins's connection.

Bru didn't have to wait long for his answer. She snapped her fingers and smiled. "I think I found something on Goins that you may like. His corporations developed some large suburban towns during the eighties, Hillsborough Estates, near Tampa and others around Saint Pete, Sarasota, Fort Myers, Melbourne and Fort Pierce. A local one is located somewhere between Orlando and Daytona-- Daylando, I think it's name is."

"Jesus," Bru said.

"All that was in that material on Goins I gave you this morning. I guess you haven't got to it yet," Melba said. "Is that what's called a smoking gun?"

"Up to now I had to give Goins the benefit of the doubt on this 1,2--DCA stuff, since I had no real connection between him and the earlier canker scam. It smelled like a rat, but now we have the rodent's dead body. If he made money out of the canker, he has a plan to make it out of the 1,2--DCA too."

"That's the way I see it," Melba said.

Bru felt overawed by the magnitude of the job facing him. "You know what they say about having a heart attack, that you feel like an elephant is sitting on your chest. Well, I feel like a Mack truck loaded up with elephants just ran over me."

Melba leaned close to Bru. She extended her hand, touched the corner of his eye. "Your black eye is gone," she said. Her hand dropped and took hold of his. She squeezed. "What do you have to do to make your case?"

"First thing is prove 1,2--DCA occurs in the new orange juice containers."

"What's the second thing?"

"Research the literature. I'm getting behind as you showed when you told me I'd been carrying around what I'd been seeking all day, proof of Goins's involvement in the development of those suburban towns."

"I take it that junk upstairs in the kitchen is what you used to conduct a test for 1,2--DCA," Melba said.

Bru agreed that it was.

"I guess that's easy, then. You read and I'll test. But first I suppose we'll have to go get some more supplies. Don't bother telling me I shouldn't do this. It's all right. I don't have to go in to work tomorrow until one. I can work on this all night if I want. On the way to getting that stuff we'll stop by my place and get my gun. It's just a twenty-two pistol, but a twenty-two hollow point long at short range will make just about anyone stop and think."

"I'm not in a position to say no to anything except getting the gun. I want no weapon around."

"How'd you come up with ideas as strange as that?" the Texas cowgirl asked. "Aren't you the one who told me about friend Leroy. Not to mention Arbuthnot and goodness knows who else."

"I can't imagine the circumstance that could be made better by shooting someone."

"Even if your life was threatened?"

"Not even then, Melba. I learned my lesson about guns long ago."

"What if my life were in danger?"

"I suppose this is the reason I'm telling you this now,

so you'll know."

"What if it took shooting someone to solve the riddle of the KiDS epidemic?"

"I think that's being overdramatic," Bru said. "I'm a scientist. I solve problems by my intellect, not with guns. I don't think any problem ever gets solved with guns."

"You must have killed a man to talk like that," Melba said. The words just seemed to have tumbled out of Melba's mouth, and both Bru and she appeared to look at those portentous words in the space above the table. Bru felt his face registering shock--and the truth of her assertion. "I shouldn't have shot from the lip like that," Melba said. "It's time to go get the stuff we'll need."

Bru agreed that it was.

Bru drove Melba's truck to four supermarkets. They bought sixty containers of various brands of o.j., both frozen and reconstituted. They also bought the requisite equipment--nine more iced tea jars--and laid in a supply of distilled water and liquid bleach. Then after Bru showed Melba how to conduct the test, she exiled him to the basement and the stacks of material she'd brought home from the library.

Bru started with Goins's files. Mostly the stuff in them was the same kind of junk he'd sampled yesterday, newspaper clippings about the effects of drinking orange juice and the like. After an hour and a half, Melba brought Bru a fresh cup of herb tea. "You look like you nodded off," she said.

"You don't look all that bright-eyed yourself," he said. "Any luck?"

"Nope. How about you?"

"At least I'm through all the papers Goins gave me. Some of that material could have been incorporated into the final report Goins wanted as padding, but none of it told me anything I need to know. I was hoping to find another

136

bombshell in there like the canker paper."

"Try to stay awake."

"Maybe there'll be something in your material that'll cue us as to how they could have contaminated the o.j. crop."

"I'm trying a new wrinkle myself," Melba said.

She went up the stairs. Bru took a moment out for a sip of tea and a look of appreciation at how Melba's long, well-formed legs filled out her jeans. She was still very young, by Bru's lights, so no wonder she looked like that. But he vowed he wasn't going to touch her, no matter how inviting her legs looked or how good he felt about her or how she twitched her butt, which he had to admit she did very nicely indeed.

Bru took another sip of tea and opened the file folder Melba's material was in. The first sheet of paper was a faxed memo. Probably something for Melba that she slipped inadvertently into the file, Bru thought. He set that fax aside and began reading the abstract of an article. Halfway through the abstract, Bru shook his head and let out a chortle of laughter. The citrus canker's official name was *Xanthomonas campestris* sp. *citrumelo*. The article that Melba had brought him was about the same Xanthan gum that was used to thicken that hot pepper sauce Melba had brought. Oddly enough, that thickening agent was of the same genus as the cankers, *Xanthomonas campestris*. It was a cousin to the cankers. His laughter was rueful and ironic.

Suddenly he stopped laughing. A fax had come in on his machine that morning. He'd scooped it up and put it among some papers. Was it the fax that he'd just set aside before he began reading the Xanthan gum paper? Bru picked up the fax. He read it.

If you want to know about William Arbuthnot, show up at Canaveral Seashore in the afternoon. Park in the fifth lot, go down to the beach and take a right. After fifty yards, strip naked. Even take your sunglasses off. Walk south toward the VAB. When you are accosted, say the word "kinko." You will be told everything.

Bru stared at the paper in his hands. His paranoia level shot up a couple hundred percent. He could see Jerry Wiley showing up at his place. He could even see Melba and Billy Goins learning where he lived and Elizabeth and Kimberly phoning him. But notes like this faxed in on his phone line? How'd they know he had a fax? Even better, how'd they even know about him?

The only good thing Bru could see in this was that he had missed the appointment. Just as he came to this conclusion, Melba let out a shout upstairs. It sounded as though she were being attacked. The initial blast was followed by three or four shorter but louder yips. Bru burst up the steps and across the bedroom. The mattress was still on the floor, the corner of which tripped him. He staggered into the kitchen and was attacked--by Melba. She threw herself at him, locking her arms around his chest. She danced away, faded back, kissed him on the chin and let out a rebel yell. *Ya-hoo.*

"I thought you were being molested," Bru said. "Now I don't know what to think."

"Bru, look. It's tested positive."

Four of the six iced tea jars were the color of orange juice. Two had turned a dingy lavender tint.

"I tested the juice instead of the plastic in the carton," she said.

"Good girl. So the 1,2--DCA evidently develops when the concentrate comes in contact with the plastic. Pretty clever."

Melba beamed proudly then yawned. She brought a hand to her mouth and said, "Now the question, Bru, is what are we going to do about all this? I mean who's going to believe you and me when we say that 1,2--DCA contamination of the new orange juice container is causing the KiDS epidemic?"

Bru did not answer for a moment. He thought about Amber dead and in a grave. He also thought about Professor Khoury's injunction to let his intuition guide him but back it up with hard physical evidence. "All we've proven so far," Bru said, "is that 1,2--DCA occurs in o.j. We still have to show it is the causal agent for KiDS. That's a long step away, mainly because we have no idea how they did it. There has to be some second agent that the 1,2--DCA activates. I haven't a clue what that is. Or how it is introduced into the juice." Bru suddenly quit talking. He noticed the call light was blinking on the fax/answering machine. "I missed a call this evening. Probably happened when we went to the supermarket."

"No," Melba said. "It was blinking when I arrived with the pizza. I should have told you."

He pushed the button. A vaguely familiar voice said, "The fax. Why haven't you done anything with the fax? Get on it. That's the key."

"Do you know what fax that person is talking about?" Melba asked.

Bru didn't answer. After the tape rewound, he pushed the button again and listened to the message. He decided the unusualness of the voice came from a faint singsong accent. It was the kind of accent that those who speak fluently but who've learned English as their second-language sometimes have. He couldn't figure who that person would be, perhaps because he concentrated on the message. "Yeah, I know what fax that person is talking about." Bru went downstairs and retrieved the paper. When he returned up the stairs, Melba had replaced her top with one of his shirts. She had one leg of her jeans off. Turning her back to him, she kicked the jeans off and removed her panties and went to the sink and put the panties under the torrent of tap water and took a bar of soap and scrubbed them out.

"I don't mean to be presumptuous, Bru, but I'm going to have to crash here. I'm too tired to drive. That happens to me. When it's time for me to conk out, I conk out. Now quickly tell me about that fax."

"You can take the bed," Bru said, thinking bedding down at his place without so much as a "may I?" was a pushy thing to do. But she'd lent him her truck, brought him research, and worked like a navvy on the 1,2--DCA experiment. "I'll sleep on the couch downstairs."

"You'll do no such thing," Melba said. "You need a good night's sleep. You're going to sleep on the mattress. Now tell me about that fax before I collapse." She took the pair of panties and hung them over the back of one of the kitchen chairs.

Bru knew he should concentrate on the fax. Instead, he stared at her panties, so much larger and, yes, so much more provocative than any pair of underwear Leta had ever left out.

"I'm sorry about that, Bru. But when I get excited I flow pretty heavily and since I'm going to leave here and go straight to work tomorrow probably, I don't want any odor--as they say on the TV commercials--to upset the girls at the reference desk. I think even those old biddies would be able to recognize that smell, and I wouldn't want to get them all excited. Now tell me about that fax."

Bru handed her the fax without comment. *Outrageous* was the word he'd always used for Melba, and it certainly seemed to hold now. To underscore that point, Melba crumpled the fax paper in her hand and hooted with laughter.

"You know where this is, don't you?" she asked Bru.

"Not really."

"It's a nude beach."

"I'm glad to hear that because I'd hate to be the only guy wandering around in the buff."

"You won't be the only guy in the buff, because most everyone else there is gay."

24

When Elizabeth cracked the door to her room, she saw a sheet of paper, folded to an inch square, fall to the floor. Someone had slipped her a note. She watched the folded paper flutter like an injured butterfly without a great deal of interest. Elizabeth was dejected. Her man Leroy was dead. The man she selected to replace him--for the night, anyway-- Professor Bruton had given her the air. Even that dried up old college president who she was working for, sort of, had refused her. She'd called him to report, she said, but what she really wanted was to get laid. But the wimp was afraid of his wife and told Elizabeth to call him at the office, code for showing up at their motel the next afternoon. That had just annoyed her more. The hell with him. She needed to get laid now, tonight. Imagine, stopping at two bars during Bike Weeks, and not finding a man she wanted to fuck, or who wanted to fuck her.

Elizabeth unclasped her purse and took out her vial of pills. No reason not to help herself to another one or two. She shook a couple of reds into her throat and swallowed them dry and felt sorry for herself. Leroy'd always been an unreliable asshole. She could never tell when he'd go off with some other woman or do something dumb to let himself get locked up in the slammer, but he'd always come back. This time the dumbfuck wasn't coming back. Elizabeth could hardly imagine anything so inconsiderate.

Elizabeth got the air conditioner going, turned the TV on, muted it, and dialed Klassik 96.5 on her boom box's FM dial. Grace Slick was doing "White Rabbit." Good. She fired up a cigarette and thought what the hell and reached for the note. She knew it was going to be from her pasty-faced little daughter--who else in this dump, where she was barely spoken to, would send her a note? Didn't that little bitch know she was the one that got Leroy blown away. If she'd have just left him alone. If he'd just left her tight little pussy alone.

Elizabeth unfolded the paper. It read: *Come see me no matter the hour you get in. Bring this note. The motion detection system will be disabled in my wing. JR*

It took her a while to puzzle out who J.R. was. Partly her problem was drugs. Her brain box was a little foggy. But also, the problem was Juan Robert had never sent her a note before. So far as Elizabeth could recall he hadn't so much as said hi to her. Finally, though, his identity sunk in. She crumpled the note and threw it on the floor. *Fuck him.* She wasn't going to have anything to do with that little weasel.

When she first came back to Florida last fall, everything was fine. The old man actually thought she had given Leroy the shove. The old fucker had let her set up her little office and had allowed her to buy the furnishings-- unheard of expenses for him. But Juan Robert turned her father against her. Leroy's attempt to shake the old fart down about the citrus canker didn't help. She never had any idea how Leroy thought that citrus canker thing could work. And now he was dead on account of it and she was left with nothing.

Nothing but a stinking note. From a stinking little

faggot who expected her to slink around in the big house at night and possibly compromise herself. But if there was one thing Elizabeth was good at, it was sneaking around houses, even ones with motion detection systems in some of the wings. Elizabeth got up from the bed and stubbed her cigarette out. She took a hit off a bottle of Listerine, swished it around her mouth, gargled with the stuff and finally swallowed it. She gave her hair a couple of licks from a can of hair spray and touched up her do and she was ready to move out.

At the first touch of Elizabeth's knuckle to the wood, the door flew open. Juan Robert, in a pair of jeans and a black turtleneck sweater, stood in the way. His finger was pressed against his lips. His lips moved. "The note," he said silently. Elizabeth held it in her hand. He took it from her and stuffed it in the pocket of his trousers and motioned with her head to follow him. He closed the door and stepped into the hall. As the door shut, Elizabeth noticed Juan's room was lavishly appointed. She saw a poster bed and a wide screen TV and expensive drapes on his windows.

If Elizabeth had had a knife, she probably would have stabbed Juan in the back. Why did he have all those things but the daughter, the rightful heir, did not? Leroy was dead and Elizabeth was unfucked--and Juan Robert had all that. It was enough to make her cry. She was crying. Tears of hot rage poured from her eyes.

Clunk. She bumped into Juan Robert. He was stopped at a door, unlocking it. Then he was outside and he reached back and pulled her along. It seemed cooler now than when Elizabeth had come home less than an hour before. "Why all the secrecy?" she said in a street voice.

"Hush up," he whispered in her ear. "The old man has listening devices all around this place."

He led her across the lawn to a bathhouse in the corner of the property that the razor wire abutted. He unlocked a door and turned and put his finger over his lips. They went across a room and he unlocked another door and went out. Elizabeth followed. She came out on the beach on the other side of the coiled concertina wire. He led her north for three houses. He came to a piece of driftwood. He motioned for her to sit. Elizabeth sat. He dropped down next to her. She could see in the tight fitting clothes that he was wiry, almost athletic.

"Now what's the deal with all this secrecy?"

"You can't sneeze in that house without being detected." Juan sat very close to her. His face was turned toward her and he spoke in a low voice, as though he thought the beach was bugged too. The surf was pounding fifty yards away--it was a winter ocean, angry and cold, that was lashing the beach, much different from the summer-like, almost dull seas of late. A distant flash of lightning showed his face. His eyes, dark and flat and somehow oriental, were large and liquid in his face. That lightning bolt also showed the sky above was half clouds--half open sky.

"That is not important now," Juan Robert said. "The important thing is that the old man is losing it."

"What do you mean?" Elizabeth asked.

"His brain isn't as tight as it used to be. Like that scene at the dinner table when he berated you and me for trying to fuck him over. He was thumping his chest and bragging. In the old days he never gave anybody any notice, he just struck like an avenging angel. His mind is going and so is his body."

"Yeah, so?" Elizabeth said, not catching the drift.

"And then those murders he ordered the past couple of days were equally uncouth. The guy he had do them points right back at him. The old man is rich and powerful, but it is doubtful even his money can keep him from stepping off if he keeps doing stuff like that."

"I still don't get why you want to talk to me about

this," Elizabeth said keeping her cards close to her chest. If he thought she was going to get all het up with moral indignation because her father killed a couple of guys--well, he had another think coming.

"He's going to cut you out of his will."

"How do you know that?" Elizabeth said--suddenly, she was boiling with indignation. That little faggot knew everything. Besides it's about what she expected from the old fuck.

"He's going to leave everything to your daughter."

"It was that Leroy play that did it."

"That's not important. What's important is that you have no future with the old guy--as long as your daughter is alive."

"That little bitch has been cutting me out with him ever since she was a little kid--ever since she got the old man to steal her little baby ass away from Leroy and me in California. What you mean is that you don't have any future with this organization, if the courts award her control of everything."

"I'm thinking of your best interests."

"I rather doubt that," Elizabeth said.

"All right," Juan admitted. Maybe I do think it would be easier to work with you than an underage minor who the court will take an interest in." Juan added, "Here take these pills. They will make you feel better." His hand floated in front of her face. The fingers opened.

Elizabeth never passed up free drugs. She popped them in her mouth and swallowed. "What are they?" she said after they were down her throat.

"Never mind," he said. "What you have to do is figure out how you are going to protect your interests." The line of clouds had pressed on. Now they were blotting out the stars over the ocean. A bolt of lightning zigged between the clouds. "It's going to rain," Juan said. "If you

145

want me to help, you will have to formulate a plan fast."

"What I need to do first is know whether I'm throwing in with a guy that has any sense. That's my trouble, the guys I get never have any sense."

"Do you know what a sociopath is?" he asked her.

"Of course not. Why would I know a sociopath? I'm healthy as a horse."

"It's not a doctor. It's a mental condition. Your Leroy was one. It means a guy who has no moral scruples holding him back."

"That sounds better, I suppose," she said.

"I'm the perfect sociopath," Juan Robert said. "I don't give a fuck about anybody."

"So you say," Elizabeth said.

"I started with your father. I acted like a lap dog. He could do what he wanted to me or with me. I didn't care just as long as he let me get inside. Well, I got inside and now I've planned against him. This whole orange juice thing. That wasn't his idea. It was mine--with the idea of destroying and taking control of his enterprises, through you, of course."

"You're fucking with my head."

"No, I'm not. Even your friend Leroy had a part in this great scheme. How do you think he learned about the canker? I gave him that information, just as he gave me the information about Bruton."

"So you killed Leroy."

"How could I get to the prize," Juan asked, reaching a hand out and plunking it on Elizabeth's thigh, "with his still being around? But as it happened, your father saved me the trouble of disposing of him."

"So this orange juice caper will finish off my old man?" Elizabeth said skeptically.

"That's right. He won't be tough enough to handle it."

"And why's that?"

"Because hundreds, thousands of children will die on account of it. Maybe tens of thousands. Perhaps hundreds of thousands."

"Orange juice can't kill hundreds of thousands of kids," Elizabeth said.

"America's children may as well be drinking watered down strychnine with their sugar-frosted flakes every morning."

And you've figured a way to make money out of screwing with o.j.?"

"You bet we have."

"Well, killing off that many kids won't bother the old man. Believe me. He doesn't give a shit about anyone," Elizabeth said.

"Oh, but he does. She whom he has left--or shortly will--leave everything to. Once she goes. He will go. I've made a lifetime study of him."

All Elizabeth said was, "Hm."

"But she has to be got rid of. And soon. I would be pleased to lend my assistance--"

Elizabeth cut him off. "I don't need any help. I know exactly how to handle the little tramp. I've planned this one out for months."

"That's the pills talking. You couldn't really do it. You really wouldn't do it."

"Oh, yeah, listen to this. I got a bottle of thalidomide. You know what that stuff is used for?"

"Making three headed babies? What?" He sounded impatient--annoyed.

Vaguely, Elizabeth realized she could be in danger. She'd taken some pills from him. She was on the beach--a deserted, stormy beach with a man who'd been her enemy. But the glow of the pills--and the thought of doing Prissy in--made her oblivious. Still, she wanted to get that impatience

147

out of his voice. "No, it's a muscle relaxer and a sleeping tablet. You take three, four of those and you feel no pain. I'll dose a coke, that is a Coca-Cola, and feed that to the princess. Then I'll lug her down to the basement and throw her in one of pop's fleet of sport cars. I'll take a garden hose and duct tape it to the exhaust system and run it into the passenger cabin and start the car up and let nature take its course. To top it all off, like the olive in the martini, I'll tuck a stuffie doll under her arm. I've thought about this one, believe me."

"If you are going to do it, you need to do it soon-- very soon. Once he changes that will, you will be out. And there will be no getting you back in. I can disarm the motion detector in her hallway. There may be some questions about that, but it's a necessary risk. We need to act soon."

Elizabeth's arm reached up, touched Juan's shoulder. The expression on his face did not change. "We shouldn't get involved like that," he said. "It never works to mix business with love."

Elizabeth laughed. She remembered who put his hand on her thigh a moment before. She knew what that was all about. "Who said anything about love? Just fuck me, Juan Robert. Show me you can get it up. I always thought you were a fag."

He looked at her, his face impassive for perhaps thirty seconds. "This is ridiculous," he said. "It is stupid. What if we are discovered in the act?"

Elizabeth just laughed. She knew she had him. She knew that he wouldn't let her go back without fucking her. That screwing had been the reason for the note and all the chest-beating about what a master brain he was. Leroy was hardly gone, and now he comes beating a path to her door. Elizabeth wondered if he understood he wanted pussy as much as control of the family estate. She guessed the answer to that was probably no. Men might rule the world. They might even rule Elizabeth. But Elizabeth had always been able to rule men--at least the ones she never gave a shit about.

25

Deputy Hank Smith knew he should wipe the smart ass smirk off his face. The sheriff, who was staring up at him from across her football field desk, had a cup of coffee by her side and a frown on her face. When he was ushered into the office he wasn't invited to sit and she didn't shake his hand, and for damn sure he hadn't been offered any of that coffee, which smelled awfully good this cold early morning.

"You know me," the attractive blond law woman was saying. "I don't much give a shit if some miscreant gets knocked around by a wayward billy club, providing it doesn't fuck up a case. I don't even much care if one of my boys whacks some bad guy--if the guy is dead you know no pinko judge all soft on constitutional rights and due process is going to turn him loose on the streets again. The people of this county elected me to stop crime, and by god, that's what I set out to do. I hate crime and I hate crooks. I'm not talking about penny ante stuff. I'm talking about the real thing."

The sheriff quit talking so Hank said, "Yes'm," as he supposed he was meant to do. He did his damndest to hold back his grin but he could feel it spreading across his face.

"Why do you look so god damn smug, Hank?" the sheriff asked.

"Because I like what you are saying, ma'am," Hank said.

"You haven't heard everything I have to say yet."

"Don't matter," Hank said in his best good-old-boy southern accent. "You're a lawman's law woman, that what everyone says."

Shelby Buckett gave a little possum grin, a grin that was meant to say you can't smarm your way out of the mess you're in. And Hank's response was to just smile and smile.

That grin Hank couldn't suppress came partly because he didn't figure he was in any very big mess. Had his dick really been in the crack he wouldn't be talking to the sheriff at all. He'd be braced by some asshole internal affairs bull. Had he been halfway up shit creek his sergeant would have had to bring him in, and the room would be filled with flunkies, all of whom would be salivating for the opportunity to get a hunk of his sergeant's and Hank's butts. But instead he was in here having a cosy little heart to heart with the sheriff, only the two of them. That meant some of Goins' money was going to the old crime-hater, pure-as-the-driven-snow Shelby Buckett herself. *Knowing the sheriff is corrupt is a pretty good reason to have an ear to ear grin on your kisser,* Hank thought.

"The people elected me to root out crime--like a bad tooth. Tear it out and cauterize the wound."

"Yes'm, everyone knows you are the most hardass sheriff in Florida. Tough on crime. And tougher on criminals."

"You got it, Smith. And to do that you have to play square with your men. Those boys are out there putting their asses on the line, and you have to back them up--even if they don't always deserve it. Like those two shootings of yours. Do you think that I think that either one of them was worth putting my neck on the line for?"

"I want to thank you for going to the well with me on them, ma'am."

"I could have had your balls on either one."

150

These were not funny words. Hank was not smiling now.

"I could still hand your ass over to the state attorney."

"But you won't," Hank said.

"And why is that?"

"Because, like you said, you back up your men."

"I want to know what's going on, Smith. Some guy by the name of Arbuthnot buys it--and you are the first officer on the scene, but we don't hear word one of it in this department. Furthermore, you were not assigned to patrol that area. And a rather large bag of goods was seen exiting the premises in your company?"

"Lies, ma'am. All lies," Hank said.

"And then the next day a biker by the name of Wisnewski checks out. The day before this happens you investigate an assault this guy pulls. You filed no complaint affidavit. You were the last person to see Wisnewski before he clocked, yet you didn't come forward with that intelligence. I want to know what's going down."

"You left something out of there, didn't you ma'am? I had a cup of coffee with Billy Goins. You never said nothing about that."

"For your information, that was noted too. But I didn't bring it up because I couldn't see how it was related."

In a pig's eye, thought Hank. Shelby Buckett might be a woman. She was also sheriff and a cop. The truth was Hank didn't have much use for women cops, including Shelby Buckett, but in her case she was cop enough to know in her guts when something was up. She knew it all right. What she wanted was an angle. A way to work old man Goins for even more loot. So Hank decided to give it to her.

"Mr. Goins was asking me if I would like to run for sheriff. I told him I'd think about it."

Hank liked the totally flabbergasted look that blitzed her face, as she started figuring the odds of beating Hank, backed by Goins's money, in a knock-down and drag-out election.

"Don't be a smart ass, Smith. If you get implicated in any of those shootings, I'm cutting you loose."

In response, Hank just beamed, like a headlight.

"Don't you get it? I'm dead serious about this, Smith."

"I know you are, ma'am," Hank said as he continued to smile.

"Go on. Get out of here. I'm through with you for right now."

Hank knew it was incumbent on him to wipe the grin from his face and to scuttle from the sheriff's presence with a certain humility. But he couldn't make himself do it. He flat felt too expansive. He saluted the old girl--or rather young girl--with a cross between an up-yours sign and a military salute, his hand shooting up from his forehead and fingers opening as they went.

The funny thing was the smile had nothing to do with the sheriff and their little chat. He'd heard from the Goins corporation. There was a little chore he'd been assigned to take care of. Nothing pleased Hank like taking care of those kinds of chores. Well, perhaps one thing warmed the cockles of his heart more.

That other thing was taking risks--of putting his balls on a board and offering anyone in sight the opportunity of taking a two by four and smashing them. He was offering the sheriff that chance. He would see if she was good enough to mash his balls flat. His bet was that she wasn't. But the odd thing was he didn't much care either way. The fun thing was to take the chance, and that he damn sure was going to. Later that day, as he'd been instructed by the Billy Goins's company.

26

When Bru woke it was full light out, and it was cold. A body snuggled beside him on the mattress. For a time he thought it was Leta, and that Amber was dozing peacefully in her room down the hall and that he'd had the strangest dream. But then his head cleared and he realized what he had thought was a twisted nightmare had actually been his life since Amber died. As a consolation, he had to admit the body cuddling next to him felt very pleasant and smelled even nicer. She gave off the odor of ripe guava, easily the most fragrant and fecund smelling of all the common Florida fruits.

Last Bru had seen of this guava, she had been parked on the couch downstairs. Bru had a hard on. He thought it was a just piss hard on, but the idea of rolling over and taking his pleasure was much too seductive for any piss hard on. There was some reason why he shouldn't help himself to the guava. *How about that I've been faithful to my wife for going on twenty years?* Bru doubted that was the reason he slipped off the mattress, tiptoed into the bathroom and dressed instead of helping himself to the guava.

Bru fancied he could see his breath, meaning it was below forty-eight degrees, the condensation point for carbon dioxide. No wonder that Melba ended up in bed with him. Bru found a windbreaker jacket which he pulled on and a heavier tweed sport coat which he threw over Melba. He tiptoed into the kitchen. He opened the yellow pages and looked for orange juice canneries. There were a dozen listings. He needed to find the source of the new orange juice can. He also needed to determine how a second agent could be introduced to the juice.

Bru told the receptionist at the first number that he was a professor from Lawson College doing some research on the citrus industry. The call was thrown around like a hot potato and finally stalled when Bru reached a voicemail box instead of a human. The next three calls turned out the same way. On the fifth call, to a plant toward the beach over in Okeelanta County, he got through to the plant manager's office. The manager, Don DiCicco, said his daughter was attending Lawson. He told Bru he was welcome to stop by whenever he wanted to and that he'd be happy to tell him anything he wanted to know. Bru said he'd be by as soon as he could get there, probably in about an hour and a half or so.

On the back of an envelope Bru worked up a list of things he wanted Melba to check out for him. First was any connection that linked Goins to his own firing at Lawson-- any hard evidence whatsoever should mean he'd get his job back. Next on the list was finding out the company that made the new plastic orange juice containers. Bru hoped he'd learn that himself at the concentrate plant, but it was such a key piece of information they had to search out every means to learn it. And then, shooting the moon, Bru put down Arbuthnot's employment record via W-2 forms or social security payments at the orange juice container manufactory. He doubted if Melba could access personnel records, but why not try? He looked at the list and realized it was tilted in favor of his personal interests so he rewrote the list putting the determination of the plastic company in the top spot and the Lawson connection with Goins in the bottom. He slunk into the bedroom and turned the pockets of Melba's jeans inside out. No car keys. He went down and checked the ignition of his Fiesta. Nada. When he went back into the bedroom, Melba had a shiteating grin spread across her Texasy face.

"I hid them," she said.

"Why'd you do that?"

"So you wouldn't go rambling all over the countryside in that wreck of yours. Take my truck."

Not a great deal of persuasion was required, what with the cold weather, the significant driving Bru had to do and the breezy side windows of the Fiesta. "I left a list of stuff that I need looked up."

"No problem, Bru."

He left without kissing her. A little peck didn't seem all that much to a woman who'd shared your bed--albeit in a platonic manner. Still, Bru decided it was best if he left her unkissed.

Bru coaxed the big truck through downtown traffic, stalling only once--at the busy intersection of Orange and Robinson just as the light changed. Finally the F-250 lurched into the bank's parking lot. After filling out the paperwork for the best part of a half hour, Bru was escorted to a little room and showed how the double key of the safe-deposit system worked. He put his contract with Goins and the copy of the paper with the notation, "Bruton, Check this out" in the drawer and closed the metal top and slid the box into the bank of numbered slots. Then he got into line and transferred the twenty-five thousand he'd put in the joint account yesterday into a new account. He was surprised at how badly he felt about taking that money out of the joint account, almost as though he was taking sustenance from Leta. He wasn't fool enough to leave that sum in a joint account with a divorce pending. The judge wouldn't care about the explanation, and Bru wasn't loyal enough to split the sum with her, but he was loyal enough to feel bad about removing it.

Hiking back to the truck he went by a store that sold cell phones for one cent. Bru went in and for just one cent

155

and a major credit card number and a lifetime commitment, a young fellow in a ponytail and earring fitted Bru up with a portable phone. "Now this thing is ready to go, right?" Bru asked after the transaction was completed and the phone was in a plastic bag.

"Just as soon as you charge it up."

"And can I do that in the car?"

The ponytail, who had made all kinds of blithe assurances while selling the phone, had to check with the manager who told Bru an adapter that plugged into the cigarette lighter would be necessary. The price was forty dollars; however, the manager told Bru on the q.t. he could get a generic item at Circuit City that would do the same job for about twelve bucks. Bru was on the sidewalk heading for the carpark when he turned around and went back and bought the adapter.

Back at the truck, Bru thought about hooking the phone up to see how it worked, but immediately trashcanned that idea. He slipped the phone still in its carton under the seat and headed for I-4. In a half hour he got off into suburban traffic and picked his way through a spaghetti skein of two lane roads until he came to the Pioneer Agribuz, Inc. plant.

The plant was brightly painted with orange paint and the air was perfumed with the essence of orange--more like the smell in the little bottles found in kitchens to give orange flavoring than the fruit. The operation looked more like a small gasoline refinery than an establishment having anything do with food processing. Large cylindrical towers shot a hundred feet into the sky, and these towers were connected by large steel tanks and huge pipes. Even in the very bright--because of the cold front--light, Bru could see lamps burning throughout the plant, the way gasoline refineries were lighted. As Bru slowed to turn into the office complex, a semi-trailer truck loaded with oranges passed

Bru and turned at the next drive so he knew there had been no mistake and he hadn't arrived at a sweet-smelling, strangely painted gasoline refinery by some mistake.

Don DiCicco was a hairy, bald-headed man with an easy grin and not much given to asking embarrassing questions. He seemed to assume Bru wanted the routine tour of the plant, the same one the grade school kids of the neighboring towns took on the years they didn't go to the soda bottling plant. "May as well start at the start," Don said, leading Bru out of the one-story, brick administration complex and directly through those large towering cylinders connected to each other by looping pipes that looked like a giant-scale lab experiment. Don led Bru to a loading dock. The semitrailer which had passed Bru was backing into it.

"That's the raw product," Don said, indicating the oranges the truck was dumping into a large bin. Bru noted thirty similar bins occupying the loading area.

"We want the finished product to be as uniform as possible, on a month to month, year to year basis. In order to do that we blend the fruits in each of these bins. The guy that tests the oranges in the bin for sugar and acid is employed by the state, even though we pay his salary indirectly. In the days when Florida produced most of the concentrated o.j. in the world, we could say we produced the best product, mainly because no one else took the trouble to compete with us. Nowadays, any serious player who wants to sell his product on the international market, has to maintain pretty much the same standards. This industry was invented in Florida after the second world war and it pretty much serviced only the American market. Believe it or not, until fairly recently hardly anyone else in the world drank orange juice in a big way. But in the last generation, Europe has come to consume more o.j. than the US, because there are a lot more Europeans. Japan and the Pacific rim are a good market too."

"All that is your way of saying you can produce a uniform product year around?" Bru said.

"Actually, Dr. Bruton, that was more my way of explaining why Brazilian orange juice is just as good as Florida orange juice. It wasn't but twenty-five years ago that just about all the export orange juice in the world came right here from Central Florida. The price was set in this state. The standards were set in this state. But nowadays you can't even tell whether the orange juice you're drinking is Florida or Brazilian. The Brazilians ship their juice to the states in huge tanker ships. And we ship some of our juice out of state the same way, sometimes frankly to get around the restrictive Florida standards. Sometimes, we import Brazilian juice--especially up here in the northern end of the citrus belt. My company is based out of Chicago. Next year I might be anywhere from Sao Paulo to Portland, Maine.

"Let's move on here, Bru. The oranges in the bins get loaded onto belts and are run by inspectors who cull out rotten or split fruit. If we were selling fresh fruit, the small oranges or those with poor color might be culled, but any fruit that can produce juice is okay by us--you might say we never met an orange we didn't like. The fruit is then scrubbed with detergent and dumped into the extracting machine. The machine inside that stainless steel vat--you're going to have to take my word for it--is a FMC In-line Extractor. It has metal mandibles which smash the orange from both sides while a steel tube is injected into the fruit and through which the juice squirts into the pipe venting below the apparatus.

"Next the juice goes into this network of looping tubes above our heads. This process both pasteurizes the juice and reduces it to the desired sugar content--all occurring in about eight minutes. We use the term 'degrees Brix' to express the sugar content of the concentrate. As a scientist you must know about degree Brix."

"A degree Brix," Bru said, "is the equivalent of one pound of solids in one hundred pounds of water. It is usually used to measure sugar, especially in grape juice when making wine or the barley wort when making beer."

"Very good, Bru. You get a big gold star to take home to your mother," Don said. "The sugar content of fresh orange juice is about twelve degrees Brix."

"Or in other words o.j. is about twelve percent sugar."

"Exactly, but that varies from variety to variety. I told you earlier that the Hamlins are the earliest orange. They mature as early as October. Since the fruit only hangs on the tree seven or eight months, it stands to reason the fruit will be somewhat less sweet than a Valencia, say, that hangs for more than a year. Therefore, we pay the growers less for Hamlins and not just because of the lower sugar content. The Hamlin also is lighter in color. We need to maintain uniformity in color as well as sugar, acid and flavor. In days gone by we'd keep big tanks of last year's crop of Valencias around to blend with the Hamlins. Nowadays we just import Brazilian Valencias--in frozen concentrated form, of course. Because of the seasonal difference it works out better. But to return to the vacuum-evaporating process, the juice enters at approximately twelve percent sugar or twelve degrees Brix. In about one and a half minutes it is up to nineteen degrees Brix. This is what we call stage three and that valve right there gives a taste of what nineteen degree Brix o.j. is like."

Don opened the valve and let an inch or so of brightly colored juice flow into a styrofoam coffee cup. Go ahead and taste it. But it's hot."

Bru brought the cup to his lips. Actually, it was about as hot as a cup of coffee and the fluid was as thick as a cup of java that had been left on the burner too long. But the flavor was good--rich but not too strong, if strange because of the unusualness of tasting orange juice warm.

"When we get up here to the fifth stage or valve, the juice is at forty-six degrees Brix." Don unscrewed the valve and let a bit of the juice gush into the cup, which he'd taken back from Bru. "You can taste this if you want but it won't be a pleasant experience. This is at about the consistency of the juice you buy in the six ounce cans in the supermarket--the grocery store stuff is in fact forty-two percent Brix. The flavor now however has a nasty aftertaste and also the stuff is hot."

Bru took the cup from Don. He could see the juice was about as thick as thawed concentrated o.j., and he didn't need to taste it to tell it had a bitter aftertaste. He could smell it. Bru could see now why Harry griped yesterday about how concentrated wasn't much like what he termed "real orange juice." At least the stuff in this cup didn't bear much of a resemblance to the Temple oranges Bru had savored in the grove with Harry.

"So how do you get this stuff to taste like reconstituted orange juice?" Bru wondered out loud.

"That's a trade secret, Bru. But since you are a resident of Florida and, since the people of Florida own that secret, I'll let you in on it in a minute. But for the time being, let's get back to the vacuum-evaporator. After eight minutes and the seventh valve, we have a product that is about the consistency of very well chewed gum and has a degree Brix reading of sixty degrees." Don shot a little of the product out of the seventh valve. It was frothy and hot but in the cool morning air became almost immediately as thick as chewing gum. The color was a gorgeous cadmium orange, as deep as the color of a Temple orange.

"Any chance a bacterium could survive your process?" Bru asked. That the canker could operate in conjunction with 1,2--DCA to produce KiDS seemed a long shot to Bru. Still, it was the most obvious means of bringing two agents together.

"Absolutely none, Bru. That pasteurization process is exactly our problem. In order to destroy any possible disease organism, we also destroy all orange flavor. If you took what's in this cup and added enough water to take it back to twelve degrees Brix, you'd have a product that tasted very much like sugar water, with almost no orange flavor at all."

"So the evaporation process destroys all bacterium."

"You got that right."

"But orange juice is billed as a one-hundred percent natural product so you don't mix in any additives. Or do you?" Bru waited with baited breath for the answer.

"Everything we put in the finished product comes right from the orange tree, nothing more, nothing less," Don said. "Now the guy that discovered the means of reflavoring was Dr. Louis MacDowell. He made the Florida citrus industry what it is. I met Dr. MacDowell, when he was an old man and I was just starting out in this business, and he just laughed at the inflated claims that have been made for his accomplishment. He claimed it was dumb luck and that he hadn't really invented anything at all."

Bru listened to Don's history lesson with only half an ear. He was disappointed that he hadn't found the obvious opportunity for the introduction of a second agent.

"The process for evaporating juice wasn't Dr. MacDowell's invention. All he, and a team of two other scientists, did was introduce what we call 'cutback' to the concentrate. Orange juice is one of those very strong flavors that can be cut quite a bit without losing full flavor, so a little fresh juice gives the concentrate a great deal of true orange flavor. But not enough to make the consumer beat a path to the frozen foods case.

"We figure we lose in the evaporation chamber eight hydrocarbons, four esters, fifteen carbonyls and sixteen

161

kinds of alcohol. We don't know which of those agents are responsible for true o.j. flavor so we recover some of them in condensation chambers in the evaporator and add them to the juice, but mainly we add d-limonene, which as you probably know, is a fancy way of saying peel oil. It's the stuff that makes your lips tingle when you get careless with a fresh orange and it's the stuff that has made this industry possible and as a citizen of the Sunshine State, Dr. MacDowell bequeathed his secret to you."

It was just as Harry said yesterday, concentrated orange juice was basically soda pop without the fizz and with the rind flavoring. But as interesting as all this stuff was, it was only the window dressing for what Bru came to learn about.

"Tell me, Don, what do you do with this product after you have made the last blend?"

"The one thing we don't do is keep it around. We get rid of it."

"And how do you do that?"

"In a variety of ways. We can shoot the product, still at sixty degrees Brix, into tank trucks and ship it out of state. Or we can dilute it to forty-two degrees Brix and put it into consumer-friendly cartons."

"Why forty-two degrees Brix?" Bru asked, to keep Don from thinking he was too anxious to learn what he indeed was anxious learn about.

"Dr. MacDowell set that standard way back after the war when he invented the process. It was his feeling--and obviously he was right--that six ounces of concentrate diluted with three cans of water would produce a reconstituted drink that was still refreshingly cold. Our consumer product could just as easily have been sixty degrees Brix, except it wouldn't make the final drink as pleasantly cool."

"So really this industry hasn't seen a great deal of

change in fifty years or so?" Bru said.

"That's right. The rise of Brazil as an orange producing country for a time seemed to upset things, but it turned out that was mostly an ego problem as far as Florida was concerned. The market is expanding and there is plenty of room for new growth, but yes, you're right, Bru, the basic elements of the industry have stayed the same for quite a while. The plant you are standing in was built forty years ago and we still use pretty much the same processes and equipment."

"With one notable exception," Bru said, hoping he was slipping this line in a cool way. If Don had heard the stories the health-food crowd were retailing about that new carton, he might not want to provide a frank answer. "I've noted the old cardboard carton has recently changed to plastic."

"Yeah, you're right, Bru. I guess we do have a pretty conservative industry here. I'm not sure we would have made that change either, but some outfit came in and made our parent company an offer that couldn't be refused. I happen to know this because we discussed this at the last general board meeting which I was invited to--I hope that means I'm being groomed for bigger and better things."

"Do you know what company it is that produces the plastic container?"

"As a matter of fact I do. It's one that operates in North Florida in the panhandle town of Port Saint Joe. I understand they make these cartons out of the pitch of sand pine trees. The process is cheaper than using a petroleum based plastic, and I understand they have beat out all the competitors, not only for concentrated cartons but for those gallon and half gallon jugs that fully reconstituted juice is sold in and also fresh-squeezed juice, which for your information, is fresh squeezed but usually frozen full strength and then thawed and doctored up a little unfrozen juice."

"The name of that company, Don," Bru coaxed gently. "What did you say it was?"

"I don't believe I did say it because I'm not sure I know it. Why, is it important that you learn it?"

"It could be the most important thing I learn today," Bru said.

"In that case, let's go back to the office and look on the bills of lading. Finding it shouldn't be any big trick."

27

Melba didn't pick up when Bru called his apartment from a 7-Eleven near the beach so he called Lawson and connected with her voicemail. He told her the name of the plastic works and asked her to glean as much information as she could about the outfit, including anything it had to do with Goins and Arbuthnot. Then he drove south along A1A until the highrises gave out and a man at the kiosk set up in the middle of the road made him pay five bucks to enter the National Seashore. Suddenly both sides of the road were given over to windswept saw-palmetto scrub.

Two cars were parked in the last lot where the road dead ended. Off to the west was a large lagoon--Bru could barely see the mainland several miles distant. Bru got out of Melba's truck and locked up. He went to the boardwalk and ascended to its highest point. The wind was snapping off the ocean, from the northeast, at a brisk clip and the surf was crashing onto the beach, which here was steep and narrow and of deep, red sand. The wind was cold and, even though Bru still had on the windbreaker he'd put on after getting up in the morning. He was freezing. The sky was an azure blue with a pale washed-out look around the horizon.

Bru looked south down the beach. This sandy strip, which was the largest sea turtle nursery in North America, stretched on for miles. In the far distance, the VAB or vehicle assembly building at Cape Canaveral jutted up. At one time, Bru hazily recalled--and possibly even now--it was the world's largest building, as measured by volume. At a distance of eighteen miles or so, it was just a blot on the horizon. A lone surf fisherman sat on a stool pouring himself a cup of coffee from a thermos. That fisherman occupied the spot where Bru had been instructed by the note to strip to the buff before heading off south along the water.

Bru sauntered toward the fisherman. A flock of sanderlings, small plover-like birds, stumped like windup toys just ahead of the surf line--and just ahead of Bru. Bru skipped a shell off the water and shambled along until suddenly a fishing rod in a holder blocked his way.

"Doing any good?" Bru asked the fisherman.

"Nah. The change of weather didn't bring 'em in like I thought."

Bru wandered down the beach another fifty yards and tried to pretend that he had business there--something not easy to do on the coldest day in weeks. Then Bru gave up and began to peel his clothes off. He took off everything but his shoes. He wrapped his clothes up in the windbreaker and secured the bundle from the wind with several large sun-bleached whelk shells. Carrying the car keys in his hand, he continued on down the beach toward the VAB.

Bru turned around every now and again to look down the beach toward his clothes. Bru saw a man emerge from the saw palmetto on a high sandy bank a hundred feet behind him. He was a slight fellow, hunched close to the ground. When he saw Bru looking at him, he froze to the spot. Then as though overcome by his own resolve, he slid down the sand dune and trudged with grim purpose toward

Bru. His hand was thrust in his pocket as though wrapped around a gun.

"Turn around, smart guy," he ordered Bru. "Bend over and spread your cheeks."

"Fuck you," Bru said. He was angry at having his nudity taken advantage of. The man bracing him stood about five ten and had wispy ginger colored hair and was about as big around as Bru's thumb. He wore large plastic frame glasses. Bru thought of him as Mr. Peepers. He doubted there was any gun in the man's pocket.

"You hadn't ought to talk to me like that."

"I'm not going to be talking to you at all in about ten seconds unless you begin making sense. Now why did you call me out here?"

"I never called anyone anywhere, fella. I received a call telling me that my--er, my--friend Billy Arbuthnot was dead, that he'd been murdered."

"Who was the caller?"

"I haven't any idea. Scared the bejesus out of me, not that I wasn't already out of my mind with grief and fear, Billy being killed like that."

"How'd I get in the picture?"

"The guy that called told me to clear out of my apartment for fear that I would get the same treatment as Billy. I was told to hide out and that a man would come to help me. I said all right, but he had to come where I said in the way I said. Hey, how do I know you are the right guy, anyway?" Mr. Peepers said. "You didn't say the password."

"I'm not going to say 'kinko' either. Now tell me about Arbuthnot."

"I ought to get something out of this," the little man blubbered.

"Buddy," Bru said, "What I'll give you is some excellent advice. Get out of the area. Go visit friends or relatives."

"You mean somebody beside Arbuthnot has been killed."

"Tell me how Arbuthnot rigged this citrus juice scam."

"I want money. Billy was always a cheap lover. Say, a thousand dollars."

"All right, I'll give you a thousand. Just tell me what you know."

"First, the money."

"Where the hell you think I got a thousand bucks on me?"

"So where is it?"

"In the car. I have it in the car."

"Let's get it."

Bru was turning blue from cold. But he wanted the answers first, especially seeing how he was going to have to give the guy a check written on the temporary checks he'd gotten from the bank that morning. "You talk first."

"You have the money, don't you?"

"Sure," Bru said.

"Billy was a real bright guy. Had he put his mind to it he might have gotten somewhere in the world. But he was only interested in what he called flimflamming the system. He hated this country and this society. Sometimes he and I would get in big arguments and he wouldn't talk to me for days. Back in the eighties he figured out a way to make the citrus canker harmless then he introduced it to thousands of acres of citrus. He made a lot of money out of that. Enough to live comfortably the rest of his life, but I think he would have released those disease spores for nothing. That was the kind of guy he was."

"That was in the eighties," Bru said. "A long time ago. Tell me what he was doing now--with orange juice, was it?"

"All I know is that he went away for stretches of time. He had a job working someplace. Does New Port Richey sound right to you?

"How about Port Saint Joe?" Bru said.

"That could be it," Mr. Peepers said.

"What was he doing there?"

"He called it adding a cat, cata. . ."

"A catalyst?" Bru suggested.

"Yeah, that was it, a catalyst. He claimed he added that to the raw product," Mr. Peepers said.

"Adding a catalyst to the raw product to produce 1,2--DCA?" Bru said. This was not the answer he was expecting exactly but it did seem to fit the data.

"I don't know a thing about the initials. All I know was what he said one night when he got drunk. He started bragging about how what he was doing would cause wholesale death and mayhem, especially among kids and old folks. Then he cussed that he didn't have enough money to fund his idea of putting it in the food chain so he went to Old Man Goins, the guy who helped him with the citrus canker."

"How did the two of them get connected in the first place?" Bru asked.

"I don't know. That happened long before I came on the scene. But evidently Goins tumbled to Billy's new idea right off. It took them a long time to put all the pieces in place. They kept it all very close to their vests. Billy wouldn't even tell me what he was doing, but he and Goins fooled with the plan so long--two, three years after that time he was drunk--I couldn't help but get an earful now and then. Finally, last year Goins bought a plastic company and also started selling the new orange juice container to all major o.j. distributors. Then this past summer Billy got a job and began doing what he called 'pitching' that catalyst or whatever you called it 'into the product.' He figured he would have the entire Florida o.j. crop contaminated by Christmas. See, the longer juice sits in the can, the stronger the effect. Anybody who drinks o.j. two three times a week is headed for bad trouble."

Bru's body was numb from the cold wind--and this knowledge the ginger man had imparted. "I need some proof of all this. You haven't given me a thousand dollars worth of information yet."

"Keep your shirt on, big boy," the Mr. Peepers said. "I know where Billy's experimental lab is located. That's what you will get for your thousand."

"Where is it?"

"At his mother's place."

"That old shack out off Camptown Spur Road?" Bru asked.

"That's it all right."

There's nothing there. I've been there," Bru said.

"But there is. His mother and those dogs guarded it for him. Billy was a sly one. Believe me, it is all there."

"Have you seen it?" Bru asked.

"Of course not. But he let on to me several times and I know he went there a lot. It's there. Now let's get my thousand bucks."

Bru turned on his heel and began walking back toward his clothes.

"Hey, where are you going? Where's my money."

"Fuck you and your money," Bru said. "You don't think I'm giving anybody any money for information like that."

"A deal's a deal," Mr. Peepers shouted. Bru was walking fast back toward his clothes. Mr. Peepers was running alongside of him, hollering into his ear. "Darn it, you promised."

Bru reached his pile of clothes and quickly pulled on his trousers and shirt. He buttoned the windbreaker jacket as he walked toward the ramp to the parking lot. He ignored Mr. Peepers's tirade. Talking sense to the old girl and her dogs wouldn't be easy. Without the evidence in that supposed lab, Bru couldn't possibly hope to get anyone in authority to believe him.

"I performed a service for you and now you are stiffing me," Mr. Peepers cried. "I didn't think a nice man like you would do that."

Bru made for the boardwalk to the parking area. The fisherman shouted, "Watch it, mac. He has a gun." Immediately a pellet whispered by Bru's ear. The training his father had inculcated in him years before kicked in. Bru lurched about, facing his assailant, and dropped to the side and down on all fours. Then he charged Mr. Peepers, who squeezed off another round. That shot was aimed at the standing Bru. It zinged harmlessly over Bru's head.

Bru came at Mr. Peepers, who was waving the pistol around, like a scrambling linebacker. Piff. Another round went zinging above Bru and then Bru's shoulder hammered into Mr. Peepers's flabless gut. Bru and the slight man went down in a heap. The guy tried to bring the gun up to Bru's face, but Bru's hands fastened in a death grip around the man's arm. Bru slung the arm against the sand. The fisherman stepped over and put his foot on Mr. Peepers's wrist. Bru grabbed the gun, which the little man's hand clung to. With the heel of his hand Bru clubbed Mr. Peepers's fingers around the pistol butt. The fingers relaxed their grip. Bru took the weapon.

"What a chickenshit weapon," Bru said, looking at the short-barreled, .22 caliber pistol in his hand. "You hit someone with this thing you wouldn't do much more than make him angry." Still Bru wondered about the advisability of pocketing the gun, of having some defense when he went up against Arbuthnot's mother and her dogs. Immediately that idea tasted rotten in Bru's mouth--as he'd warned

Melba. He knew about guns. He knew they only got you in trouble. He opened the cylinder and shook the rounds out. The shells dropped like small bombs released from a plane. Then Bru hurled the pistol beyond the foaming surfline into the ocean. "Believe me, friend. I discarded that gun for your own good. It could only get you into trouble."

The little man sat with his head in his hands crying silently and snuffling. The fisherman just shook his head and said, "He had no call to shoot at you, mac. But you should have paid him. A man provides a service for you, whether it's a blow job or mowing your lawn, you ought to do right by him."

Bru was too taken up by what he'd learned from Mr. Peepers to set the fisherman straight. He strode across the sand to the ramp over the dune vegetation. He wondered how he was going to secure that evidence. And what he would do with it once he had it.

28

When Bru turned onto Camptown Road Spur, he saw a plume of smoke rising above the pine flatwoods. He stamped on the gas pedal. The gate which he'd forced the day before yesterday hadn't been repaired. Bru drove through it into the pasture. The tongue of smoke was rising from behind the house. He rocketed down the tire tracks along the fence. Coming around the house, he saw a deputy sheriff's cruiser parked in the middle of the yard. The blue lights were going. A man in uniform was standing in the middle of the yard with a gasoline can in his hand. He was looking at the blazing outbuilding, the one that supposedly housed the lab.

"Come on out, Ruby," the deputy hollered toward the house. "I ain't gonna hurt you none." The deputy was Hank Smith.

Bru reached under the seat and groped for the plastic bag with the cell phone. He fumbled with the box and popped the cardboard tabs that held the top in place. He shook the box and a styrofoam collar, encasing the phone, slid out. Bru's fingers pulled the phone eagerly from the base. The smart money was on making a quick U-turn and getting the hell out of there. Bru could go out to the road and call for help. A sticker on the box said, "For Emergencies, Dial *FHP."

But a phone call wouldn't save that burning shack. It wouldn't save the secrets presumably burning inside it. The building was a roaring contagion. Bru threw the gearshift lever into first and stamped on the gas. The big Ford truck charged right up to the sheriff's cruiser. He slammed on the brakes at just the last moment. Smith turned and looked at him as though in a daze. "Who the hell are you?" he asked, as Bru jumped from the truck and ran to the cruiser. He swung open the driver door. Sure enough, there was a fire extinguisher. Bru grabbed the canister by the top and with his left hand unbuckled the straps that secured it. He pulled the safety pin on the lever as he rushed to the fire. He aimed at the base of the fire and mashed the lever. Foam spewed onto the flames. The extinguisher gurgled and quit spewing foam. Bru tried to peer inside. He saw a large vat. There was sort of an explosion. Bru hustled backwards as the roof collapsed and dropped into the fire. The storm window, which Bru had noticed the first time here, exploded. Bru realized it wasn't a storm window, but a solar panel--the means of power for Arbuthnot's secret lab.

"How do I know you?" Smith hollered at Bru. His face squinted in thought, giving the short, heavy-set man a

172

resemblance to a pig.

"I'm was the guy whose car was ravaged by the biker the other day."

"Yeah, Bruton. The Fud, as the old man calls you. Put that fire extinguisher down. Just drop it." Smith pulled his pistol from his holster. "I don't know what you're doing here. But I don't like it. Turn around and put your hands behind you."

Bru didn't budge. Smith was one guy Bru didn't want to put his back to.

"I advise you to turn around, sonny," Smith said in a cordial tone of voice and giving a Warren Oates smirk. "For your own good. I got work to be doing here and you're obstructing it."

Bru stood his ground.

Smith's hand with the pistol in it flew at Bru's face. The heavy 9 mm automatic smashed against his cheekbone. Bru staggered. Smith slashed at Bru on backstroke. The handgun caught Bru on the chin. His feet went spongy. He keeled over. His nose was pushed up against the sandy Florida soil. Pine straw mashed against his nostrils and mouth. He could feel Smith fumbling with his hands, pulling them into the small of his back. Click. One of the bracelets snapped around Bru's wrist. Then the other was secured behind his back.

At that moment Bru heard a deep in the throat tiger growl. Bru's skin crawled. His hair stood up. He could hear the footfalls of the dog thudding in his ear. Then they were past him. The dog caught Smith just as he was opening the cruiser door. The beast clomped down on Smith's right wrist and gave his arm a fearful shake. Had Smith not been compactly built and heavily muscled that shake would probably have snapped his arm.

Smith calmly grabbed the dog by the neck with his left hand and squeezed the brute's throat. At the same time, he kicked at its gonads. A complete flurry of bodies--human and dog--shook and kicked and growled, and the noise emitted from Smith's throat seemed more demonic and animal-like than the mutt's.

With a gargantuan effort Smith threw the dog off him. Blood sprayed, glinting in the sun. The animal flopped to the ground. Its chest heaved. Smith ran a couple of steps and slammed his foot into its crotch. The beast whimpered and made an effort to crawl away, but Smith's pistol drew his pistol. BANG! BAM! A pitiful cry squeaked from the dog's throat. Shortly it would be dead.

Then Bru realized the pitiful cry was coming not from the dog, but from the old lady. She bounded off the porch and tore across the yard toward Smith. "You sumbitch," she screeched. Her fists were doubled and flailing the air. "Killing my son. Killing my dog."

Smith just let her come. He had the most self-satisfied smirk on his face. He looked perfectly pleased. Bru knew what was coming. There was nothing he could do about it. There was no way of stopping brute force unless you had an equal or greater amount of brute force. It was simple as that. No, it wasn't. *I bragged I was smarter and brighter than the forces of evil. Now is the time to prove it.* Yes, there was something he could do. He needed to get to his feet. He discussed the matter with his body. It didn't seem interested. *Snap to,* he argued with himself.

Finally his body responded. He rolled over onto his back and sat up. Pushing himself to his feet, with hands manacled required about the same amount of energy as climbing a small mountain. Plus he couldn't call attention to himself. No bumping into things. No noise. He tried getting up silently--his left arm couldn't stretch far enough to give him the leverage needed. The old lady--still in her black dress--was tearing toward Smith, howling like a

174

banshee. Bru decided, fuck the noise. He had to get up. He thrust up and slammed against an old rusted piece of farm machinery. Its rust-thin walls dented but held. They supported his weight and he was able to pinion himself there until he got his bearings and stood alone.

The woods, with their tangle of saw palmetto underbrush, came right up behind the shed. He had only to duck into the woods, make off a hundred yards and jump into a clump of saw palmetto, and Smith would never find him. The pine trees beckoned to him. But that wouldn't help the old lady. Bru sneaked around behind the sheriff's cruiser. Smith was twenty yards in front of it and showing no interest in anything but the old lady who now was bracing him ten feet away.

"Why'd you go and kill my Butch? I ain't got nothing left." The old lady waved her fist at Smith then turned and threw herself on the carcass. She kissed the animal's face, blood flying.

Bru hoped against hope that the passenger door of Melba's truck was unlocked. It was. He opened the door and put his foot on the running board and hanging onto the armrest, hiked himself the three feet up into the passenger compartment. That maneuver was no mean feat. The blood drummed in his ear as he lay panting, resting up. *Hurry,* he told himself. *Hustle it up.* The cell phone was out of its box on the seat, but Bru had to undo the packaging from the charger cord--not easily done in the confines of a pickup truck--even a big one--with your hands behind your back. Finally, he got the cord plugged into the lighter and into the phone. He pushed the dial button. Did the machine have to charge up or be activated somehow? Just before Bru gave up all hope, the call button lighted up. He pressed it and dialed star, FHP.

A crisp voice came on the line, "Florida Highway Patrol."

"Can you hear me?" Bru asked.

"Roger. I mean yes, go ahead," the dispatcher said.

"Do you know where Camptown Spur Road is?"

"No, in which county?"

"Okeelanta. I'm afraid a woman is about to be murdered. Get a car or better yet a helicopter here as soon as possible. Just follow Camptown Road until you come to the spur. This place is the first, possibly the only place, on the spur road."

"Wilco," the dispatcher said. "We'll get a vehicle there as soon--"

BANG! The percussion rocked the truck. Bru poked his head up. Mrs. Arbuthnot's body lay limp on top of her Butch. Smith's pistol was in hand down at his side. His bloody right hand was digging in his crotch.

"Was that a shot?" the dispatcher asked.

"Just hurry and get someone here," Bru told the dispatcher. "I don't want to end up like that old lady."

29

Bru lay on the seat of the truck, passenger door open, tracking Smith's movement by ear. Smith's footfalls stamped in aimless circles, as though strutting around then stopping to thump his chest.

Then finally, he started hollering, "Bruton, where are you? I want you."

Bru hied his body off the bench seat and his feet dropped to the ground. He landed on his feet. Smith stood over the lifeless carcasses of the old lady and the dog. His eyes were glassy. The face, though still triumphant, seemed apprehensive. His trouser crotch was daubed with a crimson-brown color--blood. His right wrist was trickling blood. His pistol, Bru was pleased to see, resided in the holster on his hip.

"I already called the incident in," Bru said. "The dispatcher said a car would be along pronto."

"I reckon I ought to get them bracelets off you," Smith offered. "You saw I had to do it. I had no other choice."

"You had no reason to kill that old lady, Smith," Bru heard himself roar.

Smith blinked his eyes. One brow shot up. Bru smelled the odor of pine straw and dirt--sharp and fecund and oddly northern in the cool afternoon air. Smith thrust his face at Bru and looked at Bru hard.

Bru's impressions of the scene were very sharp--of the dilapidated farmhouse with its unpainted but priceless cypress sideboards, of the grove of deciduous citrus leaking their perfume into the air, of the burning embers of the collapsed outbuilding over Smith's shoulder, of a mockingbird singing its fool head off in the saw palmetto on a cool but otherwise fine spring day. Of Smith, looking at him with a wolfish grin on his pig face. "The old man probably ain't gonna like this," he said going for his holstered weapon as a distant thump-whack, thump-whack sound rapidly became louder and clearer--a helicopter. Shortly the green and gold machine with the sheriff's star shot out from the pine tree tops.

It gyrated about in a circle, looking for a suitable landing spot, then settled to the earth. Bru could see the sunglasses and cocky grin on the pilot's face. He wondered if he'd ever seen a more welcome face. Smith gave a sour grin. Bru noticed the words "Okeelanta Sheriff Department" painted on the side of the helicopter. As the pilot shut down the whirlybird's power plant, a sergeant jumped out and ran over to the pickup. The sergeant shot Smith's uniform a nasty look and barked, "What went down here, Smith?"

"He shot that woman and that dog," Smith said, indicating with his head Bru. "Killed them just dead as hell." A mischievous grin played on his lips.

"Bullshit," Bru said, sticking his handcuffed wrists out from behind his back. "I was nowhere near a pistol. Smith shot that old lady down."

The sergeant scowled. "What was it, Smith? Who did the victim?"

"Did I say he did it?" Smith said, just pleasant as he could. "I meant I shot them--her, in self defense. He'll tell you."

"All right, not another fucking word out of either of you. Bill," the sergeant shouted to the pilot. "Take Smith over there and get his sidearm and secure it. Turn the recorder on and question him. I'll talk to this honyock."

The sergeant sat Bru down on the running board of the pickup. "Now what the hell happened?" Bru indicated his hands. The sergeant gave no indication that he saw. "Come on. Spit it out. What went on," he snarled.

Bru related the story. The sergeant listened to Bru with a skeptical frown on his face. Then he conferred with Bill and talked with Smith for a while. Then the sergeant went to the helicopter and talked on the radio for a time. After a while Bill, the pilot, came over and took a handcuff key from his belt and released Bru's hands. Bill was carrying a square case that said, "Mobile Evidence Kit" on the side. He made Bru put on a pair of gloves, which were then stowed in separate plastic bags and filed with Bru's name and the date. Then he took the index finger of each of Bru's hands and ran the point of an instrument that looked something like a knife and something like a scalpel under the nails. The scrapings were deposited in separate bags. The sergeant came over then and filled a form out which was a write-up of what Bru had told him. He made Bru sign it.

"There's no fooling about this being your address where we can get hold of you?" he asked Bru.

"No," Bru said.

"All right. You can go. I thought for sure they were going to take you in and sweat you for a while. But I guess there's some big stuff going on, what with Bike Week and all. It'll be a while before the FDLE evidence unit gets here."

"What are you going to do about him?" Bru asked meaning Smith, who was standing in his blood-stained clothes chatting friendly-like with the other cop. "He shot that woman down like he shot her dog. In cold blood. And don't forget the stuff in that building Smith was trying to burn. You need to secure it as evidence. When things cool down perhaps something can be reconstructed."

"The law will take care of things."

"You haven't done very well so far, have you?"

"Do yourself a favor and disappear," the sergeant warned Bru.

Bru got in the truck. At the intersection with Camptown Road, he told himself to turn left--toward Orlando. The thing Bru needed to do was get with Jerry--or some other lawyer. He needed to make sure his ass was covered.

Bru turned right--toward the beach. He didn't stop until confronted by the guard at the gatehouse of Goins's place. It was the young man with the toothpick in the Sam Browne belt, although he didn't have a toothpick in his mouth now. He shot Bru a strange look. But then Bru gave him an odd look too. Bru wondered how it was that guy was still working there after his revelations to Elizabeth. "I'm not sure they will let you in," the guard said to Bru.

"I'm not asking," Bru told the young man. "I'm insisting."

The young man slid the window of the booth closed

and picked up the phone. Bru looked straight ahead. To his surprise he saw the gate was open. He stamped on the gas and drove up the winding lane toward the big house. When he got within sight, he was surprised to see three Okeelanta sheriff's sedans and a cube truck, which also bore the sheriff's logo. What the hell happened here? Bru wondered.

30

Rock music blared in Elizabeth's office as Juan's knuckles bashed on the door. He tried the knob, locked. Noise was ravening in Juan's ears. Elizabeth's music? No, the sound of his own mind howling. *How could she be sitting in there listening to music? At a time like this,* he thought. *When the house is crawling with police.*

Bang, bang, bang.

When she cracked the door to look out, he burst in the room. "We have big trouble," he said.

"How's that?" she said taking the joint from behind her back and sucking smoke into her lungs. She offered it to Juan.

He took a step to the air conditioner embedded in the wall and hit the exhaust button. His left hand clamped around her wrist. The index and thumb from his right hand vise-gripped the joint. He went into the bathroom and flushed the roach down the toilet. "What the hell are you dressed like that for?"

She had on a gauzy blouse and peddlepushers. Her hair hung down in sexy ringlets.

"I'm celebrating," Elizabeth said. "You should celebrate too."

What was there to celebrate? The ravening noise in

his head? It screamed at him. "Paul just called from the guard booth. Bruton just showed up. He didn't wait permission to come up to the house. He just drove in. What do you suppose he's found out?"

"It's probably nothing," Elizabeth snarled. "He's probably just learned that little warm cunt checked out and he's come to bill and coo. It was always like that with that damn kid. Right from the moment I had her, the old man, Leroy, all of them, made a bigger deal over that kid than me. I was the one whose body was ruined and got ugly bearing her. They came and ogled little miss shitbritches, and they're still doing it, now that she's clocked."

"Your father is really a mess. I'm worried about him."

"That was the idea, remember?" Elizabeth said. She opened the tray drawer of her refectory table-desk and took out a bottle of nail polish. Juan grimaced as he recalled her cutting that priceless antique to install the tray drawer. Now he watched, with hopeless rage, his new partner as she began painting her nails. "We were going to drive him round the bend by killing her. Looks to me you are not holding up so well either. The complete sociopath you told me you were and here you are running around like a chicken with its head chopped off. Just because little snookums bought the farm."

There was more truth in that assertion, Juan knew, than he would like to admit. Her death had come so suddenly. He had never much liked Kimberly, he'd thought, but she been around for so long and she was sweet in a nice innocent way. Her sudden termination did bother him. Or maybe he was just scared by the house full of cops, including the sheriff, no less. "I don't think Bruton would have run the gate if he was just concerned about Kimberly," Juan said.

"Probably not," Elizabeth agreed, her brows knitting

in concentration at the job in hand--painting her nails. "So it took Bruton three days to figure your scam," Elizabeth said in a bored tone as the brush daubed paint on her middle fingernail. "One of the dumbest ideas I ever heard of was hiring a scientist with the idea that you were going to fool him about a scientific scam."

"Your friend Leroy had something on Bruton that was going to make him see the light of reason, in case he caught on."

Elizabeth considered the nails of her right hand. Juan's head sounded like a coyote was yowling in it.

Elizabeth looked at Juan and gave him a sour grin. "Don't worry about Bruton. He's a man. I know how to make men do what I want."

Those words were arrows of rage and envy wounding Juan's heart.

"When I get done with Bruton he won't remember there ever had been an orange-juice plot or a Kimberly. You get back to the old man and the sheriff. Make sure the old fart keeps telling the same story. And you remember to keep your yarns the same too. As long as you keep your stories straight the heat can't catch you up."

She flicked her hand. "Go on, get. I'll see to Bruton as soon as my nails are dry."

31

The maid Guadelupe answered the door. Her face was long. Her eyes were red. She had difficulty meeting Bru's eyes. But when her eyes did lock with his, her dark Spanish irises seemed to plead for help and consolation.

"What's wrong?" Bru asked.

"Mr. Bru, it's *Senorita* Kimberly. She di-ed last night."

Then it was Bru who needed the help. His feet buckled and Guadelupe's arm went around his waist. She led him to a circular staircase and he sat on a step. She left and brought a glass of water which he drank.

"I'm sorry," Bru said.

Guadelupe just looked at Bru and he knew from the expression on her careworn features, he needn't have apologized--that she felt the same way herself. "You are a good man, Mr. Bru. It's too bad you weren't able to save Kimberly. Thank you for bringing her to me that night."

"What happened?"

"She killed herself. In the car. With the exhaust you know."

"How is the family taking it?"

"The *senor* is pretty broken up. You came to see him? You might have to wait for a while. The *policia* are with him."

Bru nodded and got to his feet. He was a bit shaky. "I have to talk to him immediately. It's important. Very important."

Lupe gave him her arm and, for a moment, they embraced. They broke apart. "I might get into trouble, but I'll take you to him. I'll probably quit now anyway with Miss Kim gone." They passed out of the foyer. Lolling in her office door was Elizabeth. Her arms were behind her back thrusting her more than ample breasts out to ever greater and more ample volume. She was smiling broadly. When Bru came within arm reach, she snatched him from Lupe and pulled him into her office. Bru let himself be deflected from his mission partly out of respect for Kim's mother and partly because he was still dazed by news of the girl's death.

The air conditioning was running and it was very

cold in the little room. Elizabeth put both her hands on Bru's chest and pushed. He plopped into the antique French chair. She plunked her butt on the refrectory table, hiked her leg across Bru and spiked her foot on the chair arm.

"You have to be nice to me today," Elizabeth said, wiggling her toes in her open-ended sandals. "My daughter, little Miss Snookums, clocked out. It's hard on a person when her daughter folds like that."

"Yes, it must be--" Bru searched for a word, "difficult," It was only then Bru became fully conscious of her dress and thought back to her outlandish breast thrusts. He thought, *This was the woman I stiffarmed Melba for. God, how could anyone be so brazen?*

"It was so inconsiderate of her," Elizabeth said.

"What I don't get," Bru said, "is how she did it. Her grandfather kept her cooped up here. She didn't drive."

"That's right, she didn't."

"Yet she started the car and monoxided herself. That seems a strange thing for someone who didn't know how to drive to do. Did she just let the thing run?"

"It was awful," Elizabeth said, snickering a few sobs and a tear. "Kimberly, the poor dear's complexion turned a bright pink--like a crab after it's been boiled. The carbon monoxide does that."

"So she just let the car run and the entire garage space filled with fumes?"

"She rigged a garden hose to blow the monoxide into the passenger compartment," Elizabeth said.

"That doesn't sound like something a girl would do, would know how to do."

"What are you getting at?"

"I'm getting at nothing," Bru said. "And that guard with the toothpick is still on the job."

"I didn't have time to take care of that last night. This morning we had other things to think of. Fuzz was all over the place."

"Yes, I suppose now it doesn't matter whether you keep him on the guard booth or not. If you'll excuse me, I have to talk with your father."

"Don't leave me, Bru." The calf crossing in front of his eyes knotted and bulged. Bru got a whiff of her cunt odor, meaty and rank, like a can of cheap dog food after the top has been roweled off. Just the night before this women- -in retrospect at least--had seemed so incredibly attractive to him and her pussy smelled so enticing. Now the thought of her touch gave Bru shivers. Bru pushed her leg out of his way and stood. "I'm sorry about Kimberly. She was a fine young lady. I have an important matter to discuss with your father." Feeling his body was wooden, he pushed through the door.

32

Guadelupe was waiting. "Mr. Bru, Mr. Goins is with the sheriff. Maybe we shouldn't break in, not even today."

"The sheriff is exactly the person we need," Bru said. "Take me to them."

Guadelupe made a face but led Bru across the big room and to the Florida room where Goins had received Bru the first time. The rude little guy in the suit, Joo-an, was there as well as the sheriff and Goins. Juan looked startled by Bru's sudden appearance. He popped to his feet.

"What are you doing here? Get out," Juan shouted.

"I have to talk to Mr. Goins," Bru said. The sheriff turned and cocked her head toward Bru, looking puzzled. "I'm glad to see you here, sheriff. You may find what I have to say interesting."

"Sheriff, please help me get him out of here," Juan shouted. "This is highly irregular, bursting in like this, after a death in the family."

"Why are you here, Bruton?" the old man said from behind the desk. "I thought I told you to stay away from my family." From the way his face perked up, though, he seemed to squeeze some comfort out of Bru's presence.

The sheriff stood and pointed a finger at Bru. "Place your hands on your neck and turn around, mister," she said in a command voice. "I knew this guy was trouble from the moment I laid eyes on him. He just doesn't seem to get the picture."

"I'm sorry about Kimberly," Bru said, directing his words to Goins. He padded closer to the desk. "I liked her very much."

"How'd I go wrong with her?" the old man blubbered. "I tried to give her the very best--and she does . . . Well, you know what she did. I don't understand it. Look, I suppose I should thank you for what you tried to do for her the other night. Perhaps if I'd taken a page out of your book---"

In the corner of his eye, Bru saw Juan nodding. The sheriff's voice barked in his ear, "I told you, mister, to put your hands on your neck." Bru turned toward the sheriff. He saw her pretty face contorted with rage and concentration as her hand made a downward stroke. A sap was in her hand. Bru stepped back and the sap clipped him on the cheekbone at about the same spot the big biker's blow landed. Bru's vision flickered. He saw stars. He shuffled. His sight came back in time to see the sheriff's arm come up again. Bru heard the old man shout, "What the hell did you do that for?"

The sheriff's arm stayed the second blow, which was good because she had dead aim on Bru's temple and his body was too deadened by the first shot to dodge out of the way. "He didn't comply with my command," the sheriff said, unrepentant.

"Jesus, sheriff, Shelby," the old man said. "This man works for me. He's here to give me a report. You don't beat up a man's employees in his presence."

"I don't like that guy, Bruton. I think he's a shakedown artist. You just told him to stay away from your family. And I got a report about a half hour ago that he was at the scene of a violent death, out in the country somewhere."

"Forget it," the old man said. "Forget everything. Bruton looks like he's in all right shape. Why don't you just run along and let me handle it? You are okay aren't you, Bru?"

Bru's hand was on his cheek. He was going to get a shiner this time, no doubt of it. But this time he was still on his feet. He supposed you got used to getting clopped in the face, just like you got used to other bad things--like young women dying.

"Yeah, I'm okay. But I'd like it better if the sheriff stayed."

"You're right. Maybe she ought to hear what you've turned up."

Now Juan burst between Bru and Goins and the sheriff. His arms were exxing in front of him. "No, no way. The sheriff has to go. We don't discuss our business in front of the law."

The old man shrugged. "Juan's right. We talk about bidness with them who are in the bidness. I guess it's best you head on out after all, Shelby."

Bru looked at the sheriff and said, "I think you'd better stay. We need to talk about your man, Smith, among other things."

"Are you saying you have a crime to report, Bruton?"

"I'd say I have more like a genocide to report--the death of a hundred kids. And many more will be forthcoming unless we do something fast."

Juan was jumping up and down saying, "The man is off his head. You don't want to listen to his garbage, sheriff."

"Look, Mr. Goins," the sheriff said. "I think this guy's a flimflam artist. You sure you don't want me to chill him out for you?"

"He's talking about that damn 1,2--DCA shit," the old man said.

Juan jumped between Bru and Goins. "Sheriff," Juan called, "Mr. Goins is clearly distraught from grief and this bunco man, Bruton, is trying to take advantage of the situation. Please do something."

"Joo-an, god dammit, get out of the way. I know exactly what I'm doing. Okay, so what did you find out, Bruton?"

"I know for a fact that Arbuthnot distributed a catalyst in the plastic stock that the Port Saint Joe Plastic Company produces for citrus containers. That catalyst makes the plastic product secrete 1,2--DCA on contact with citrus juice. I've also learned that Arbuthnot knew or believed that 1,2--DCA contamination would make for a health problem."

Bru looked at the sheriff. Her pretty face, which had been uglified with anger, now looked quite plain.

The old man's head snapped out of his hands. "That son of a bitch Arbuthnot lied to me about that 1,2--DCA. He told me it would only have the perception of causing a health problem--just enough of a problem to cause a bruhaha, to stir up the loonies. I wouldn't have done anything to knowingly harm kids. I swear."

Bru looked at the sheriff. "You heard that, didn't you?"

Juan said to the sheriff, "1,2--DCA is harmless. Ask him. Don't listen to the old man. He's suffered a shock. He'd confess to the kidnaping of the Lindberg baby and the World Trade Center bombing right now."

"What about it, Bruton? Is this 1,2 stuff deadly?" the sheriff asked.

Bru remembered what Professor Khoury told him about being able to drink a tumbler of the stuff. The truth of the matter was he hadn't turned up any evidence that the compound was dangerous, only that it was present in some o.j. containers. "Sheriff, stopping this KiDS outbreak will be the biggest case of your career."

"You didn't answer my question, Bruton. Is this 1,2 compound deadly poison?"

"It's producing this KiDS epidemic," Bru said, but his voice sounded lame in his own ears.

The sheriff shook her head. "I don't know what's going on here," she said. "I advise you--all of you--to get yourselves lawyers before you talk like this around a lawman."

"This Bruton's trying to coerce my employer, sheriff," Juan said. "I plead with you to call your men in and restrain him."

"Juan, put a sock in it," the old man said. "Bruton's right and you know it."

"I most emphatically do not know it," Juan said, looking at the sheriff.

"As Bruton claims, over a hundred preteenage children have been stricken by that KiDS disease already," the old man said.

This thing has to be stopped immediately," Bru said, "and you're the only guy who can do it."

"Stopping the disease will bankrupt me," the old man said, looking right at Bru. His eyes were the color of blue chalk. "I leveraged my entire fortune in order to control the orange juice stocks outside the United States. If this deal doesn't go down, I wouldn't even be able to pay off that silly bonus I promised you."

"You heard that, sheriff," Bru said. To Goins, he said, "You're going to have to pull the plug on this thing, no matter what it costs."

"I suppose in my gut I always knew Arbuthnot wouldn't rely on some silly internet rumor to cause the run on orange juice. In case things went way wrong, I even bought you a million dollars worth of o.j. futures and phonied up records of your working as a consultant for the plastic company, fixing you up as our fall guy."

"And that's why you tried to get me to work on this deal without a contract or upfront money. So you could pretend I was working on my own," Bru said.

"Yeah, that's right. But you and Wiley were too clever to fall for that simple trick." the old man said.

"Sheriff, ask him if he has any evidence that 1,2--DCA is a harmful substance?" Juan demanded. "He keeps dancing around that question."

"Answer the man's question," the sheriff demanded.

"Bruton's right. The stuff is killing off America's kids," old man Goins croaked out in a pained wail.

"Sheriff, my employer's overwrought," Juan said. "Bruton's trying to shake him down in your presence. Arrest Bruton."

"Leave Bruton alone," the old man said.

"I can show that Arbuthnot worked at the Port Saint Joe Company and that he contaminated the cans," Bru put in.

"Are you dead certain you can do that?" Juan asked.

"You know I can," Bru said.

"No, I don't," Juan said.

"If you have evidence produce it," the sheriff demanded.

190

The only witness Bru had, Arbuthnot's sidekick from the beach, he had chased into hiding. He should have given that little weasel the thousand dollars, he saw now. Bru said, "There'll be plenty of both in good time."

"And in the meantime, you expect me to do a tune on Mr. Goins on your sayso. Forget that, mister." The sheriff took a step toward Bru and shook her finger under his nose. "Bruton, I don't know what your game here is, but I don't like it. Mr. Goins has testified that he's put a million dollars in your name. A teenage girl is dead, along with three other persons you more or less have a connection with. The next time I see you you'd better have some hard evidence in hand or I'm going to lock you up. You smell like a bullshit flinger to me." The sheriff spun on her heel and clumped for the door. Going fast as she was, the metal cleats on her boots made a strange sort of tatting.

The old man waved his hand in front of his face. "I suppose I'll go to jail as well as lose all my money," he said.

"What I know is that we have to take that orange juice off the shelves," Bru said.

Goins put his closely shaved head in his hand and Bru watched his body shake. Bru did not really believe that Goins had been deceived by Arbuthnot. The old man's crimes were unimaginable--on a scale with something a Hitler or a Pol Pot would commit. The worst street criminal was practically a babe in arms compared to him. But Bru couldn't help but feel for Goins all the same. Kimberly's loss had shaken him. Maybe the old guy really did feel for the suffering he'd inflicted. Finally Goins looked up from his binge of dry heaving and said in a weak voice, "Call old P. Rogers Gresham then, and tell him what the deal is."

"Would it be possible to wait a day or two so we could begin to eliminate our positions overseas?" Juan asked, squinting daggers at Bru.

Goins looked at Bru, who moved his head sideways

about an inch. "No, we want that recall order out today."

"Yes, sir," Juan said. "Will there be anything else?"

"Get on this, Juan, right now. By tomorrow morning we want every can of bad juice in this country out of supermarket reefers."

After Juan left, Bru stood. Since he couldn't think of anything to say, he simply made for the door. Goins said, "I want to thank you for making me do this, Bruton. I'm glad you did."

"I'm sorry about Kimberly," Bru said. "She was a nice kid." Bru crossed the room to the door. On the other side of the door Bru had trouble with his knees again. They felt rubbery and weak. He wasn't certain they'd support his weight all the way out to the truck.

33

Serendipity, a happy chance occurrence, was the word for it. In research, it seemed to Melba, serendipity was an essential way of turning up the information she was looking for. She'd bust her butt on a problem, going through the computer registers, breaking or stealing passwords, trading information with a network of like-minded hackers and, then suddenly, there the info she sought would be delivered to her from out of leftfield. So far this afternoon, Melba had gained none of the items on Bru's wish list. She and Miss Tibbs'd been kept going by patrons's queries ever since she came on at one. Then the slack period just after midafternoon rush kicked in. Miss Tibbs went off on break and Melba booted her computer up but instead of concentrating on breaking Lawson's innermost secrets, Melba found herself wondering if she would go directly to

Bru's place after she got off work at nine. Or should she go home and shower first? She supposed she should go shower first, even though that'd get her to Bru's place well after ten, on a week night no less. Still, she had high hopes this would be *the* night and she wanted to make sure the prize she offered Bru--ut oh.

These thoughts were interrupted by the sight of Irma coming through the heavy oak library doors. Irma was a gawky middle-aged widow with protruding teeth who always wore a blue turban on her head. Some thirty years before she had had the great good fortune of slipping on a banana peel and breaking a leg on a Lawson sidewalk. As part of her settlement the school attorney gleefully granted her the right to take classes tuition free in perpetuity, figuring they had gotten the better of Irma. To date it was claimed Irma'd run up a tab of almost three quarters of a million dollars in tuition waivers. But she was a harmless soul if you overlooked the malicious but inevitably true gossip she purveyed around campus.

Irma stopped at the circulation desk just inside the door. Georgina, the circulation librarian, was almost never to be found at circulation, but by some psychic power, she appeared. Melba watched Irma bend and put her hand to Georgina's ear. She whispered something and then both women gave the other a shocked look. Georgina's hand went to her face and she bustled back into the wilderness of cubicles. A few minutes later Collie Collier came shooting out of the office cubicles, her little snake hips going for all they were worth. A lock of Collie's iron-gray, never-mussed hair had fallen over her forehead and her eyes were popped and her mouth a perfect circle of astonishment. She bustled toward the reference librarian's office.

Miss Tibbs came back from break ten minutes late. It was the first time in Melba's memory that the head reference librarian had been late for anything. And Melba could see she was bursting at the seams. Miss Tibbs batted her eyes at Melba. Her adam's apple worked in her throat. Melba betrayed no interest in Miss Tibbs's secret because she didn't want to be disturbed from working on Bru's wish list.

"My dear, if you insist I will let you in on a little secret."

"I don't insist," Melba said with her usual forthrightness. "I'm busy. Let me do my work."

Miss Tibbs rattled on anyway. "I have it on unimpeachable authority that Dr. Newcombe, our president, has AIDS."

"Didn't you hear me. I have no time for idle gossip-- what?" Melba whooped.

Miss Tibbs gave Melba a stern look--for making noise in the library. Melba looked appropriately apologetic and Miss Tibbs went on. "He learned of it this morning during a routine examination for insurance."

"Just like Magic Johnson," Melba said.

"Whoever that is," the head reference librarian said.

"How did your source learn of this?" Melba asked skeptically.

"Right from the horse's mouth. Eva, the president's secretary, told someone whose name I would never divulge who told someone who told me. But there's more. The president took the day off on learning the dreadful news. He left Eva, poor dear, with the difficult job of informing his how-should-I-call her? His lady love. Now don't go rushing to judgment when you learn the president wasn't true to his wife. I'm sure it was just an impulsive one-time fling. The president was working for us, dealing with the woman, trying to get money for the endowment."

"Huh?" Melba said, puzzled by Miss Tibbs manner of speaking.

"It was someone you never heard of. Her name is

Elizabeth Chapman."

Miss Tibbs was right. Melba had never heard of her. "So how did she take the news?" Melba asked, distinctly crestfallen at not having come up with a name of significance.

"You'll be relieved to know," Miss Tibbs said, "to learn she didn't arrive for her appointment with the president this afternoon so Eva was spared the difficulty of informing her."

It was only then that the word *serendipitous* flashed in Melba's head. *Elizabeth.* She'd heard that name the night before from Bru. "Now who exactly is this woman the president was, er, involved with."

"She's the daughter," Miss Tibbs said, sniffing, "of Billy Goins, the richest man in the state of Florida. Can you imagine the scandal should word get out that our president exposed Mr. Goins's daughter to HIV."

"I won't tell anyone," Melba said, suppressing the rebel yell she wanted to cut loose with.

"I won't either," Miss Tibbs said, just innocent as she could possibly be.

Melba considered phoning Bru with the big news that she'd found another secret Goins's link to Newcombe, possibly the one that could be milked to produce that smoking gun Bru sought. Just as important to Melba, Elizabeth as her rival for Bru's affections got shot down by this intelligence. But the news was too important to impart over the phone. Besides, nine o'clock would come soon enough.

34

As soon as Bruton left, Juan made a beeline for Elizabeth's office. When she saw him, she got a bored look on her face and began sawing away on her nails again, which Juan noticed had been redone in a two-tone half moon pattern since he'd last seen her less than an hour before. "Now what?" she asked.

"Bruton accused us in front of the sheriff of contaminating the entire country's orange juice supply? The old man confessed to the plot, but Bruton didn't have his story straight. He's on to the fact that Arbuthnot worked in a plant, but he got the wrong one. Bru supposed it was the Port Saint Joe Plastic Company. That's where the juice containers are produced. We had that catalyst seeded into the plastic as part of the process. But the process requires a second stage, and the factory that Arbuthnot worked at was elsewhere."

A look of annoyance crossed Elizabeth's face. "Why are you bothering me with this?"

"Your old man ordered me to make a complete recall, which means Billy Goins Corporations--meaning you--goes broke."

Suddenly Elizabeth quit sawing on her nail. "We have to stop him," Elizabeth said.

"The question is how."

Elizabeth thought for a moment and said, "Kill the old fart?"

"Make it look like a suicide? Two of them in the house of a billionaire in twenty-four hours, leaving the out-of-favor daughter with all the money. That sounds like a sure way to end up in the penitentiary."

"Do you think it would help matters any if Bruton disappeared from the face of the earth?"

"I think that would help matters a lot."

For a moment Elizabeth's face narrowed in concentration as she gave her nails a final couple of whacks. There she finished the job to her satisfaction. Her face brightened. "You want to come up to my room for a quick one before I dress to go croak Doctor Bruton? He didn't seem impressed with my pedal pusher outfit this afternoon. I s'pose I best become Miss Scarlett from Tara plantation again," she said in a heavy southern accent. "You're a pretty good lay," she said, "considering how small your dick is."

35

After her shift ended at the library, Melba didn't go home and shower. She went directly to Bru's place. As soon as the tires of Bru's Fiesta crunched the shells on his drive and she saw the old Chevy Caprice parked next to her truck, she realized she had miscalculated. She should have called first.

Not knowing what to do, she killed the lights and sat in the car for a moment looking up at the lighted window of the upstairs kitchen. Suddenly the silhouette of a woman appeared in the window. She was enormously bosomed and her hair was swept up in the sort of hairdo that the thumbnail sketch of Miss Manners in the newspapers sported. She seemed right at home there. She had a tray of ice cubes and Melba could hear her calling to Bru in the living room--or rather bedroom.

Melba's stomach churned. It was the same kitchen

where she had performed her experiment the evening before, where she'd uncovered the secret of 1,2--DCA in the orange concentrate. Tonight, it was the domain of someone else--the daughter of the richest man in the state of Florida. Bru had told her about her upswept hair--and Melba had smelled her on him the night before. She was the woman Melba had thought she'd aced with her serendipitous piece of intelligence.

Bru hadn't made a move for Melba last night, though she had crawled into bed with him, offering herself to him. Melba refused to feel sorry for herself. Bru wasn't the first man she'd failed with. There'd been Darryl out in San Angelo. She'd thought he was hers until she found him enjoying the comforts of one of his own heifers in the barn. Darryl claimed it was no big deal. All the horny young bucks on the ranches did it. He'd even bought her the F-250 to show how much she really meant to him. For a while, she thought perhaps she could get beyond it. But finally the answer was no she couldn't. That's how she felt about Bru and this woman now. If he wanted the daughter of the crookedest, er, richest man in the state, one who consorted with the president of Lawson College, he could have her. Melba found the spare keys she kept in a magnetized key safe in the fender well. She unlocked the driver door, cranked up the big V-8 engine and backed out of the driveway. Goodbye, Bru Bruton. Good luck with Miss Rich Bitch.

36

Once Bru got back to the furnished rental, he collapsed in what passed for an easy chair--it was vinyl covered--and didn't move. Bru wasn't even weary. He was beyond weariness. His body felt waxen, dead, corpselike. The thing that really got him was Kimberly's suicide. It was as though all the darkness that had surrounded Amber's death had come back and was assailing him.

Outside daylight faded and cold came. It was cold enough that a little heat would have been welcome. Or at least a jacket or blanket pulled over him. Bru couldn't care less. The kitchen light was on and it shot a trapezoid of depressing yellow light onto the bedroom floor. Suddenly there was a woman in that spot of light. Bru had no idea how she got in the room. He supposed he'd locked the door when he came home.

It took him a while to identify the woman as Elizabeth. Partly, he was that far out of it. And partly she had changed her hair. Rather than the sexy, frizzy style she'd worn at her father's house, she now wore her locks long and straight. Her lipstick was a subdued dark red shade and she exuded a manner of concern. "Bru," she said. "I'm worried about you, about the abruptness with which you left today. I was afraid for the way you were taking Kimberly's passing."

For his part Bru just stared at her. This was the woman who got him off in her little office and seemed to be trying to seduce him just hours after her daughter killed herself.

She took one hand in the other and cast down her eyes, looking demure. "Maybe what I mean is that I'm worried about myself--about the way I acted this afternoon. I'm afraid I acted a slut." She came and knelt in front of Bru. She put one hand on the arm of his chair and the other on his leg. "Everyone handles shocks like that in their own way. I was trying to deny that Kimberly had passed on. You more than anyone must understand that."

She was right about that, Bru thought. Bru knew about the denial and the strange rituals one acts out to pretend what happened hadn't. He knew too that life must go on--or must it? Bru shut his eyes. He felt her hand rise from his leg and he was aware of her flying across the room to the kitchen.

He heard her fooling with a tray of ice cubes. "Do you want coke or orange juice?" she called. Then she was back pressing a glass into his hands. Coke. He could tell by the carbonation bubbles fizzing on his hand. "Go on, drink. It will make you feel better."

How did coke arrive in the house? Bru wondered. He hadn't bought any. Maybe Melba had. He took a sip of the soda.

Elizabeth watched him closely. She nodded as he swallowed. "That's a good boy," she said.

"Where's your drink?" he asked.

"Hey, you're talking now," she said. "That's an encouraging sign. Have another sip. See what it can do for you?"

Bru pushed the glass into her hands. "I'm not thirsty any more."

"No, you don't," she said. "I fixed that glass special for you. You're going to drink it all the way to the bottom, if it's the last thing you ever do."

Bru put the glass on the dresser. He was tired. He wished she would go. He yawned. His eyelids wanted very badly to close. He lidded them. The last thing he saw was Elizabeth looking at him intently, as she had when she was encouraging him to drink.

Then he heard the clasp of her purse open. *She's going, great,* he thought. But her footsteps treaded into the bathroom. He heard the window slide shut and he could hear what sounded like tape unraveling from a roll. Then he heard the window rattle as though Elizabeth were taping the cracks in the window. Why would she be doing that? Then the footfalls went into the kitchen and there were more tape tearing sounds and windows being fooled with. Now Elizabeth's hands were on his arm. "Come on," she urged. "Get out of that chair and lie down here on that mattress that you so thoughtfully placed for me on the floor. Since gas is heavier than air, it forms a nice thick layer on the floor."

Bru's body flopped onto the mattress. The shock startled him awake. His eyes opened but the effects of the drug she'd laced the drink with made him lid them immediately. With his whole being, he wanted to sleep. He just wished she would go away so he could snooze.

Bru could hear her heels tatting on the kitchen linoleum. Then he smelled that telltale dead-mouse odor of natural gas. Elizabeth came back and knelt on the mattress. She kissed his cheek. "Sleep tight, Bru," she said. There was a click. The door latch locking on her way out.

Bru told himself he needed to get up. And then he was getting up--but not to his feet. He floated right up to the ceiling and looking down he saw the shabby, furnished apartment. The yellow light from the kitchen was still spilling onto the bedroom floor and on the mattress was his body snuggled in the covers. He looked perfectly content lying there.

Suddenly he felt his spirit being sucked from the room. He was alarmed at being made to abandon his body.

He tried to cling to the walls--but no such luck. He was dragged out into the night. The compulsion pulling him along was mild enough and pleasant enough and suddenly Bru found himself hurtling through the cool Florida night, enjoying the hell out of himself. Then he wasn't in Florida anymore. He seemed to be zipping through the solar system--there went the moon and off to the left or rather port was Mars. And then he was beyond the galaxy. He was even beyond three dimensional space as Bru understood it. As a scientist Bru was making observations about this new condition of dimensionless space. It made perfect sense to him. It made no sense to him.

Then he could see what he had been drawn toward-- like an elevator car heading for the top floor. It was a light shining through a hole. Bru wanted to get through that hole into the room with the light. He wanted to get there with all his soul. He wanted to gain entry into that room more than he ever wanted to do anything ever before. He somehow intuited that he was inadequate to gain entry, that getting in would be on a par with one of the labors of Hercules. That it would require all the wiles he could summons.

Suddenly a wraithlike form appeared at his side. No, there were two. One of each side of him. They wore flowing gauzy gowns and they were brightly lighted and he felt very comfortable with them. Then he understood why. They were women, or rather girls. One was brunette, the other blonde. "Daddy," one called. "Bru," the other said. "We're with you, Daddy--Bru," they called in unison and each was under an arm, guiding and propelling him toward that light in the hole he had to burst through. Amber was kissing his cheek and Kimberly was hugging him. "Bru, I want you to know I didn't kill myself. I wouldn't do that. Mommy murdered me."

For a moment all three of them were sorrowful and then just as suddenly they were joyous. Bru was together with the two people he loved best in the world. This went on for an instant or an eternity. It was hard to say which, but Bru's soul was nourished and refreshed and suddenly there was a chorus. The hole with that white light was just above them but all around them were these kids making a hellish racket, sighing and moaning like tortured souls in hell.

"You're going to have to go back, Bru," Kimberly said.

"I don't want to go back," Bru said. "I want to stay with you girls. I want to get through that hole with the light."

"I'm sorry, Daddy," Amber said. She was crying. Her tears wetted Bru's cheek. "You have to go back for them."

"You have to stop Mommy and Grandpa and them. You can't let them ruin the orange juice. It's not the 1,2--DCA. It's the gum. Remember that."

"I don't care about that stuff. I'm not going back. I'm not," Bru said, but the light in the hole dimmed. And Amber and Kimberly began to fade away. They were screaming, "We want to be with you, Daddy, Bru. We love you. We'll be with you later. Don't forget it's not the 1,2--DCA. It's the gum--in the shed."

Then they were gone and there were only the little people all around Bru, their arms writhing, saying, "Stop them, Dr. Bruton. Stop them. Find out what it is that killed us."

And it was as though Bru was on an express elevator car and he was going down and he didn't like it. Far above him he saw the two girls' faces and they were waving to him and above them was the light he had yearned for. The light was very dim now indeed.

37

Leroy's doctrine was "Go out different from the way you came in." This applied to highway routes as well as the dwellings he sent his girls to burgle. So instead of taking the straight shot home on I-4, Elizabeth hooked a right on the East-West Expressway, which she took to the coast then headed north on I-95, altogether at least twenty-five miles out of her way. To make the best of the situation, she stopped off at Earthquake Magoon's in Edgewater, not far from where Leroy's crib had been. Her tasteful southern matron outfit was greeted in that establishment with all the warmth and friendliness of a turd in the punchbowl.

Elizabeth slugged down a beer and ordered another one. Although pissed that she had to buy her own beers-- that no he-man big belly biker stepped up and bought her a drink--she didn't want to have to go back and fuck Joo-an again. He was already getting on her nerves. As soon as he figured a way to get rid of the old man and she got all the money, she would shitcan Juan too. She had to fuck somebody though. Killing always did that too her, got her horny and excited. The stool next to her was occupied by a skinny chick, all black hair and tattoos. Her face was wrinkled and lined like a prune and both her elbows were on the bar and she was staring into her drink as though it was a crystal ball.

"Buck up, sister," Elizabeth said, wondering if she was going to have to settle for licking a little dried up pussy tonight. "Life can't be as bad as you look."

"Oh, but it can be," the woman said with just a hint

of a foreign accent. "My boyfriend died, I'm HIV positive and my connection didn't show up this week."

"I've heard worse," Elizabeth said consolingly.

"Hey, I know you," the shriveled up woman said. "You used to fuck Leroy."

"I sure did," Elizabeth said. "Were you one of his girls too?"

"Yeah," she said elevating her head and patting her hair. "I guess you could say that."

"Let me have another beer," Elizabeth told the bartender. "And give my friend one too--give her a double," she said, liking this turn of events. If the sister had been Leroy's girl for long, she was certain to be bi because Leroy always insisted his women sleep together. It'd be a sure thing to get in her pants.

"To Leroy," the woman said, holding up her glass. "He really knew how to treat a woman. He made me feel I was a queen."

Elizabeth did a double take at this skinny hank of a woman. She couldn't imagine Leroy keeping her around very long, much less treating her like a queen. Elizabeth wondered why she hadn't heard of this chick before.

"But then I had something he wanted. That's why men always treat you well, when you have something they want. Now that he's gone, nobody could much need what I have to offer."

Elizabeth got a sly look on her face. Elizabeth broke open her purse and rummaged around looking for her pillbox. "A couple of Percodans brighten your mood, honey?" Elizabeth asked.

The woman's prune face burst into a smile. She reached for the pillbox. Elizabeth pulled the container back.

"Oh, I get it. I have to spill what I know. Well, it ain't much. Just some guy I used to fuck by the name of Bruton killed a guy in Miami a long time ago."

"Shit," Elizabeth said. It was the information her friend in Orlando had sent her to Bruton to find out and which Juan had been desperate for too and which, oddly, could have saved Bruton's life. "You're right. That isn't much." She gave the woman the pills and thought, had she learned of this earlier she could have had a lot more fun with friend Bruton. He was out of the picture now. Well, at least, Elizabeth decided, she'd get some sex for her pills. That was something.

38

After Melba pulled into the street from Bru's place, her Texas ire went off like a volcano. *Let him sleep with her,* she thought. *It'll serve him right. See what he thinks when he learns she was exposed to AIDS. Hell, maybe she's the one that gave Newcombe AIDS. Maybe Bru will pick it up too. That'll show him.* She cussed Bru every way she could think of. She called him a lousy no-good coyote and a hound dog and various kinds of skunks and polecats and when she got through with all of those, she wheeled the big truck around and headed back for Bru's place. She couldn't let Bru be exposed to AIDS. Besides she could hardly wait to see his face when she told him about the Newcombe-Elizabeth connection and the president's health status. She bet that would frost his balls. She especially looked forward to telling Elizabeth off to her face. Seldom had she been offered a richer opportunity.

The trouble was Elizabeth's car was gone when Melba returned and the upstairs door was locked. Melba rattled the doorknob hoping that Bru had simply nodded off, that he hadn't actually gone off with Elizabeth someplace.

No such luck. She was annoyed with herself for being so slow. She should have marched right in and given Elizabeth what for when she was here the first time.

Melba went downstairs, tried the door down there. Locked up tight. She sat on the bottom stair for a while and ran her fingers on her knee. She was impatient and it was cold out--she could see her breath. Melba supposed the only smart thing to do would be to go home and wise Bru up tomorrow. But first she'd try the old credit card trick. It'd never worked for her before. She got out one of the half dozen credit cards with astrological credit ratings that had appeared, unsolicited, in her mailbox and which she had stowed away for just such an emergency. She thrust it between the door and the jamb. Nothing. She jiggled it the way the guys on TV and in the movies did. Still nothing. She put her eye up close to the bolt to see if she was missing something. She got a faint whiff of gas. She stuck her nose to the crack in the door. That mouse turd smell of natural gas was overpowering.

The place smelled as if it was about to blow. *Get out of here quick,* she warned herself. She ran down the steps, found a lawn chair, ran back up. *Don't throw that thing through the window. A spark could ignite the gas.* Melba heaved the chair through the window. She reached through the hole and unlatched the bolt. The gas smell was sickening. A body lay on the mattress--a man's body. Bru.

Melba hustled to the bed. "Bru, god dang it. Get up from there," she hollered. Nothing. Not even a moan. Melba was five eleven in her stocking feet and weighed almost 140 pounds. And she was athletic. She grabbed Bru by the shirtfront and hoisted him to his feet. She slung an arm over her shoulder. He was dead weight but Melba was motivated. She lugged him to the outside landing and, hanging onto the rail with one arm and the other around Bru, she tripped down to the lawn. She dumped Bru's body onto the Saint Augustine grass and threw herself on him, cleared his tongue out of the way, held his nose and blew into his mouth. After about six such breaths, Bru's hands lurched up and kicked her away. "Leave me alone. I want to stay with Amber and Kimberly."

Melba laughed and said, "No, you don't, lover boy. Not until you tell me what's going down here. You trying to do yourself in?"

"Huh-uh," Bru spat out. "Elizabeth helped me--tried to kill me."

"You mean I saved your life. Now you are mine to do with as I please."

"That's not the way it works. Now you're responsible for me," he said. "In all ways financially, morally, physically."

"I like my way better," Melba said, going suddenly suspicious. "She seduce you?"

"She dosed me--with thalidomide, I think."

"Thalidomide," Melba chirped. "I thought that stuff was illegal."

"It was only became legal recently in the States when it was cleared to treat leprosy--not exactly a garden variety disease. Also, it was okayed to treat wasting in AIDS patients," Bru said. "Those women who had the deformed children back in the sixties had gotten their drugs overseas, where it had been prescribed as a first-rate sleeping tablet and for morning sickness. I saw a vial of the stuff in Elizabeth's office and wondered what it was for. Now I know. She kept it around to slip her enemies Mickey Finns."

"Maybe not entirely, Bru. She was Newcombe's lover. He has tested positive for HIV."

Bru slapped himself as though to clear his head. "Everything is foggy from that drug. I thought you said Newcombe had HIV."

"That's what I said. Maybe Newcombe gave her the disease and she was taking the thalidomide to keep from wasting."

"Close but no cigar. The thalidomide was for Leroy, a junkee and biker friend of hers."

"Isn't that the smoking gun you've been looking for connecting Goins and Lawson?"

"Probably," Bru said. "Look, my head is all foggy. And I'm cold."

"Should we get you to a hospital?"

"No, gas isn't poison. It merely acts as a blanket that suffocates its victims. Now that I'm conscious, I'm all right. But I'm still groggy from that thalidomide. I only took a sip or two of the coke she forced on me. I need to walk. Burr, it's freezing out here. I suppose we're going to have to call the gas company to get back inside my place."

"No way, Bru. I'll just find the main valve and turn it off there. It's usually near the meter. I got a wrench and a flashlight in my truck. Then I think you'd better come over to my apartment for the night, just in case Elizabeth should come back to check on her job. She might do better next time."

"I think that's a great idea," Bru agreed. "Besides there's nothing like almost being murdered to make you horny as hell. I'd like to make passionate love tonight and I think your apartment is the best place to do that."

"While I turn off the gas, you take a little walk, mister," Melba said. "I don't want to get you over to my place then have you pooping out on me."

39

As a professor Bru often wondered how students could have the wrong proof but the right answer--without cheating, that is. That's how he felt about ending up in Melba's bed. It seemed to Bru he'd done practically everything to keep from ending up right where he was. He'd tried to take up with Salome the night Melba'd brought him pizza--but Todd Tolson beat his action. And Bru was too honest to lie to himself about his infatuation or semi-infatuation with Elizabeth. Her sexiness and her daughter and, yes, let's not forget her money, had him going for a while. Then too there was Leta. Bru had not slept with another woman for more than twenty years, going all the way back to Ileana. Mentally, breaching that wall was not lightly done.

Except it was. Melba threw Bru in her truck, wend her way into the darkness of the new buildup out east around UCF and carried him into a townhouse apartment almost as she'd toted him out of his own garage apartment. Bru had very badly wanted to drive his own car but he could see Melba was right in not letting him drive. His head was fouled from that drug, which the early exhilaration of coming back from the near dead had masked. His body felt like putty.

Melba guided him to her bed, which he collapsed on. When she came out of the bedroom, showered in a nightie, Bru was conscious but still dressed on top of the covers.

"Am I going to have to undress you too?" she said.

Bru made a whine in acknowledgment.

"So you like that idea, eh?"

Bru was tired. He just wanted to get under the bedclothes and get to sleep. It seemed to him he was now suffering from a reverse effect of that sleeping potion. His body was asleep but his mind alert. Bru made another whine. Melba's large competent hands began undoing his shirt buttons. Her hands felt warm against his cold body. She shucked Bru out of his shirt and pulled his trousers off.

"Should I leave your u-trou on?" she asked rhetorically. "I think not," she said and tugged his trunks off.

Bru wondered how his entire body could be in a state of deep massage relaxation, except for his equipment, which Melba fingered as she nodded appreciatively.

"Am I embarrassing you, Bru?"

Bru made that whinnying sound again.

"I take that to be a yes. I suppose I'd better stop."

Bru whinnyed even more.

"Must be an emphatic yes," she teased.

Then suddenly, like a ninety-pound gymnast, she flipped her body over his and lowered onto him. In one fell swoop. She sucked him right up. And then clamped around. She wrapped her arms around Bru and suddenly Bru felt warm and amazingly comfortable.

"I got you now," Melba said, "and you're never getting away."

Later, much later, Bru woke and tiptoed into bathroom. He peed and found a washcloth and sponged Melba's dried juices from his body. She smelled good on him. Bru regretted removing the odor, but back under the covers she still gave off that guavay smell. Her hand snaked into his and squeezed his fingers. Bru returned the pressure.

"Are you happy?" she asked.

"Yes," he said.

"But what?"

"But nothing."

"There was a hitch in your voice. Something's bothering you," she said.

"I was afraid I was going to feel bad about being disloyal to Leta."

"But you're not?"

"No. That relationship was over. I knew that in my head the evening she told me she was going to live with Jerry. But I didn't know that in my gut--and my heart--until you took me in hand."

"Come on, Bru. Don't be an old prude. I took you in pussy."

"I like the way you smell," Bru said. "I liked the way Amber smelled. But I never really liked Leta's raw body odor. I didn't dislike it. But to me, it was just a signature. I never reacted to it positively. I'm not sure I ever really did love her--"

"Sure you loved her, Bru."

"Of course, I loved her. She was my partner and the mother of my child. What I mean is there is that kind of love and there is whole-body-and-soul-immersion kind of love."

"Are you telling me I'm whole-body-and-soul-immersion kind of love?" Melba asked.

"Possibly," Bru said.

Then Melba did something that really surprised Bru. She began to cry. Bru felt the shivers through her hand, still linked to his, and the mattress. He didn't think she was the type. "Hey," he said. "You don't have to bawl just because some guy tells you something like that."

"That's not why I'm crying, Bru. I'm crying because you think you might get killed today and you want me to know that it was as good for you as I always thought it would be."

Bru took in air to deny it but said nothing.

212

"You're not the kind of guy who tells a woman he loves her after he makes love to her once."

"Look, I need to use your computer. Can I get on the net without a password?"

She told Bru the password in a leaden voice.

"And then it might be handy to know the location of that twenty-two pistol of yours," he said. "You never know."

"God dammit, Bru. Don't do this. Let the authorities handle it. Remember, you told me just a couple of days ago that you'd learned that violence never accomplished anything."

"Sure. Just say go lock up a multibillionaire. As far as that goes, explain in a mild-voiced way about orange juice contamination. That ought to impress the authorities almost as much as it did the sheriff yesterday, who by the way was probably right in the skepticism she showed. I came home last night and somehow I just didn't feel good about my scene with Goins. I had to have a near death experience to get it. Professor Khoury warned me about running off half cocked. I did that yesterday. I didn't have the evidence. I just thought I had it after I talked to Arbuthnot's friend. He told me he knew for a fact that Arbuthnot was planning to contaminate o.j. He's the only evidential link I have and I scared him into hiding. It's a long way from knowing these guys are behind the KiDS epidemic and proving it.

"Yesterday, I naively thought," Bru continued, "I had the whole thing taken care of. The old man told me he'd pull those polluted cans from the nation's supermarkets. Instead he sent his daughter over to kill me. These are not the kinds of people that are going to give up because you ask them to."

"Nor are they the kinds of folks who are easily persuaded by the means at your disposal," Melba said.

"Then it looks like I got my work cut out for me,"

213

Bru said.

"It sure does," Melba said, yawning. Then she rolled over on her belly. "The pistol's in the bottom dresser drawer. There's a box of hollow-point longs there too. Don't forget to take the ammo. And don't take my truck. I don't want it getting all shot up. Leave it at your apartment and I'll pick it up later." Her voice was angry. "And please don't come in here and wake me up before you leave. I want to go back to sleep remembering what it was we had--what we could have had. You are going to go and get yourself killed. I know it."

Bru bent and kissed the top and her head. He patted her rump almost perfunctorily--he was already thinking about that weird revelation he'd gotten in that near death experience with the girls telling him the answer was in the gum and the shed. Melba too seemed already to have forgotten about him. She turned on her side and pulled the covers over her head, without saying a word. He supposed he was a little disappointed in Melba--but she had acted like a champ when she saved him earlier. Bru knew you could only expect so much from a person. Had the stakes been smaller, he supposed he could be angry with himself for abandoning her. But he had to break this case.

The .22 was easily found in the bottom drawer. Its ammo was a different story. Bru almost walked off with a box of .222 shells instead, before he wised to the fact that the latter were ammo for a deer rifle. He discarded that box but in his impatience was unable to find the box of hollow points. He checked the cylinder. All nine chambers held a round. Bru hoped nine shots would be enough. He expected that the .22 would just be his backup weapon anyway.

Bru went into Melba's living room. The clock on the wall said it was five, too early to make the phone call he needed to make. So he called his apartment and checked his own phone calls, something he hadn't done earlier. Sam Goldstein of the Lawson business school had left a message. "Bru, give me a call. There's some weird shit going on in fcoj--that is frozen concentrated orange juice--futures. The foreign market is bid up almost double the US one. Let me know what you know. I've never seen anything like this--ever. This sort of thing isn't supposed to happen."

Bru said, "Hm," to Sam's message then he turned the monitor of Melba's computer on and got on line. When Melba's internet browser booted up, he clicked the mouse on the "search" button and typed in the word "gum" preceded by another word. The search engine listed only 31 entries. Bru opened the first url listing--a dud. The second and third also provided nothing of interest. But when the fourth opened, he said, "Bingo." He'd hit pay dirt.

He printed out this information then he took from his wallet the card Don DiCicco, the manager of the orange juice concentrate plant had given him the day before. He dialed the home number. A woman's voice, equal parts sleepy and startled, answered the phone. She said she'd call Don. After a while, Don came on the line. "Holy smoke, Bru, you took me literally when I told you to call any time."

"Sorry, Don, but this is important. Yesterday, you told me nothing was added to orange juice concentrate. There must be an exception to that. There has to be," Bru said.

"Actually, Bru, I said *we* added nothing to the juice. Some plants do add an emulsifier to make their juice product a bit thicker. As long as they stay under one-half of one percent by volume, the feds will allow them to call their output one-hundred percent natural juice."

Bru hung up and snapped his fingers and pumped his arm and said, "Yes."

Bru cracked the bedroom door and looked in. The wedge of light showed Melba as just a bundle on the bed.

The covers were still over her head. Bru respected her wishes and left without waking her. He wrote on a stickem pad note, "Keys will be on floorboard under the seat. Truck at my place," and left that in exchange for her key ring. It was still dark out and early enough that the city hadn't begun to wake up. On the way, Bru stopped at a twenty-four hour Walmart Superstore and bought the smallest tape recorder in stock. It was about the size of a deck of cards and used the kind of microcasette that is found in answering machines. The clerk assured Bru it was voice activated. He bought batteries and left the store with the machine operational in his breast pocket.

In the truck Bru played back the tape of his conversation with the check-out guy. The tape worked all right and so he headed to Winter Park and the home he'd left just a handful of days earlier. It seemed like a lifetime before. The flourescent light was on over the sink. Bru wondered whether he left that light on or if Leta had been back and forgotten it. Most likely the latter, he reckoned, even though forgetting a light wasn't the sort of thing she'd normally do. He went to the kitchen phone and dialed Goins's number in Daytona.

It was faint light out now. Still before seven. Juan picked up after five rings. "Get me Goins," Bru said.

"Who is this?" Juan asked.

"It's Bruton."

There was a dead silence at the other end.

"What's the matter, Joo-an? Didn't you expect to hear from me again?"

"You can't talk to Mr. Goins. He's indisposed." Juan's voice betrayed his origins for the first time since Bru'd known him. The words rushed out in a sort of pidgin.

"I don't want to talk to him. I want to talk with his friend, Hank Smith."

"Smith?"

"That's right. I'm going to call you back in about fifteen minutes. Then I'll tell you where I expect him to be. I'm talking this morning. Like in about an hour." Bru slammed the phone in the cradle and turned around and there stood Leta in a bra and slip. She was working on her hair. Her face looked older than he remembered. The smell of hot water and soap rushed him, as though she'd just stepped out of the shower.

"Bru," she said. South Pacific islanders are supposed to have a dozen words for coconut, each one specifying the nut in a different stage. Leta had almost as many inflections when calling his name. The inflection she used on this "Bru" baffled him.

"What are you doing here? Are you shacking up with Jerry in our own house?" Then after a moment, he added, "It's okay with me if you are."

Leta's face fell. Her brows knitted. "You have found someone already?"

"Yes, I certainly have."

"That Texas cowgirl, of course." Leta's hand went to her face. "She called when I was here. I gave her your new number and address. I thought I was being clever and assuaging my guilt."

"You didn't answer my question," Bru said, not sure he liked the way this conversation was going. "You spent the night here, didn't you?"

"Yes."

"Did you get cold feet? Or was it Jerry wanting his kids back?"

"A little of both, I guess. Probably, Jerry pining for his family mostly though. It wasn't as good an idea as it seemed."

"Oh, god, I'm sorry it didn't work for you, Leta."

"But you think things will turn out all right with you and Melba."

217

Bru couldn't suppress the grin spreading across his face. "I resisted for a while. I told myself she was too young for me, by which I think I meant that she was too wild and Texasy. But I like her and we get on in ways you and I could have used some improving in." Bru suddenly shut up. He remembered the purpose of his visit here. He reminded himself this was not a time for truth telling. It was possibly a time for taking leave in the right way. "But I'm not griping. We--you and I--had a good relationship."

"I never regretted marrying you, Bru. I was physically infatuated with Jerry in college and perhaps I still am, but I never would have wanted to be Jerry's wife."

"Thanks, Leta."

"Life can be shit," Leta said. Each took a step forward. They embraced. Bru could feel Leta's tears on his collarbone or maybe those were his own tears. Bru knew her tears were for Amber and their lost relationship and maybe somewhere down at the bottom, for Leta herself. Pressed against him, Leta felt comfortable but her body odor, even smelling mostly of soap and hot water, did not-- as he'd come to realize earlier--attract him.

Bru backed away from her. "I came here to get something. I think I'd better get it and go. I'm in a hurry. It's in the bedroom. You stay here. I don't want you seeing what it is."

Leta's eyes were full of tears and her head was averted. She sniffled and said, "Okay."

The M15 was on the top shelf in the closet, way in the back and stuffed under numerous shoeboxes filled with god knew what. Bru had always thought he should dispose of it--for obvious reasons. But it was his father's most prized possession, given to him as it had been by old Westy Westmoreland. Going up against Smith, Bru needed something that would knock a big man on his ass and keep him there. That .22, although all right as a back up, was

218

worthless against a guy like Smith. The pistol was in a wool bag with a drawstring. Bru hooked the drawstring and pulled it out in a crack in the boxes. He undid the magazine. It was full of rounds. He didn't have any spare ammo. But that was all right. He wouldn't need anymore than what he had here.

40

Bru parked his Fiesta under a corrugated metal canopy at a fish camp on the Saint Johns River. He went into the bathroom, which didn't have a lock on the door or any water in the toilet bowl and changed into his jungle boots and the set of desert camo fatigues he'd found in the garage, the latter dusty and cobwebby. They'd been left over from a walk-on part he'd had in a skit at Amber's middle school and which had not gotten back to the property department. He tucked the .22 in the top of a jungle boot and put the .45 in this fatigue pocket, went inside the store and gave the old timer with a prospector's beard a ten spot so there wouldn't be any trouble about where he parked the car and headed up the beaten path alongside the river.

This path had been trod by fishermen and Bru knew of this place because he'd brought Amber here to fish for bream and catfish. He hoped it'd be deserted on a cool weekday morning. A couple of elderly black women were canepoling from the bank. Bru wasn't happy to see them but he gave them a curt nod and hustled on. The path went around a bend. As far as Bru could see there was not another human in sight. As far as that went the only thing he could see in the distance was Lake Monroe. The channel shot straight as an arrow toward it. The river had been canalized here in the name of some civic-improvement swindle at a point in the past, and the banks on both sides of the river were grown up with a thick stand of maiden cane and other tall grasses, dun colored--like his desert camos-- this time of year.

Bru hiked along the bank for what seemed a long time. He turned around and the bend in the channel was only two hundred yards away. He hiked another two hundred yards and then he saw motion up ahead--a boat turning into the river--he ducked into the grass. He could hear the prop vibration making a shingle-rattling sound. An airboat--something he hadn't planned on. Bru's idea had been to get Smith on the river in the open where he had the drop on him. Bru ducked below a corrugation in the spoil bank. The airplane-like noise grew louder. When it sounded like thunder rolling beyond him, Bru stuck his head up.

It was an Okeelanta sheriff's airboat. Smith was sitting in the high chair at the controls, his hair whipping in the wind. Bru had ordered that he come in a boat, unarmed, and that he stand at the controls. The airboat threw Bru off balance. Seated as he was in the airboat, the engine blocked a clear view of him. But it was safe to assume he had weapons up the yingyang. Bru leveled the .45 and squeezed one off at the propeller. The slug hit the cage and then deflected into the prop. Unbalanced, the prop noise was even more thunderous but off key, then it died to an idle and both Smith's hands were pointed skyward.

"Goddammit, Bruton," Smith hollered above the chuffing of the unmuffled airplane engine, "I came out here to talk. So show yourself and let's talk."

Bru formed his hand into a megaphone. He directed at a spot behind Smith to prevent him from spotting his location. "Come about, Smith, and go up the river at idle speed." The airboat hove around and the big aircraft engine puttered along, like a thoroughbred race horse straining at the bit. Smith was lightly clad in the cool morning air, having on a tee shirt and jeans and a baseball cap. Love handles hung over his belt. The idea, Bru supposed, was to proclaim no concealed weapon. Smith made a big production of showing that he was looking straight ahead and not trying to ferret out Bru's location on the bank.

"That little spic said you wanted to palaver, Bruton. So let's hear it. I'm a get myself in a heap of trouble stealing this here boat to come out and confab with you, seeing how they put me on suspension yesterday. But I did like I was asked to make you happy. Look 'ee, I'm getting out of earshot of you so's if it's all right I'm a turn around and putter back toward you. Don't go getting an itchy trigger finger again."

Smith turned the boat wide in the narrow channel. Now most of his body was concealed behind the engine. The boat couldn't make the turn. Smith goosed the engine and the flatbottomed craft ran up on the bank and came back down in the water. The bow was on a trajectory with Bru. Smith opened the engine up full bore and craft thundered across the relatively narrow channel on a collision course with Bru. The noise was stupendous and terrifying. Bru watched, almost as though horror-stricken, as the boat flew across the river. When it hit the sloping shoreline, he dropped behind the spoil bank and the craft went skidding on bent-down stalks of cane over Bru's head and got lost to sight in the canebrake behind.

Bru listened to the groaning engine of the airboat as it maneuvered in the tall grass. Without a built-up head of steam, he doubted the craft would be able to push through the mature stand of cane, which meant Smith would come out on the same path he'd gone in on. The aircraft engine screamed like a banshee, thundering as it bore through the stalks. Bru stuck his .45 in the waistband of his jeans. He jumped on the other side of the ridge of spoil and crouched in wait.

The plan wouldn't have worked had the boat not gone semi-airborne and slapped down right in front of the berm. The bow nosed into it and the boat went catywampus. To regain control, Smith applied more power as Bru leaped onto the gunwale of the boat. Bru grabbed Smith, in the high chair, by his belt and the deputy came shooting off the stool. Bru smashed into the cage and then he and Smith plunged into the water. The boat fishtailed but kept on a more or less straight line course, hit the bank and went careering off into the cane. Bru crashed into the water, half stunned. The coffee-colored water was cold. Bru could touch bottom on tiptoes. He looked around for Smith. He was about twenty feet away, floating face down. The current was dragging him toward the center of the channel and downstream toward the lake, away from Bru.

Bru took a stroke toward Smith. The artillery and electronic gear in the camos held him back, tended to pull him under. The gap between them had widened. Smith was still face down. Bru tried to touch bottom. It was over his head. Bru considered letting Smith's body float off as bait for gators or vultures. The man may well be bluffing. And if he weren't, Bru could hardly think of a person whose death would more improve the world. Bru flutter-kicked back to shore. Then from automatic impulse, Bru ran along the bank at a point well past where Smith floated, unloaded the hardware from his pockets and jumped into the stream. By the time he swam to mid channel Smith's body had floated within grasp. Bru dragged him back to the bank and pulled him up on land and left him face down while he reinstalled the tape recorder in his pocket, put the .22 into his boot, bloused his pantlegs, extracted the magazine from the .45, placed it in one pocket, popped the chambered round and tucked the automatic in his belt. Then he turned

Smith over. His face was blue. Bru supposed it would be impossible to fake a complexion change.

"Shit!" Bru said, dropping to his knees. He clamped Smith's nose between thumb and forefinger and, opening his mouth, moved his tongue to one side. Then Bru put his lips on Smith's and, mindful that Melba had performed his same operation on himself not more than twelve hours before, blew into the deputy's mouth and alternately massaged the short, chunky man's heart. Each time Bru blew into Smith's mouth it became more physically repugnant. *Let the son of a bitch die,* Bru thought, telling himself that was the last exhalation he'd give, but each time he bent and breathed again. Then suddenly, Smith sputtered, turned on his side and drizzled a little water out of his mouth.

"Jesus Kee-rist. Why did you have to go and do that for?" he asked.

"Hey, asshole, you were trying to kill me with that fucking boat."

"Now that you mention it, I guess I was," Smith said, still groggy. "What did you want with me anyway?"

"Nothing," Bru said. "I'm going to go have a nice little chat with your friend and employer, Billy Goins, and I want to make sure you aren't going to be waiting for me when I come out."

"Jesus, Bruton, you don't have to kill me. I just work for Goins. I'm not in love with him."

"Why shouldn't I kill you?" Bru said, bitterly amused by Smith and the disorientation he was showing. "How about you telling me what you know about Goins's attempt to kill off half the young people in the country by poisoning their orange juice?"

"I really don't know nothing about anything like that. All I know is the old man told me to croak that guy Arbuthnot for him so I did it. And then he wanted that Wisnewski done too. So I did that. I'm just a soldier,

Bruton. I do what I'm told."

"What about old lady Arbuthnot? Did he tell you to do her too?" Bru's indignation flared thinking about the senseless death of that old woman.

"I suppose so. That dago that works for him said she had to be taken care of. And to burn that outbuilding," Smith said getting haltingly to his feet. He nodded curtly and gave a Warren Oates grin. "You wouldn't happen to have a hit of speed on you, would you, partner? I'm having a little trouble getting going."

"Look, asshole," Bru said, "the deal here is figure how to tie you up, so to speak. If you got some ideas about that, start talking."

"You ain't gonna croak me. You just brought me back to life. By the way, I want to thank you for doing that. It wasn't very pleasant there while I was knocked out. It was all hot and fiery and I was being sucked into this hole in the ground." He gave that possum grin.

"My ingrained values got in the way of good sense," Bru said. "I should have left you face down in the river."

"You won't take my word that I won't waylay you after you have your little powwow with Old Man Goins?"

"Would you take your word?" Bru asked.

"You got a point there, all right," Smith said with another smarmy, up from under smile. "Well, I'll give it to you whether you want it or not. I won't bushwhack you after you meet the old man."

A plane droned in the distance. Time was running out. Soon witnesses would be about. Bru had to act. "That's not good enough, Smith. The only way that old bastard will take the orange juice off this nation's shelves is if I physically force him to. I can't do that as long as you're around," Bru said more or less thinking out loud.

"You should have left me in the river, all right, Bruton. Now you're going to have to kill me right here and now." Smith laughed at that prospect.

"You like killing so well you even like the idea of your own killing," Bru said.

"You're trying to work up the nerve to do me, Bruton. I'm laughing because you don't have it. You're not man enough to do it."

"You're helping."

"But not enough. See what this does for you?" Smith put his hand in his back pocket. The action was performed slowly, deliberately giving Bru time to insert the magazine in the .45 and work the action, chambering a round. Smith produced a pair of handcuffs, which he held out to Bru as an offering. "You can lock me up and leave me here. Call the sheriff's department. What with the unauthorized use of that airboat, which thanks to you, has no doubt been plentifully damaged, Sheriff Buckett will lock me up. I won't be able to stand in your way."

But before Bru could react to this plan, Smith threw the handcuffs into his face. They clunked into Bru's forehead and immediately Smith bounded for him. Smith was a couple of years younger than Bru but he was plump and out of shape and Bru's reaction time was better. Bru sidestepped him. Smith stumbled harmlessly by. Then the training his father had inculcated in Bru years before kicked in. He made a sweep with his right leg knocking the props out from under Smith. He plunked face down onto the river bank. Immediately Bru was on top of him, pinning him to the ground. Then Bru went for the thorax, dislocating his neck and pinching his windpipe. In a jiffy Smith was right back to staring into the yawning maw of hell, flames shooting up around him, Bru calculated. Bru popped the man's wisdom knot with his clotted fist. Smith's forehead bounced off the sand and he was out.

Bru fetched the cuffs and got the key out of Smith's back pocket. He opened the manacles, pulled Smith's hands

225

behind his back and clamped them on. In the distance he could hear the prop drone of an aircraft coming toward him. As the plane neared the engine popped and crackled like an old fashioned radial. Bru had little time. He grabbed Smith by the cuffs of his trousers and lugged him into the cane. He dropped him behind the spoil mound and reemerged from the brake. Across the river the light plane--it was a yellow biplane--was circling above the spot where the airboat had probably come to rest.

This chapter had not worked out as cleanly as Bru would have liked. It was by no means certain Smith was completely neutralized. But short of killing Smith he supposed it was about as good an outcome as he could expect. Now the task was getting to Goins.

41

Bru had the Fiesta pegged at seventy-five. At that speed the little engine gasped and moaned and occasionally hiccupped. The two causeways that were I-4's east and west bound lanes traversed an open marsh or a prairie as it was sometimes called in Florida. The bottom of the highway levee was marked by a growth of willows and beyond that was a plain of saw grass and cattails and the stubble of marsh mallow hibiscus plants. Yonder a hammock of very tall cabbage palm trees came to within a few feet of the causeway.

Bru wondered if just killing Goins would solve the problem as he became aware of the sound of popping and then of pinging, like sand hitting the hood of his car. Then suddenly the shadow of an airplane--it was a biplane-- crossed his car and again he heard pinging and the popping sound of a radial engine's manifold blast. Then a new starburst appeared in the windshield and a series of metal rents stitched across the hood of the Fiesta. Bru's head snapped around. To his amazement a sedan was pressed up close to him in the passing lane--its speed seemed to match the Fiesta. Then even more amazing, he recognized the face in the passenger window. It was laughing, leering at him. It was Smith and suddenly the sedan veered into Bru's car. The Fiesta caromed onto the shoulder.

Rather than try to brake, Bru downshifted into fourth and gave it some gas. He managed to keep the little car from going down the embankment. He stabilized his position, one set of wheels on the blacktop and the other on grass. He was about to pull onto the paved shoulder when the sedan sideswiped him again. This time the Fiesta shot off like a billiard ball at a thirty-degree angle. It went down the side of the levee, through the wall of willows and onto the saw grass prairie. Bru felt as though he were on a toboggan. The Fiesta skated across the marsh, which now in the early part of the dry season felt slick rather than slushy. Still the car oversteered badly--the least touch of the wheel and the rear of the vehicle began to swing forward. Bru tapped the wheel to correct this problem and immediately the vehicle swerved into line and overcompensated just a touch. Which of course called for another correction.

Bru's consciousness was taken up with the problem of steering and keeping and eye out for that plane. Suddenly he heard the buzz of a radial engine and he could see out the driver's window the biplane bearing down on him. In that instant, the action seemed to go into stop action. He saw the old fashioned plane, its fabric body painted yellow. He even identified the model, an open cockpit Stearman trainer of WWII vintage. Bru was able to identify it because there had been one on the Army post in Hawaii when he was a kid. He'd even gone up in it for a couple of promotional flight lessons. He remembered the flight instructor saying this plane was amazingly stable. "Forgiving," was the actual word he used. You could do almost anything to it and it would automatically rectify the problem. Partly the reason was because of its biwings--it had twice the control area of a monowing. And partly it was the happy accident of the Stearman's design.

Bru's mind snapped another photo. The pilot turned the plane on what seemed a dime. And the craft seemed to hover in the air less than fifty feet up on a course parallel to Bru's Fiesta. The mental shutter clicked. Now the pilot, who had on a pair of goggles and a leather flyer's helmet, had a stick in his hands. *Snap.* The stick turned into a rifle. It was an AR-15, the civilian version of the Army's M-16-- the plane was so close Bru could make out the characteristic trapezoidal carrying-handle rear sight. The pilot butted it against his left shoulder. He aimed the weapon. *Click.* A burst of rounds sprayed the Fiesta. Glass shards flew. A couple of the rounds ricocheted around inside the engine compartment making a sort of twanging sound as they bumped off the fenders and firewall. Snap. The plane pulled up and cleared the tops of the tall cabbage palms by just a few feet. The pilot gunned the engine and banked and made to come around.

Cabbage palms! Bru's attention had been on keeping the Fiesta from flipping over and then on that plane. He hadn't even noticed the copse of trees ahead. Then suddenly he was very much aware of them. He saw their trunks--graceful things, beautiful things, primeval things-- waving in front of him. Click. Apropos of nothing, he noticed the garden of air plants clinging to their trunks. In great detail he took in the colony of ball moss ascending the trunk of one of the palms. Somehow his mind was able to remind him that ball moss, like Spanish moss, was really a kind of bromeliad, the family of plants the pineapple was related to and that members of the family, including ball moss were called wild pines. He even fancied he could see the little tuftlike blooms reminiscent of the pineapple fruit.

Then it was perfectly apparent that was exactly the problem--that is that he was close enough to take in those minuscule ball moss plants in detail. The Fiesta was smashing right toward the tree. Bru slammed his foot on the brake. The car fishtailed. He pumped the brake and jerked the wheel. The Fiesta swerved, missed the tree with the ball moss going up its trunk, knocking down a bunch of wax myrtle bushes growing on the periphery of the hammock and shot into the middle of the hammock. There was no way to steer clear of the forest of palm trunks. Bru stabbed the brake a final time and pulled the wheel to the left. The car wheeled, presenting the passenger side to an upthrusting palm tree. The rear tire slammed into the tree. The trunk of the tall palm snapped off and the tree came thundering down, missing pinioning the Fiesta because it had pitched forward. Then the front end smacked into a tree, the door sprung open. Bru unclipped his seat belt and plopped onto the tacky forest floor as a second palm tree squashed the roof of the passenger cabin like a tin can. On all fours Bru crawled across the bare muck to the cover of the myrtle bushes on the edge of the hammock.

Overhead the Stearman thundered. A banana clip worth of rounds tore up the the palm fronds, the slugs plunking harmlessly down into the muck. Bru supposed the idea for that blind shooting was to terrorize him, force him into rash and stupid actions. He could feel his heart pounding in his chest. His jaw was clamped tight. *I have some advantages,* he told himself. On I-4, no more than a hundred yards away, heavy traffic flowed from Orlando to Daytona. *Just hole up and hold out. Sooner or later someone with a cell phone will call the FHP, which will arrive like the cavalry to save my ass.*

This thought had hardly been formed when a slug slammed into the palm trunk just ahead of Bru. A spray of sawdust splattered Bru's face. A small man with a enormous rifle was standing in the saw grass fifty yards distant. He brought the gun up fired again. The guy was that Juan Robert. Bru snorted at the sight of Juan Robert, the insolent majordomo, as assassin. It looked like the old man had to pull out all the plugs in order to put together a hit team this early in the morning. Bru would exact infinite satisfaction by annihilating the little wiseass. Bru checked his waist band. The .45 was gone. The .22 was still in his boot. He took it out. It was a pea shooter, completely useless at this distance. Then Bru had a really terrifying idea. Where was Smith? He was unaccounted for. Bru's eyes went back to I-4. The willows that fronted the highway berm intersected with the far end of the palm hammock. Suddenly Bru knew where Smith was. Or at least where he was heading--into the palm hammock. He had to find that .45, even at the expense of exposing himself.

The Stearman was back. Now it was circling the hammock. The AR-15 unloaded a clip, reloaded and blasted away again. Now Bru got the strategy. The pilot would blaze away at random, trying to keep Bru pinned down while the other two closed in for the kill. Like a hound with its nose to the ground, Bru retraced his path to the squashed-down car. He checked the bench seat of the Fiesta, under the front seat, what he could see of the back seat. No pistol. Finally, he couldn't stand the exposed feeling of being a sitting duck in the car. He spreadeagled himself in the mud. A slug tore into the car. Another heavy boom and a slug thudded into the engine. Bru could see Juan Robert standing out in the sun. The firearm he was blasting away with was a shotgun. More deadly than a rifle but shorter ranged.

Since the pistol wasn't in the car, he had to have lost it on the hammock floor between the car and the myrtle bushes. Using Juan Robert as a landmark, Bru retraced his path and there it lay, only a few steps (or crawls) from the auto. He grabbed the weapon, flicked the safety off and made for the myrtle brush blocking the view of Juan Robert.

He was standing in the sawgrass, a hundred fifty feet away, stuffing shells into the gullet of the shotgun. Bru snapped off a shot from a crouching position in the bushes. The shot went wide. Juan brought the gun up and fired a shot at Bru. The recoil of the weapon almost knocked the little man on his ass. Bru stood and fired at Juan. This shot went wide to the left--Juan was outside the effective range of the pistol. Now Juan got back into a shooter's stance. He leveled the shotgun and squeezed one off at Bru. It whistled by Bru--his shotgun wasn't much more accurate at that range than Bru's pistol. But this time Juan was better positioned and his gun was pointed at Bru and ready to fire again. Bru squeezed his shot off first. It caught Juan Robert in the shoulder. Bru watched in horrible fascination as the gun went flying in one direction and the small man's arm went in another. Juan's still attached arm came around feeling for its departed mate and his face bore an expression of astonishment and horror. Then he collapsed into the prairie to watch the lifeblood spurt from his artery, and to die.

Bru had no time to gloat. The Stearman attracted by the shooting had swung around wide and bore down on Bru. Bru assumed a shooter's crouch and followed the plane. The pilot didn't have the angle on Bru. He didn't even try to throw down on him. Bru too decided to let the plane pass without taking a shot. The chance of hitting a homeshot was perilously close to zero. He tried to recall how many rounds were in a M15 magazine. He couldn't remember. Perhaps he'd never known. But he counted the rounds he'd expended. One had been discarded at the river when he emptied the chamber and another to wing the airboat's prop. Three shots to nail Juan Robert. Five down. Not more than one or two to go. He had to be economical with his shots.

Where was Smith? Bru peered into the gloomy interior of the hammock. The canopy of palm trees, up fifty or sixty feet, was so thick no underbrush could thrive on the forest floor. Bru could see through gaps in the palm trunks to daylight on the far side. He could even see cars zipping along I-4. But the trunks were tightly spaced. The interior of the hammock seemed a nightmare to Bru. Trees to hide behind but open area for him to cross and show himself if he tried to flush Smith out or even slink into the middle for cover from the plane. Bru preferred to hide in the myrtle bushes and let Smith find him. If Smith had an automatic rifle, like the AR-15, he'd have no chance against him if caught outside of cover. By staying put, Bru had his rear flank covered by the open saw grass marsh.

The error in this thinking became immediately apparent. Bru heard a fluttery, popping noise as the Stearman's radial engine was gunned. Checking that unprotected flank, he saw the plane's landing gear, only a yard or so above the saw grass, coming at him on a tangent. Bru froze, not wanting to betray his position in the peripheral underbrush. The pilot sprayed the vegetation. Leaves flew and a round zipped just over Bru's head. Bru's instincts were to run off into the interior of the hammock. The urge came almost on the autonomic scale, like breathing. How many more passes like that could he survive? But he quelled the impulse.

They are in communication, he thought. *Smith and the pilot. Smith's hidden out among those palm trunks. That pilot is trying to herd you to him.*

The plane was making another pass. It was on the

same trajectory as last time and, if possible, even lower. Bru could see the pilot craning his neck, the AR-15 at the ready. He told himself to be very still. Then as the spluttering roar of the Stearman grew louder he heard the snick of a round plopping into a palm trunk. Smith shooting at him. They were trying to get Bru in a crossfire.

The pilot cut loose with a spray of gunfire. The pilot pulled out and went up directly above Bru and the spent AR-15 clip came hurtling down. It landed almost on Bru's foot. He felt the metal cannister. It was warm from operation in the rifle.

Move, Bru told himself. Slink off into the bushes-- and give Smith a better shot at you. Here came the Stearman again. But this time something was definitely different. The plane just kept coming, its gear just inches above the prairie vegetation. It was coming at the hammock at an angle--and right at Bru. This should have been salve for Bru's soul. At that angle, the pilot couldn't shoot at Bru without chopping up his prop. So Bru was immune.

But Bru's intuition told him there was something wrong with the picture. Just stay put. Sit it out, he told himself. But his intuition was faster than his conscious mind. This time he bolted to his feet and ran, exposing himself completely to the Stearman, which kept doggedly flying on. No more than two seconds elapsed from Bru's jackrabbit start to the crash. But Bru's jogger's quick physique saved him as the gigantic Stearman smashed into the palm trees. Three tall trunks dead in front of the engine sheared off but the plane's wings crumbled. The tall trunks catapulted over onto the cockpit crushing the pilot. A mist of avgas came up from the ruptured fuel line, poured over the hot engine and turned into a black vapor. A few seconds later flames began licking greedily at the fabric fuselage.

Bru was standing on the saw grass prairie drinking all this in horrid fascination. Then he saw a muzzle flash in the darkness of the hammock. He was being shot at. He knew where Smith was. But, worse, Smith knew where Bru was. Thank god, the guy's a lousy shot, Bru thought. Then suddenly the gas tank in the Stearman exploded. Tracers of fiery flame shot out onto the saw grass and into the hammock and paper dry fronds on the floor caught fire and began to burn. Bru used the cover of the explosion to duck into the hammock and secrete himself behind a pair of palm trunks that made a sort of box. His eyes were sunblind. When they adjusted to the dark he saw movement ahead at one o'clock moving toward two o'clock. *Smith.* Not more than fifty feet away, no doubt bearing on a tack that he miscalculated to bring him to Bru.

Raise your weapon and shoot, Bru instructed himself. But he couldn't. It was almost as if in cold blood. Then something occurred that made Bru wonder if he was losing his sanity. He heard an automobile horn honking and what sounded like a heavy truck engine growling in granny gear and four-wheel drive. The bleeping was incessant and he heard a voice, a female voice hollering. "Bru, Bru, get your silly ass over here," she twanged out in an identifiably Texas accent.

It had to be Melba and her truck on the marshy prairie. How could she have gotten here? Bru didn't look. He didn't want to spoil his vision. He knew what Smith was making for--Melba and her truck.

Bru stepped out from behind his covert. "Smith!" he hollered.

Now Smith was momentarily blind, having gazed out of the dark hammock onto the prairie. He squinted at Bru out of scrunched up eyes. Bru lifted his arm. The M15 blasted. The slug caught Smith in the throat. His body recoiled against at palm tree and stayed pasted there for a moment, as though impaled. Smith's upper lip with the Clark Gable mustache twitched and he gave a smarmy grin.

"Good shooting, Bruton," he said, then added, "I told you I wouldn't come looking for you *after* you saw the old man." Suddenly he made a gagging sound and the death rattled bellied out of his mouth.

"Bru Bruton, get the hell away from that dead man and come here this moment. Let's get out of here before my truck sinks in the soup and we never get out."

Smith's body slipperslid down the sloping trunk of the palm tree and ended up almost at Bru's feet. *Just the way Etienne did,* Bru thought. He looked at the .45 in his hand a moment and then with disgust he chucked it at Smith's corpse. Then like a puppet on a string, he turned and did as Melba said.

42

Melba ramrodded the F-250 to the edge of the hammock and held the passenger door open. Bru jumped in and they were off. The big pickup's wheels shot out roostertails of mud and then tromped down the wall of willows as it scaled the highway berm. Melba put on her left blinker light and edged into traffic on I-4. Bru noticed a high-powered rifle, a .222 Remington, slanted toward the floorboard between them. It exuded a faint smell of spent cordite.

"Why'd that plane smash into to the palm trees?" Bru asked.

"Because I shot the pilot, silly."

"But how did you get here?"

Melba gave Bru a dreary look. "My mommy didn't raise any stupid children. Why do you think I told you not to wake me when you left? I knew you'd never let me ride shotgun with you so I stuffed a couple of bolsters under the bedspread. I fetched the deer rifle my daddy gave me and sneaked down and got under the naugahyde cover of the pickup bed. Jeez, it was cold out there waiting for you."

"How come I didn't see your truck at the fish camp?"

"I hid it in the canebrake. I couldn't very well run around with a rifle there and I didn't know where you went so I just stuck tight by the truck. I figured--hoped--you knew what you were doing out on the river."

"I thought if I insisted Smith come immediately, he wouldn't have the time to mount a very effective operation. As it was they seemed to be scraping the bottom of the barrel with that Juan blazing away with a shotgun."

"That airplane seemed a fairly efficient touch," Melba said dryly. "How do you suppose they managed that?"

"Maybe the pilot was standing by for orders. In any case, he was able to grab his weaponry and get in the air and cross the county all in an hour and a half or so. The thing about rush jobs is that everyone gets going so fast they always forget to cover all the bases."

"Yes, like my hanging back so far that I lost you in the traffic on I-4. I missed seeing your car scoot off into the hammock so I crossed the median strip and was heading back when I saw that plane circling the copse of palm trees and firing at something--you."

"Jesus," Bru said.

"My first inclination would be to stop and wait for the police," she said, even though they were swallowed up in traffic and long past the scene of the action. "I suppose you still are wanting to head for Old Man Goins's place."

"You damned right. Take I-95 up to the Ormond exit."

"How are you planning on gaining admittance to Goins's estate?" Melba asked.

"I'm not sure you are going to like my plan," he said.

Bru directed Melba to the Granada Avenue beach approach. Bru forked over five bucks at the beach toll booth and Melba drove onto the sand. Bru pointed out Goins's place. Without another word from Bru, Melba shifted the truck into four wheel drive. She hit the gas. The big pickup shot up the dune, and into the coils of razor wire that were laid along the periphery. It rolled over the wire onto the Saint Augustine lawn. In Goins's Florida room/office Bru saw the tall man's figure slumped in his green throne chair.

Bru made for the door, tried the latch. Naturally, it was locked. He hammered on the door. Goins's looked up, came slowly to the door and let Bru and Melba in. Only then did Goins seem to notice the truck on his back lawn. "Why did you come up like this, Bruton?"

"As though you don't know," Bru said.

Goins gave Bru a sharp look. Then his look softened. "I don't get it. What's going on?"

"For starters, I'm still alive--after your people tried to kill me twice since I last talked to you."

"My people tried to kill you twice since yesterday-- what are you talking about?"

"And the orange juice, presumably, is still on the shelves."

Goins gave Bru a slack jawed look. His eyes were a chalky blue and confused. He turned and tottered-- looking very old--to his green chair, which he collapsed into. He put his head in his hand. "What the hell do you suppose is going on?"

"That's why I came here. For *you* to tell *me*."

"I gave the order to get the orange juice recalled. You heard me tell Juan."

"For what good it did."

The old man looked at Bru, his eyes narrowing. "So

it was Juan who was fucking with me? I thought it was Elizabeth and that no-good Mansonite she took up with out in California, that Wisnewski."

"You were right on both accounts," Bru said. "Both of them tried to kill me. Juan attempted to shotgun me to death this morning. I'm happy to say he missed. Elizabeth came by last night, slipped me a mickey, then turned on the gas. Does that sound familiar?"

The old man emitted a mournful moan. He covered his face with both hands. "What a monster I bore. She killed her own daughter."

"I'm afraid that's the way it stacks up."

"But at least Kimberly didn't do herself by her own hand. That's more of a relief than you can imagine," the old man said. For a moment the trace of a smile flickered on Goins's thin lips, then, as though the grotesqueries he'd been living with caught up to him, he seemed to shrink in the chair. His stature now was much less than Bru's six feet. Also, he seemed to age before Bru's eyes. Bru couldn't help but feel sorry for him, even if Goins had been ultimately the author of his own troubles. Still, no man should have the death of his beloved granddaughter visited on him. Not even someone who did the evil things this man had done.

"We still have the matter of those tainted orange juice cans to take care of," Bru said.

"What do you want me to do?" Goins asked.

"That's a good question," Bru said. "I've learned I was wrong about 1,2--DCA, by itself, being the cause of KiDS. Strictly speaking, there is no good reason to recall all orange juice, just that contaminated with a second agent. The trouble is I have no idea how to identify the tainted batches."

"I don't believe I understand what you are talking about," the old man said. "Nor do I think I need to know. We elevated the level of 1,2--DCA in the orange juice cans.

That right there is enough reason to pull the cans from the shelves. If you don't mind, Bruton, I think I will call P. Rogers Gresham at Port Saint Joe Plastics right now in your presence so I don't change my mind later."

"That sounds like a good idea," Bru said. "If you know the number I will dial."

Goins looked at Bru out of narrowed phlegmatic eyes, as though he were trying to hard to recall how to find the number. He shrugged.

Melba brought a phone. Bru called directory assistance, got the number and by striking the one button, and an additional fifty cents let the phone company dial the number for him. Bru asked the receptionist for the head man and, by free use of Goins's name, after a while he came on the line. He handed the phone to Goins, who said, "P. Roger, did you get a call from my man Joo-an last night? I was afraid you hadn't. Well, I got some news that isn't very pleasant. However, I think it best you get right on it and issue a recall before the Feds or one of them do it for you. I'm talking about those orange juice cans you've made these past few months. They contain a contaminant. You need to get them out of the nation's reefers. Like I said, this is a bitter pill, but it got to be done. Get going on this." The old man put his hand over the speaker. "Does that satisfy you, Bruton?"

"Tell him you'll send him a fax explaining the situation in writing in a few minutes. Get his fax number," Bru said.

Goins passed the phone to Bru. "You do it."

Bru took the number and told Gresham, whose voice sounded extremely perplexed and not the least pleased by what Goins'd told him, that a written statement would arrive shortly.

The old man nodded. "You're right about getting this in writing. No one will take it the least bit seriously any other way."

The door flew open and the security guard that had shaken down Kimberly for sexual favors burst into the room. He had a pistol in hand. "What do you want?" the old man growled.

"There has been a perimeter breach," the young man gasped.

"Put away that pistol and get out of here. Bruton, get going on that statement, please. I want to get this over with. I want the matter settled."

"Bru sat down at the keyboard and typed: "As a means of cornering the world orange juice market, I, Billy Goins, acquired Port Saint Joe Plastic Company. The product PSJPC made had an artificially elevated 1,2--Dicitrolaminealdehyde (known as 1,2--DCA) content which in concert with a tainted emulsifier in some orange juices is responsible for the incidence of the so-called KiDS disease. Because of our actions all orange juice in containers produced by the Port Saint Joe Plastics Company should be regarded as tainted and recalled immediately. All parties will be fully indemnified by me, Billy Goins and the various corporate entities I control.

"In order to conceal my conspiracy to contaminate frozen concentrated orange juice I colluded with President Wilmer Newcombe of Lawson College to force Dr. Rupert Bruton to write a report which I hoped would be favorable to our cause. To do this, I agreed to contribute monies to Lawson College's endowment fund with the understanding President Newcombe would terminate Bruton's employment with the college. Also, I employed as a contract killer Deputy Smith of the Okeelanta County Sheriff's Department to eliminate Arbuthnot (a longtime confederate and the person responsible for the contamination plot on an operational level), Leroy Wiesnewski and Bruton. Smith and my aide Juan Robert, with the assistance of an airplane from which an automatic weapon was fired, engaged in an attempt to take the life of Dr. Bruton this morning, an attempt which failed.

"I, Billy Goins, and my corporate holdings take full legal responsibility and hereby agree to whatever recompense the proper authorities recommend."

Bru read the statement to Goins, who nodded in agreement with all the provisions until the part about taking full legal responsibility. "It's not fair of me to burden my stockholders with this assertion. There are widows and orphans dependent on those companies--" then the wind seemed to go out of his sails and he nodded wearily. "I didn't really send Smith and Joo-an after you this morning, but you may as well leave that in. As far as that goes, I wasn't really aware of all of Arbuthnot's activities but you're right I had him killed by Smith when I suspected he had collaborated with whoever was trying to blackmail me with that citrus canker thing--and if the truth be known I also figured he was responsible for that KiDS epidemic and hadn't fessed up. Arbuthnot was a despicable--if extremely bright--human being. The world lost nothing when Smith disposed of him. But I set the ball in motion for all those other crimes. I may as well own up to the responsibility." Also, he had Bru add the letter "L" in front of his name and then Guadelupe, the maid, and Ken, the senior security guy on the shift, were called. Goins dated and signed five copies of the note and his staff dated and witnessed each of those copies. Bru placed four of the copies in envelopes, which he sealed. He gave one envelope to the head security guard, one to Goins, one to Melba and he kept one for himself.

"This copy needs to be faxed to this phone number," Bru told the guard, a thin graying man of about forty. Then turning to Goins, Bru said, "There's one thing you have to tell me. Why did you do it? You had more money than you could spend in a hundred lifetimes. Why risk everything for

241

nothing?"

"I thought they counted not by what you spent but what you had. I thought that was the only game there was. I wanted to be the tenth richest man in the U.S. I would give it all, every penny, if only I could get Kimberly back." The old man's face looked ancient and preoccupied. A gray sheen showed on his face. After a moment he nodded his head and gestured with his hand for them to be off.

Bru shook his head. All the death and evil the old man had unleashed--just so he could find himself in tenth place on some imaginary list. He didn't know whether he should loath Goins for his evilness or pity him for his shallowness. The guard and Lupe made for the door. Bru motioned for Lupe to stay. "You don't let him out of your sight," Bru said, supposing the answer to that question was that mostly he pitied the old guy. Her expressive Latin eyes darted wildly from Bru to Goins. She crossed herself and sat. Bru took the guard aside, "What's that kid's name?"

"You're talking about the guard with the insolent manner?"

Bru nodded.

"Paul."

"Call the police and then keep your eye on him. He made Kimberly do unspeakable things to let her sneak out at night. Maybe the cops can exhort a confession out of him."

"That the only reason I'm calling the cops?"

"No. Another reason is to arrest Kimberly's murderess. Melba, you go with Ken and make sure all those things are done with no shenanigans. It's not that I don't trust you, Ken, but you no doubt appreciate the fact that things have not always operated as they should in this household. I'm going to keep Elizabeth company to make sure no evidence gets tampered with in the meantime. Where is she?"

"In that little room she calls her office," the guard

said. "Be careful with her. She knows how to handle herself."

"I've already found that out," Bru said. "Believe me, I have."

43

Bru tried the knob of Elizabeth's office door. It gave. He pushed into the room and there sat Elizabeth in her antique French chair. She looked like a movie star, her hair down and frizzy and her face made up to look unmade up--no sharp, guilt lines around the mouth, none of the black patches from psychological anguish under the eyes. She had on a tight fitting top and skin-hugging designer jeans. She appeared five years younger than the matronly belle that had casually stopped by his house to kill him the night before.

"Why, Bru, I expected you much sooner," she said, taking a sip from a sherry glass set on the table. "Would you like a little something?"

"No I wouldn't," Bru said, thinking, *Jesus, what a job of work this woman is.*

"You're pissed about last night? Come on. You know how those things go. You do what you have to do. I'm glad you were able to outsmart me. I've always liked you. You know that."

"Your boyfriends, Juan Robert and Deputy Dawg won't be coming to save your ass, Liz," Bru said.

"Did you kill both of them?"

"I must ruefully admit I did," Bru said.

"Good," she said. "I never liked that Juan Robert. He was a little creep and the deputy I never even met. Of this whole bunch I always liked you best, Bru. Back in college don't you remember me trying to bed you?"

Bru shook his head.

"I mean it, Bru. The problem was I always thought you were a wimp. I don't mean then. Then I didn't care if you were a wimp. I'm talking about now. I need me a real man."

"And I made the short list. Wow, what an honor."

There came a shout, a long feminine blood-curdling hoot, punctuated in the middle by what sounded like a pistol report. Abruptly the shout stopped, was quiet for a few seconds then started again, this time as a soulful wail. Bru recognized the voice as Lupe the maid's.

"Sounds like he finally did it. I didn't think even that tough old coot could bear up for so long under the strain. How many heiresses to a three billion dollar fortune do you know, Bru?"

"Unfortunately the only one I know tried to kill me."

"Hey, I already told you I was sorry about that."

"And murdered her daughter."

"We have differing points of view about little Miss Warm Cunt," she said making a face and dismissing her daughter's death. "What you should really be pissed about is what we did with President Newcombe to get you fired. That wasn't very nice of us. But don't feel too sorry for yourself. Let me tell you fucking Newcombe wasn't much fun."

"Whose idea was that? Your father's."

"I thought you were a faster read than that, Bru. That was Leroy's play. He wanted to go at my old man in a two sided attack. See, first he started in on him with this stuff about the citrus canker, a scam the old guy pulled back in the eighties. The old fucker glommed off a whole lot of land for subdivisions. The second part was to get you involved. Leroy would play close to his vest and he never told me why he was getting you in position, but I figured it out later with that guy Joo-an. When Leroy was younger he was all right, but age and too many drugs and whatnot really slowed him down. But, look, we're getting off the topic, which was me and you. What say you throw in with me?"

"Lady, I'm sitting here making sure that none of the manifold drugs in your bathroom dispensary, some of which I'm sure will show up in the body tissue of your dead daughter, don't disappear before the police arrive."

"I could do things for you no woman has ever done, Bru."

"Oh, shut up," Bru said.

"Have it your way," she said. In a flick of her hands, she turned the tight-fitting top inside out and tossed it over her head. She wore no bra. She cupped her hands under her enormous breasts, offering them to Bru.

Bru couldn't gainsay those breasts, large, with upturned nipples. "I've seen them before, remember, when you banged them into my face. The first day I came out here to talk to your old man" he said trying to sound blase, but his throat constricted and went dry.

"Doesn't interest you, eh, Bru? Well, what about this?" She stood and undid the brass button on her jeans. She peeled them down her body. She stood for a moment, her thatch and thighs fully exposed from the front. "Doesn't do anything for you, eh? How about this?" She turned around and bent over, touching her head to the seat of her chair. Her rear was exposed to Bru's view--just butt really, with little flashes of bush coming through.

Still, the unexpectedness of this sight hit Bru like a hammer blow. Then the painted nails of her hands spreadeagled on her cheeks. The bright red against the white of her flesh gave Bru a tremor. Her fingers parted her buttocks like a flower and there was her blossom glistening in its collar of hair and just above it like a purse with its drawstring taut her pink anus.

"Come on, Bru, hurry. I want you inside me. Don't pretend you aren't hard. I can feel the heat of your dick way over here. Take it out and plug me. I want you so bad. You can have your pick of whichever hole you want. And, don't forget, you're also getting your share of the three billion."

"You have AIDS for Christsake," Bru said. "I'm not going to touch you. And it's my pleasant duty to inform you that your father has compromised most of that three billion-dollar nest egg."

"So I'm HIV positive. Big deal. I go to this doctor in Jersey every couple of months and he gives me a whole new blood supply. If you don't like that you can do that drug cocktail business. You expect to live forever?"

"Hey, what's going on here?" Melba said, slipping through the half opened door. "Mr. Goins just shot himself. Why is her necked butt sticking up in the air like that?"

"She wants me to fuck her," Bru said.

"She can do me too if she wants. There's plenty of pussy for everybody," Elizabeth said.

"Does she have all her buttons?" Melba asked.

"Doesn't appear that way," Bru said.

"Hey, I'm just trying to be accommodating, Bru. I'll take her along with you is what I'm saying. Don't worry about the money. There'll be plenty for everyone."

"Yeah, until you decide to do one or both of us in," Bru said.

Elizabeth sprung upright and sat down in the chair. She had a look of hurt on her face--as though Bru misunderstood her and she was bothered on account of it.

"Bru, you are going to have to help me. That's all there is to it. I know about Etienne. I even have a witness to that unfortunate murder you committed all those many years ago. The police might find your reasons for your recent homicides justifiable. But there's no way you will be able to get around the evidence that witness will present. You're mine, Bru, whether you like it or not."

Melba looked at Bru and took his hand and squeezed it.

"Too bad, Lizzy," Bru said. "You're going to have to face the music and there's nothing I'm going to do to prevent it."

"You had your chance, Bruton. I could have made you happier than you can ever imagine. When the cops arrive, I'm going to sing like a bird. You will go away for a long time. Maybe you'll even end up in Old Sparky, the electric chair at Raiford. As for me, with all my money, I'll beat the rap. I always have before."

"That might be, dearie," Melba said. "But for right now, why don't you put your clothes on--so you'll have something to take off to bribe the cops with."

"Oh, you rangy fucking Texas whore, I hate you," Elizabeth said, lunging at Melba with her blood-red nails flaring.

"Be careful, Melba," Bru hollered. "She was trained in hand-to-hand combat by the Manson family."

But Melba doubled her fist and smacked it square into Elizabeth's jaw. The blow connected solidly. Elizabeth's still nude body stumbled backward two steps and collapsed into the chair, out like a spent bulb.

44

When the deputies arrived, Elizabeth, who by then had her clothes on, pointed at Bru and Melba and said, "Arrest those two for the murder of my father."

The deputies obliged her but not before Bru was able

to convince them to impound the drugs in Elizabeth's bathroom cabinet. Bru was separated from Melba, manacled and put in the back of a sheriff's cruiser. His last hurried statement to Melba was, "I'll talk to Jerry about getting you legal representation." Her words were, "I love you, Bru."

Bru was driven to the facility in the swamp on International Speedway Boulevard and taken to an interrogation room. The sheriff herself came to him. "I don't suppose you will talk to me without an attorney present," she snarled. "Your kind always hides behind their so-called constitutional rights."

Bru didn't bother answering. He used his phone call to reach Leta who said, "I've already called Jerry. Your going off with that gun scared me." Jerry arrived just a few minutes later. Before he'd talk to Bru, he held up his finger and banged on the door of the interrogation room. A deputy opened and Jerry said, "Do you have the tape rolling?"

"We don't eavesdrop on attorneys and prisoners anymore. Not since the court order restraining us."

Jerry gave him a dreary look. "How about you just showing me your bank of tape recorders."

The deputy gave a shrug and he and Jerry went away then after a while he was back. "I guess their ears are switched off," Jerry said. "All right. How about giving me the skinny on what went on here. From what I heard on the outside, it doesn't sound good."

Bru handed him a copy of Goins's confession. Jerry read with a confused, almost cross, expression on his face but toward the end he looked up at Bru and grinned. Then Bru told Jerry about the tape recorder he'd bought early in the morning and carried with him and which the police had taken from him on arriving at the jail. Jerry excused himself. After a while he was back with the machine and a deputy.

The deputy watched through a glass partition, out of earshot, while they played the tape. It did a tolerable job of recording the various conversations, shootings, collisions Bru had been involved in that day despite being drowned, banged around and dragged through the swamp. Next Bru filled Jerry in on the details of the orange juice contamination. He gave him an earful of the carryings on of Elizabeth and Leroy including the murder of Kimberly, Deputy Smith's various assassinations and finally Arbuthnot's scams, not to mention Old Man Goins's role.

Jerry just nodded his head. "I don't think we're going to have much trouble clearing you," he said.

"When I tried to explain things yesterday, the sheriff went out of her way not to get the point. I'm not sure she hasn't been bought and paid for by Goins and his henchmen."

Jerry gave Bru a stern look. "Don't ever but ever make the assumption that an official of the law is corrupt. It can lead to nothing but trouble. You need everyone in officialdom in this county to smile on you. Otherwise, you can cool your heels in the clink for a whale of a long time, even if they can't prove a thing on you. That was yesterday when Goins was alive and needed a fall guy."

"That woman can't stand me. She makes no bones about it."

"Did you not hear what I said minute ago? My guess is that everyone will be real happy to dump the blame on Goins or one of the other dead guys and forget about it. Now is there anything else I need to know? I'm talking about things that could possibly be made to put you in an unfavorable light."

"There are just two things I can think of," Bru said. "Evidently Goins bought a million dollars worth of citrus futures in my name in an attempt to make it look like I was behind the o.j. scam, if it came to that. He also phonied up employment records at the plastic factory."

"Holy shit," Jerry said. "How did he get your social security number and signature and stuff?"

"From President Newcombe."

Scribbling furiously on his legal pad, Jerry shook his head and chortled. "That's the kind of thing a man could go to jail for. In Newcombe's case, I suppose he'll probably just lose his job at Lawson unless you really press it."

"Nuke'em is already paying the price," Bru said. "In one of those palace intrigues you warned of early on, Goins's daughter got to Newcombe ahead of Goins. She gave him a lasting reminder of their association. Her man, Leroy, was a needle freak and he'd presumably acquired AIDS that way and transmitted the deadly virus to Elizabeth. Now Newcombe is HIV positive."

Abruptly Jerry stopped laughing. His face turned brick red. Globules of sweat appeared around his temples and in the thinning strands of his widow's peak. After fifteen seconds of dead air, he said, "You said there were two things.

"Yes, the other one is a little harder to explain away," Bru said. "When I was a kid I killed a guy using the M15 pistol I shot Smith with."

Jerry's nostrils flared and his eyes narrowed. "When and where did this happen?"

"In Dade County in the agricultural area south of Miami. The guy was a Haitiian, probably an illegal and a drug pusher. He seduced my girl away with crack cocaine-- that was before we even knew what crack was. The only name I knew him by was Etienne."

Jerry shrugged. "You were right in letting me know about this, but it's not very likely any of that information will come back to haunt you."

"I'm afraid there's more to it than that," Bru said. "Elizabeth got onto that story. She threatened to blackmail me with it. The gun I shot Smith with was the same weapon I used on Etienne."

"Jesus, Bru, what the hell was wrong with you for keeping that fucking gun? Any coked-to-his-gills street hustler would know better than that." Jerry stared off into the middle distance tapping his index finger against his chin. After a while he said, "Well, let me go talk to them." Jerry went off to confer with the sheriff and the state attorney's people, and then after a while he and Bru and a whole slew of folks, some in uniform, some in suits, were in a room and Bru was answering questions.

A billionaire and a cop were dead. It was apparent to Bru, notwithstanding Jerry's claim, the gendarmerie and the judiciary needed a head, a live one. It was obvious in their view Bru's would do just fine, but Jerry waved Goins's confession in the air and then read it--and so long to their open enmity. Bru was amused at the way the supposed hard cases who a minute before had been all for strapping Bru in Old Sparky, waxed amiable as the ambition at somehow claiming credit for breaking the KiDS epidemic case dangled before their eyes. Before the proceedings had hardly gotten going, Jerry asked that Bru be allowed to go home and come back another time, if necessary, to answer further questions.

From the murmur in the room it seemed to Bru that the idea was on the point of carrying when the sheriff stood up. "Mr. Bruton," she said.

"Dr. Bruton," Jerry corrected.

"Dr. Bruton, our investigators have learned that you own a million dollars in frozen concentrated orange juice futures."

Jerry popped up. "Those futures were purchased in Dr. Bruton's name by Billy Goins."

"So he claims," the sheriff said. "Look, my problem is that Bruton is claiming Goins and company perpetrated a scam, yet he can't explain how it happened. Yesterday, he told me in one breath that this 1,2--DCA stuff was harmless and in the next that it was the thing causing that KiDS epidemic. Until he can give a straight story on that, he's going to be my guest in the steel hotel."

Jerry jumped to his feet again. "But sheriff, Dr. Bruton learned of his supposed ownership of those futures at the same time you did yesterday afternoon from Mr. Billy Goins himself. At that time, Goins told you both that he purchased those futures in Bruton's name so my client could be framed to appear as the mastermind of this orange juice scam."

"I want to hear Bruton," the sheriff said, "not a silver tongued rascal like you, Wiley. So far I don't see any evidence tying any KiDS epidemic to Mr. Goins. All I see is a dead billionaire and Bruton with a million dollars worth of citrus futures, bought by someone else."

"Not knowing how the orange juice scam worked completely is evidence for Dr. Bruton's innocence rather than otherwise," Jerry said, but Bru was tugging at his sleeve.

"It's all right, Jerry, let me answer her," Bru said, getting to his feet. "Yesterday Goins's henchman Arbuthnot's roommate, friend, lover, whatever told me that Arbuthnot and Goins were involved in a plan to contaminate orange juice stocks. He also told me Arbuthnot had worked in a factory on and off for a period of time leading up to the outbreak of the KiDS disease. I made the erroneous assumption that factory was the plastic works at Port Saint Joe, a community in the big bend region of the panhandle not far from Tallahassee. I made that miscalculation because I knew Arbuthnot, in clothes that might have been worn in a factory, had visited an old professor, a mutual acquaintance, in Gainesville, which is more of less on the way from Port Saint Joe to his home in Okeelanta County.

252

That factory in Port Saint Joe makes almost all orange juice containers used in the U.S., and I had found that juice stored in those containers secreted a compound called 1,2-Dicitrolaminealdehyde. This compound had long been suspected by nonprofessionals to cause health problems. The trouble with my assumption--as the sheriff quickly ascertained and as I should have known--was that this compound 1,2--DCA, for short, is completely nontoxic.

"It was no accident that in the heat of the chase I made that wrong assumption. This scam could work only if the complete Florida orange juice stock were taken out of production. To do that that KiDS disease had to be traced back to Florida orange juice and 1,2--DCA was conveniently at hand to take the blame. By the same token the perpetrators of the plot didn't want the real causal agent tying them to the KiDS disease. My informant--Arbuthnot's friend--steered me to Arbuthnot's secret lab at his mother's house off Camptown road in a rural part of this county. But just before I arrived your Deputy Smith on the instructions of Goins or more likely his majordomo, Juan Robert, completely destroyed the lab."

Bru stopped and looked up. The sheriff was squinting at him. "Had you not called me on that 1,2--DCA thing at Goins' place, sheriff, I might not have discovered how they really produced the KiDS disease. Arbuthnot's lab was a very curious building, just a large shack actually, disguised as a tumbledown outbuilding. The first time I was there I'd noticed what appeared to be a storm window slanting cockeyed on the roof--that was queer, a storm window in Florida. After the fire I glimpsed in the building's ruins a large kettle. Before I go farther, I need to give you a little background on this Arbuthnot," Bru said. "As a GI during the Vietnam War he deserted to the North. In reward for his good work he was given a strain of bacterial disease that mimicked the symptoms of the extremely dangerous citrus canker. The name of both strains of citrus disease--"

"Why is this guy wasting our time with this horseshit?" It was the Hispanic cop with the Apache eyes who had escorted Bru and Kim to view Leroy's body in the morgue.

"If you just listen for a minute you'll see," Bru said.

The sheriff motioned for Apache eyes to sit and Bru continued. "The confusion between these two strains cost the state of Florida and citrus growers several billion dollars back in the eighties--a costly error Old Man Goins capitalized on to build a real estate fortune. The scientific name for both strains of this disease is the same, *Xanthomonas campestris*. Oddly enough, a useful bacteria is also found in this genus. It is cultivated in huge vats to produce a substance called expolysacharide or EPS for short. EPS is a gooey slime which is used as a thickening agent in many foods from ice cream to sauces and juices. Commercially, this product is known as Xanthan gum and the manufacturing seat for the country's largest company is in New Port Richey, Florida, on the west coast about halfway down just above Saint Pete. Xanthan gum is added as a thickening agent to various juices, including--I learned today--to some orange juices. Our friend Arbuthnot cultivated various strains of *Xanthomonas campestris* using the nursery of illegal trifoliate orange trees he kept at his mother's house in the pineywoods off Camptown Spur Road. One of those species produced an expolysacharide that, in combination with 1,2--DCA, causes a toxic condition in youngsters, or in other words KiDS. That explains," Bru said in an aside, "why the KiDS outbreaks were clustered in pockets around the country. If 1,2--DCA alone had been the toxic agent, the incidence of the outbreaks would have been spread evenly. As Arbuthnot worked it, you needed to have both his tainted EPS *and* 1,2-

-DCA in the juice you drank to be effected. Probably you had to have the bad luck of drinking the same concentration for several days or even weeks or months in a row before taking ill.

"To get back to the production element," Bru said, "Arbuthnot used the shed Smith burned to culture the bacteria in a huge vat. Employee records will show that he worked in that factory in New Port Richey. He introduced and cultured his toxic strain of *Xanthomonas campestris*, into the company's production vats which, in turn, was distributed by normal commercial channels to the orange juice producers. And there you have the explanation for KiDS."

A hullabaloo broke out as various investigators fired questions at Bru. But the sheriff gained the floor. "Didn't I hear somewhere that no plant disease has ever been known to bother humans? Here you're claiming this Xan stuff is responsible for KiDS."

"You are correct. But it's not the EPS bacteria that is toxic. The culprit is the secretion of that bacterium in conjunction with 1,2--DCA--altogether a horse of a different color."

"This guy Arbuthnot wasn't a scientist, right?"

"He didn't hold a Ph.D.," Bru said.

"Then how'd he or whoever, come up with this very complicated-sounding idea of using a strain of the citrus canker to cause a human disease?"

"He may have discovered it on his own. But my guess is that he learned of it from the Chinese when he was a turncoat collaborator of the People's Republic during the Vietnam war. It could very well have been a folk poison which he sorted out."

The sheriff seemed to like that answer. She sat down and others fired questions at Bru, mainly about who was responsible for what. Did Goins have full control or was the mastermind Juan Robert or Leroy or Arbuthnot or even Elizabeth or Deputy Smith? The questions ran on and on. After what seemed hours, Jerry asked if Bru could be released. There was a lot of palaver about that. The guys in the suits seemed to be in favor of the idea but a man in green--a deputy--abruptly left. He came back shortly, evidently after conferring with the sheriff who'd dismissed herself earlier, and whispered into the state attorney's ear. The semi-amiable atmosphere turned frosty. Jerry told Bru not to worry. They could only keep him twenty-four hours without charging him. For some reason, the way Jerry said this didn't give Bru a great deal of confidence.

45

Bru, still in the desert camo fatigues clothes he had crawled through the swamp in, was escorted to a grubby little room with a bed and a lamp with the light bulb in a security cage. A lot of time passed. Bru never really slept but somehow he felt as though he should have. Stubble grew on his chin and his feet felt grody in his socks.

Something resembling the rap of knuckles presaged the appearance of a guard. He had a moronic grin on his face. Bru was led to a much smaller interrogation room.

After a while Jerry Wiley came in. A lock of his widow's peak hung over onto his forehead. He was all smiles. All those smiles made Bru a little uneasy. Before Bru could learn about Melba from Jerry, the sheriff bustled into the room.

Jerry rose and Bru was surprised to learn all over again that Shelby Buckett was a rather pleasant looking woman. Her blond hair, was brushed until it glistened and fell unbraided over her shoulders. She stood a full half head shorter than Jerry. She was carrying a zippered plastic envelope, about the size and shape of a bank bag. This was the first Bru had seen of her since she fired that round of questions at Bru. Bru followed Jerry's lead and stood. Bru noticed that Jerry didn't offer the sheriff his hand. He wondered if that was standard protocol for a defense attorney, or whether he was merely saving Bru from the rebuff that would have come from the sheriff's refusal to shake his hand. A man in a suit came in. Jerry called him by name. Bru supposed he was the state attorney's representative.

The sheriff said, "Gentlemen." They sat.

Shelby Buckett looked at Bru. Her eyes were very large and very brown. "I thought I would meet you in here again, Bruton," she said. "It was good of you not to disappoint me." Then she did something that surprised Bru. She smiled. When she smiled her face went from the attractive side of plain, to radiantly beautiful. It was a strange look on the face of a cop, especially a kickass cop with Buckett's reputation.

"I'm sorry we kept you locked up overnight. Given the gravity of the crimes involved here, you must understand the necessity of making sure all the facts checked out before we let any of the principals out of sight, especially after the bullshit story about expolysacharides or whatever. Did you find the food and lodging satisfactory?"

Buckett paused as though for a response from Bru. So he nodded.

"Everything you have told us about Goins and his operation has dovetailed with what we have found out. Fortunately, for you perhaps, an investigation into Deputy Smith's activities by this department was ongoing."

Bru sucked a fold of his cheek into his lips and bit it to keep from smiling at this admission. Suddenly, Buckett's eyes turned hard and flinty and her face morphed into hardass cop.

"I don't like it when a cop goes down for any reason. It's bad for the profession. But this time I have to admit Smith's end was probably timely so far as my department is concerned."

Buckett gave Bru a very small smile. There was nothing attractive about her features now. Her warm brown eyes had somehow turned gray. "However, that is not the matter I came here to talk to you and Mr. Wiley about." The zippered plastic case suddenly appeared from under the table. Buckett deposited it at a spot midway between Bru's side and her own. "Elizabeth Goins Chapman has made certain allegations about a crime that occurred in south Florida sometime in the late seventies or early eighties. She claims that an upstanding resident of the southeast coast by the name of Etienne was killed by someone using a .45 caliber pistol. She didn't know the caliber but her informant told her that the pistol the shooter used was a US Army general officer's handgun. That would make it, in the 1970s, a .45 caliber M15. A routine check with the Dade county sheriff's office showed that a subject known as Etienne, who was believed to be an illegal Haitian pimp and drug runner, was murdered in Homestead about then. The file faxed to us indicates he was, as reported by Ms. Goins-Chapman, dispatched by a .45 caliber pistol. The slug was retrieved and, according to the file, is in good repair with a significant number of identifiable lands and grooves. In other words if the pistol that fired that bullet is ever recovered, that slug can tie it to the death of this Etienne."

With that Sheriff Buckett stood. Her eyes were slits. "You are free to go, Bruton. And don't forget to take your property in that plastic envelope. By the way, for a stinking liberal you did a commendable job or getting rid of some of the biggest dirtbags in this county." She scowled and turned on the balls of her feet and made for the door. The guy in the suit followed her without a word.

Jerry stood. Bru, a bit dazed, followed his example. He picked up the zippered bag. It was heavy as though it contained coins. He took hold of the zipper but Jerry put his hand out, stopping him from opening it. He motioned with his head for the door. A deputy was waiting for them in the hallway. Bru only said one word as they walked: "Melba?"

"Justifiable homicide. Wasn't hard to prove since over one hundred spent AR-15 shells were found in the cockpit of the burned biplane. Also, a sheriff's deputy passed on the freeway and saw the plane firing into the hammock of palm trees. The episode was so darned outlandish the deputy thought it was a movie being shot or something and just kept going. Melba should be waiting in the parking lot."

Jerry was wrong. Melba was at the outside door when the deputy showed Bru through it. She bounded into his arms and hugged and kissed him. Bru pulled her close. Melba's tropical fruit odor smelled familiar and pleasant to him. Her long blonde body felt comfortable next to his. His body seemed to fit into hers and together they made a single unit. It was a good feeling.

"What's in your hands, Bru?" she asked.

Bru unzipped the envelope and looked. The M15 general officers pistol General Westmoreland had given his father stared up at him. Although Bru had suspected that the pistol was in the bag, actually seeing it made shudders pass through his body. "Why'd she do it?" Bru asked Jerry.

"Because she's a two-fisted sheriff that thinks the bad guys ought to be dead and the good guys ought to go free."

"Jesus," Bru said, "who'd ever think a left-leaning, pinko liberal like me who believes in due process and constitutional rights would be thankful a fascist sheriff was running Okeelanta County?"

"I'm not sure even a former activist state attorney like me can agree with her methods," Jerry said.

"What's the 'but'?" Melba asked. "I can tell from the hesitation in your voice, there's a but."

"Isn't there always a but," Jerry said. "She wants the million dollars in citrus futures Goins took out in Bru's name."

"I never even thought about them," Bru said, shrugging.

"Wait a minute," Melba said, "What happens if he fights for the money and goes to the mat on that old shooting charge?"

"Even if he were convicted, which is unlikely in my view, Bru wouldn't spend more than three or five years in the jug. And I would probably end up with most of the million dollars in legal fees."

"And if he gets off," Bru said, "all he is out is having his name dragged through the mud. She can have the money. I'm not interested in it."

"She'll probably use it," Jerry said, "to buy more crime-fighting gear, like the Australian software that tracked the paths of the various principals in the orange-juice plot. That as much as your story convinced her you were dragged in later on to be a patsy. On a little different tack, since you've decided you don't want to trade the family heirloom there in on the million bucks, my advice to you is to not be in any great hurry to get back to Orlando with your new sweetheart. Take her on the gambling boat cruise this evening. Get out there beyond the three mile limit and make sure that thing in that plastic bag in your hands disappears forever."

Melba looked Bru in the eyes and batted her big round baby blues and said, "Would you please, darling?"

46

Two weeks later Bru strode into Jerry Wiley's law offices. Lorraine, the two-hundred-twenty pound receptionist, stood and said, "Good morning, Dr. Bruton. Jerry said for you to go right on in."

Bru snorted at this attention from Lorraine. During the three months Bru worked out of Jerry's offices, Lorraine had never said hi to him. It just went to show there was nothing like killing a couple of guys to raise your status in the world.

Jerry was working on some papers as Bru barged in. He waved and indicated a chair across from the desk. After a while Jerry looked up from his papers and grinned a yard-wide country boy smile. After beaming at Bru for a five count, he saw the expression on Bru's face was stern. "What's the matter, Bru? That object the sheriff passed you has been deep sixed, you have the love of a beautiful woman, and it looks pretty certain Elizabeth will be declared criminally insane and will be packed off forever and anon. Not even a billionairess, which she technically may no longer be, can get off scot free when she has killed her daughter. What more could a man want?"

Bru gave Jerry the fisheye and Jerry continued talking, "The senior vice president at Lawson College called. They want 'to initiate a dialogue,' as he said, about your status at Lawson."

Bru kept the gimlet eye on Jerry. Jerry continued to talk, "I submitted to the college a copy of Goins's confession as you asked me. An emergency session of the board of regents was called. This happened yesterday.

President Newcombe was summarily fired without, I may add, the so-called golden parachute, a fat severance package, that usually cushions the fall in these cases."

"It couldn't have happened to a more deserving guy," Bru said.

"I saved that morsel back, relishing it for this meeting. Thought you might want to savor it a bit too."

"Actually, I sort of feel for the poor bastard, what with that case of HIV he contracted from Elizabeth. He didn't appear to be the type to go for a cheap strumpet like her."

Jerry shrugged. "You can never tell what fault lines track in the heart of a man. Especially when it comes to a woman. You were almost seduced by her yourself," Jerry said. "Now about your status at Lawson."

"Never mind my status at Lawson. I'll take care of that myself. What I came here to talk to you about was your HIV status. Have you taken the test, Jerry?"

Jerry's face betrayed no concern--it was a lawyer's face in the summation phase for a client caught red handed. "Why do you say that, Bru?"

"Because Leta's HIV positive, you sanctimonious asshole."

That made him crack. His jaw dropped and his eyebrows sagged like a collapsing tent.

"I always knew in my gut you had something to do with setting up that Goins scam," Bru said. "You just acted guilty too many times, like for instance that afternoon you came over to my garage apartment with Goins's check and contract. That was right after you had made off with Leta and you dawdled with a hangdog expression on your face. It was obvious you were trying to do a mea culpa about something. On my breezy ride to Daytona I ranted to myself that Lawson had taken you into its confidence before I was dismissed. And that you had cynically been there waiting to give me a job so you could get your hooks onto my wife. But in my scientific heart of hearts I knew the evidence was not really there so I didn't really believe all of that."

"Sometime you have to follow your intuition, Bru. In this instance, it was right."

"I know that now. Elizabeth seduced you first and she went through you to Newcombe. Why didn't you just stick with her? She was younger and better looking than Leta. She potentially had more money than you could shyster in a hundred lifetimes."

"For two reasons Bru. One, is because she's a piece of shit. And two because she wouldn't have had me. She knew what she wanted--to get to Newcombe. She'd gone back to school and tried to get to him that way. No dice. Newcombe was too wary a bird to fool with a student, even a mature woman in her thirties. So then she backed up and tried to get at him through me, the lawyer of the daughter of one of the richest men in the world. That way Newcombe paid attention to her. As soon as she got on to Newcombe, she completely lost interest in me."

"How many times did you pop her?"

"Just once."

"And you hoped you hadn't contracted the disease, even after you learned Newcombe had gotten it?"

"Yes, I pissed and washed very carefully afterwards, just the way they teach you in the sex hygiene classes. I cowered like the moral craven I am."

"Have there been others besides Leta and Elizabeth?"

"No," Jerry said.

"Don't lie to me, dammit," Bru said.

"I'm giving it to you straight. Elizabeth let me have her body and left me dissatisfied with my frumpy fat high-school sweetheart. And as luck would have it, for whatever reason, she was out to ruin your career and that left Leta

263

hanging like a fruit ripe for the plucking. I didn't know what they were up to, Bru. I didn't know Elizabeth was going after you when I put her onto Newcombe. Later, before they fired you, Newcombe asked me to take you into the firm as an environmental consultant. Even then I hadn't tumbled to what they were up to. I was only a step or two ahead of you in figuring out what was going on."

"Try not to act too damn smug," Bru said. "Because they were trying to maneuver me into the electric chair if I didn't do what they wanted while you were trying to bed my wife. Then to add insult to injury you tossed her out, you shithead."

"When it came right down to it, Bru, I'm just a farm-town Baptist guy. I couldn't leave the wife and kids."

Bru spit in disgust. "You make me want to puke."

"What are you going to do about it, Bru?"

"I'm not going to shoot you and I'm not going to turn you in to the state bar association. You helped me out of that jam over in Okeelanta County. I'm not sure I could have gotten out of that on my own."

"You are probably right about that. I'd imagine you'd still be sitting in jail had I not worked a little magic on Sheriff Buckett. That woman doesn't like you."

"You are going to have to take care of Leta," Bru said.

"You want me to leave my wife?" Jerry said.

"If it comes to that," Bru said. "You are going to take care of that woman. And I mean in all ways financially, medically, emotionally, even sexually if that's permissible when two have the disease. This 'Oh, I'm sorry I changed my mind,' shit isn't going to cut it."

"Jesus, Bru, what about my own family?"

"Look, I'm not asking you to fuck over Rhonda and the kids. I just want to make sure Leta's taken care of. If that doesn't happen, shit is going to fly." Bru looked at

Jerry for a moment. Jerry nodded, dropped his gaze to the floor. His head fell into his hands. Bru stood, put his hands in his pockets, kicked the door open and crossed the outer offices.

Outdoors, it was warm again, in the low eighties. A couple of feral monk parrots sat on a power line screeching and otherwise playing grabass with each other. A fragrance drifted in on the breeze--citrus blossoms. No, the time for citrus blossoms had gone. This was the odor of Confederate jasmine, the smell of noble battles long passed. The sun felt good on Bru's skin. He looked at his watch and hurried away. He didn't want to be late for lunch with Melba.

Author

Steve Glassman was nominated for an Edgar award by the
Mystery Writers of America for a critical study of Florida
crime writing, which he coedited, in 1997. His other
contribution to the fiction of the state of Florida was a
historical novel set in the Seminole-Civil wars era called
Blood on the Moon. He follows the zany carrying on in
the Sunshine State from his grove of tropical fruit trees in
New Smyrna Beach.